CLEO BROWNE

Tav

Contents

Trigger Warning

This book deals with a badassery in all its forms.
Please be aware that in order for these characters to be badass,
this book contains content that some readers may find
disturbing, such as graphic descriptions of violence and
torture, grooming, sexual assault, R18 sex scenes, and an
exorbitant number of dildos.

Hey Readers!

Thank you for choosing to pick up Tav's story!
I always knew that sweet, golden retriever Tav would have his story,
but I had no idea who his Ol Lady would be.

Enter Suzanne Strickland Henry.

Suzanne won my Elizabeth's Trust character auction.
But, instead of wanting my FMC based on herself, she paid
homage to her grand aunt Blanche, who was a total badass.
From those early conversations, Tav's lady love was born.
Thank you, Suzanne, for sharing your memories of Blanche
and gifting me
a character I fell in love with. It only seems fitting that I
dedicate this book to her.

For Blanche

Who the heck is that?

Devil's Rose MC

Marx - Pres
Rhodie - VP and Enforcer + Tuesday Tombs (Chewy)
Rider - SAA
Wire - Secretary/Hacker + Remy Wright
Jovie (Wire and Remy's adopted child)
Switch - Medic
Tank - Member
Judge - Member
Sniper - Member
Fox - Member
Nitro - Member
Savage - Member (ex Death Rider) + Nat
Dex - Member (Ex Death Rider)
Jimmy - Prospect
Takoda - Prospect
Tav - Prospect + Blanche (Pixie)
Niko, Sage, Cove, Elio (Tav and Blanche's children)

Tombs Security

August (Gus) Tombs + Ana Tombs

Jules Tombs
Tav Tombs + Blanche Landry
Niko, Sage, Cove and Elio (Tav and Blanche's children)
Tuesday (Chewy) Tombs + Rhodie
Sidney (Pops) Tombs + Debs Taylor (Mother of Ana)

Bartashev Bratva

Roman Bartashev + Sasha Bartashev (BFF's of Ana)

Chapter 1

Tav

"Tav! Beer me!"

My little sister slaps her hand on the bartop, not looking in the least bit worried that she and her gang were in a fight with the bunnies and raided by police strippers. She's not even looking in my direction, her attention on her "girl gang" who are now trying to twerk on the dance floor, seeming as unbothered as their fearless leader.

Grabbing a cold one, I pop off the top and slide it across the shiny wooden bartop.

"Happy little sis?"

Dayz, or Chewy, as her cut states, turns to look at me. "Are you kidding? Look at all these peeps we have now."

"Did you just use the word peeps?" I smirk at her as she frowns back.

"Yes. Because I am very eloquent and have many formal and informal words at my disposal." She waves a hand at me when I snort at her answer.

She opens her mouth to say something else, then thinks twice. She looks at me, really looks at me. Her eyes hold mine, which is unlike her. Tilting her head, she squints a little.

"You're happy," she says it like a statement rather than the question that I asked.

"Yeah Dayz, I'm happy. This place, these people, I dunno. They're like the cousins we never had or something," I say, shrugging.

"Exactly! I'm glad I got them for us." She swipes her beer off the bar top and badly dance walks back to her girls, as a laugh bursts out of me.

My brothers and I never would have imagined that when we came to the compound in search of our little sister all those months ago, we would end up part of the DRMC family. And yet here we are. Dayz is in love with the VP, Rhodie; Gus found a woman to put up with his annoying anal-retentive personality, and Jules, well, he's in swinger heaven with Fox, Nitro, and the bunnies. Even Pops has managed to find a good woman. Then there's me. I'm happy. I have my family, and my new brothers in the MC, but I can feel something is missing. A little pixie woman that's had me in knots since the day I laid eyes on her.

9 Months Ago

The lift doors slide open revealing, inch by inch, a beautiful face attached to an equally beautiful body. Short, probably around my sister's height, with curves for days. I just know she would be soft and warm in my arms.

"Did you get eyes for Christmas?" her sweet voice says, black brow raised.

My eyes dart over her face. Dark eyes, thick lush lips, heart-shaped face topped with short, black hair in one of those pixie cuts hot alternative girls have. Like this one. I stare at her a moment longer before her words work their way through my addled brain.

"Wait, did you just ask if I got eyes for Christmas?"

"It was that or telling you to take a picture. It'll last longer." She shrugs, and I can see the corners of her lips tip up.

I'm about to shoot back a witty comeback when the lift dings and the doors start to slide, me on one side, and the beautiful pixie on the other giving me a finger wave as they close. Shit! She didn't even try to keep them open for me. Looking up, I can see she's two floors up. Taking off down the hall to the stairwell, I take them two at a time, burst through the fire exit, hit the lift button, and wait for the lift to arrive, the doors sliding open just as I suck in a breath. I want to be impressive. Rebut her smart mouth with an equally smart answer of my own, with a full breath. Not huffing like an obscene phone caller.

The doors slide open, revealing her to me again. This time, her head is down as she's scrolling her phone, but then she realizes that she's not alone. Her eyes start from my feet and slowly travel my body before her gaze lands on mine. A smile stretched across her lush mouth.

"Well, seeing as you ran two flights of stairs, do you want to join me?" She steps out of the lift and walks past me in her heels that make her ass look phenomenal and her hips sway just right.

"You know, you shouldn't ask strange men to follow you. It isn't safe." I keep my distance a little. I may not be as big as my brothers, but I'm still a fuck ton bigger than the pixie in front of me.

"Pshhh. I know who you are. Tav Tombs, one of the four Tombs Security owners. I was at your presentation. I would love to pick your brain one day, but I've got one more night on my own before I head home to Rose Grove and my kids. If I want to have sex this year, hell, this decade, then you and your obvious interest fit the bill." She gives me another once over, one hand on her hip, the

other holding the door handle to her room. Her gaze stops at my thickening length, her tongue coming out to sweep that full bottom lip that I want to suck on.

Now, I'm no prude, however the hottest woman I've ever seen is asking me to follow her into her room so she can use my cock and I feel a little weird about that.

"Look, Pixie, I'm down if you're down, but let's take it slow. Get to know each other. You know a lot about me. I know nothing about you." I hold my hands up, letting her see that I'm serious about getting to know her.

Her eyes narrow before she rolls them and then huffs out a breath. She turns to walk through her door, with me following close behind, her mumbling, "Great. The hottest guy I've ever seen wants to get to know me."

She dumps her giant handbag on a chair, throws her room key card on a built-in desk, and huffs again. OK, maybe she's a little stressed. I know exactly how to help her.

Standing behind her, I lean down, sucking on the exposed column of her long neck. She lets out a hiss before turning to me, staring into my eyes, wrapping her hands around my neck and pulling me in close enough for her to latch her lips onto mine. Her tongue pushes between my lips, sliding along mine, dueling, tangling, tasting; angling my head where she needs it. She's a fucking firecracker.

Without unlatching her lips, she jumps, trusting me to catch her, her plump ass landing in my waiting hands. She rubs her core against me, her hands gripping me, before she pulls back, her eyes hooded, pupils blown.

"We should slow down a little, maybe get to know one another?"

"Fuck that gentleman shit. I need your cock. I'll talk after that."

With that, she grips my shirt in her hands and pulls, tearing it open, buttons flying every fucking where. She latches onto my neck, under my beard, sucking, hard. Fuck! Looks like we're not taking this slow.

Turning, I throw her on the bed, her small body bouncing once, a small grunt escaping her. Before I can ask if she's OK and apologize for getting a little rough, she starts stripping, fast. By the time I remove my trousers, she's on the bed, her legs spread wide, fingers in her pussy.

She has her eyes on my cock and I've never felt more desired than I do now. That could be a girly thing to say, but shit, she looks like she wants to devour my dick and I'm very, very happy about that.

"I need your cock. NOW." she pulls her fingers from her core, swirling her cream around her clit, letting me see how wet she is.

Pulling a condom from my wallet, I tear the wrapper with my teeth, pinch the end and roll the sheath over my length to the base. Kneeling on the bed, I bat her hand out of the way, face plant into the wet curls at the top of her cunt, and inhale her sweet scent.

Before I can get my mouth on that pretty pussy, her hands grip my ears and none too gently pull me up.

"No time. Get that fat dick inside me now!" She pulls me roughly toward her, slamming her lips on mine while her hips wind, seeking my cock.

With our tongues and teeth clashing, I line myself up with her sopping wet hole, notch my dick at her entrance, and push in slowly, letting her get used to the feel of me. As with this whole interaction, she has other ideas, grabbing my ass cheeks and pulling me toward her at the same time she thrusts up. We both groan in unison, her tight pussy squeezing me like a fist, making my balls draw up in anticipation.

Resting my weight on my elbows, I pull out before I start pumping in earnest. I wish I could go slower, but all her demands and moans, her "mores" and "harders" have me losing my mind. We'll go slow *next time. Pushing myself up and off her, I lean back on my knees, grabbing her ass in my hands, angling her up as I fuck up into her. She's thrashing on the bed now, her arousal dripping down my knees onto the sheets. Two more thrusts have her shaking hard as she screams my name. Three more thrusts have me unloading into the latex, wishing I was filling her up instead.*

Collapsing next to the most beautiful pixie, my cock slips free of her tight confines. I take in her flushed cheeks, her chin pink from my beard and rough kisses, and her dark shining eyes.

Her eyes twinkle as she holds her hand out to me.

"Blanche Landry. Pleasure to meet you."

"Tav, Jimmy says there's a bunch of kids at the gate asking for you," Rhodie calls out, his phone against his chest, snapping me out of my thoughts.

Thank god I'm behind the bar, otherwise every brother would see my boner and I'd end up with "Bones" or "Woody" as my road name or something.

Frowning, I glance at the time.

"They asked for me?" pointing to myself in case Rhodie has gotten me confused with someone else. He's great and loves my sister, and because of that fact, I'm unsure how clever the man actually is.

"You're the only fucking Tav Tombs we've got, dickhead."

"He say how many?" Checking my messages I see nothing to note. Pulling up my tracking app, I check to see where my girl is. I'm not surprised to find she's turned her phone off.

"Four kids, ranging in size from Jovie to small man sized."

My lips twitch. Jimmy, the prospect who does gate duty, has a fun way with words. "I know them. I'll go out."

"Prospect," Marx barks, "It's 9 p.m. Kids asking for you at

this time means they need help. Rhodie, get Jimmy to bring them in."

Rhodie nods and says something into his phone. All the brothers are looking at me. So is the girl gang, but they look more nosey than anything.

"How do you know these kids, Tav?"

"I've been kinda dating their mom."

"Wait, the skittish woman?" Gus asks. That is most definitely not how I would describe Blanche. My siblings have respected my wishes of not looking into her, even though I know he and Jules have been concerned about my girl not wanting to be all in with me. But there are reasons for that, and they're not mine to share.

The door swings open and Jimmy walks through, ushering the kids in.

"Tav!" Cove yells out, running up to me. I pull her into my arms instinctively, her brother Elio crowding my legs.

Niko steps closer to his sister Sage, shielding her from view while eyeing up my club brothers.

"Hey, it's OK. You're safe here. This is my club Pres, Marx," I tell Niko while indicating.

Marx steps forward and smiles gently at the teens. He's met with a scowl from Sage.

"The rest of the men here are my club brothers. Their wives and girlfriends are over at that table." I point to the girl gang. Thankfully, they've settled down.

Ten minutes earlier and the kids would have walked into their brawl with the bunnies. I'm not sure what's going to happen with them, but seeing as they were scrapping with Dayz and Nat, two Ol Ladies, it wouldn't surprise me if they get the boot. The girl gang smiles and waves at the kids, like nice ladies.

Little do the kids know.

"Tell me what's going on."

Niko eyes everyone before setting his dark eyes on mine. "Mom went hunting. She told us to come here and ask for you if she wasn't back in 12 hours. She said you'd keep us safe."

"She's damn right. Nothing is going to happen to you, OK?" I look down at Elio, hugging my legs, letting my free hand rest on his head.

The girl gang gets to their feet, Nat taking the lead. "We'll get rooms set up. One for the boys, one for the girls." Marx gives them a nod and I shoot them a smile in thanks as they all traipse off down the hall, whispering about how cute the kids are.

"Can you tell us what your mom was hunting for, kid? We can get a group together. Some of us are ex army search and rescue. We'll find her." Judge says, gently, quieting his gruff voice a little.

The older kids, Niko and Sage, stare at me, unsure how to answer Judge. Tipping my head at them that it's safe to tell these men, Sage turns to look at Judge.

"It's not what she's hunting. It's who."

"What the fuck?" echoes around the room.

"OK, kid. Who is your mom hunting?" Marx asks, being infinitely more patient than I'm used to.

Niko looks at me before looking at Marx. "Royal Landry."

"The prophet's brother?" Wire asks. I know he and Remy have been watching the family closely since finding out that Hammer is working alongside them and their trafficking business.

"Tav, who have you been dating?"

Snuggling Cove closer to me, I look at my brothers before

setting my gaze on Marx.

"Blanche Landry. She's going to be my Ol Lady."

"What!?"

I expected that from Marx. But not from the chorus of voices that joined him.

"What?" I ask, looking around the room. Gus, as per usual, is looking like he's going to have a heart attack. Dayz and her girls are back, looking excited. Probably wanting to add another woman to their gang. Niko looks pissed, of course, I mean, it's his mom I just claimed. Marx looks, well, he looks like he usually looks, just with squintier eyes. How the hell does Dayz put up with him looking at her like that?

"Let me take the kids and show them their rooms, and you sort, whatever this is, *ne*?" Mama Debs' hand on my shoulder gives a little squeeze before she steps around me, holding her hands out for Cove, taking her from my arms. Her brother Elio untangles himself from my legs and follows Mama Debs like she's the Pied Piper. Even the older kids stop scowling and follow her.

Everyone's eyes follow the kids out of the room before they all turn on me.

"Tav, do you want to explain what the fuck is going on?" Gus says in the measured tone he uses with Dayz.

"I think the prospect made it very clear," Marx says, his arms crossed over his chest. "He's claimed Blanche Landry as his Ol Lady. The same Blanche Landry who got rid of Valor Landry, Hammer's business partner, leaving us on the back foot. Blanche Landry, who Tav told us was just a friend."

"Very, very good friends by the sounds of it," Pops loudly whispers to Rider, nudging him with his elbow, both giggling at the joke.

"OK. I should have come clean then, but she's got a lot going on and wants to wait a little before seeing where our relationship is going." I drift off, not wanting the whole MC to pity me. Or worse, give me shit about it. "But my claim still stands. One day Blanche is going to be my Ol Lady and, as is laid out in the bylaws, Ol Ladies will be protected by the MC. I joined for the camaraderie and brotherhood." I swallow. "And I'm hoping that if shit hits the fan, I'll have you all by my side if I have to go to hell and bring her back to me."

Glancing at my family, Gus, Jules, and Dayz, they all nod in unison. Looking back at my DRMC family, the brother's faces give away nothing. Stoic until Marx makes his decision. He's a big bastard, and his narrowed eyes are making me wonder if my bowels are strong enough to get through the next few minutes.

"She's an unknown from a fucked up family, a family trafficking god knows what with Hammer. What's to say we can trust her? You know as well as I do that family ties are strong."

"She hates them. Hates them all. Why the hell do you think she's hunting them?"

Our heads turn to the angry voice in the hall, Niko standing there, his fists clenched. At 17 years old, he still has a teenager's body, not quite filled out just yet, lanky arms and legs, nothing to be scared of. However, the fire in his eyes says something different. I've seen that look before, on his mother's face. I'm guessing so has Marx, because he tilts his head as he assesses Niko, then gives him a nod.

"Alright then. Blanche Landry is your Ol Lady, Tav." Marx nods once, effectively dismissing me to handle Niko on my own.

"Are you alright, Niko? Do you or the younger ones need

anything?" I ask, stepping toward him, ready to help if I can.

He shakes his head at me, a frown permanently etched into his face. "Mom called. The hunt turned into a rescue. She'll be back tomorrow morning. I'll pack them up early, get them home, and off to school." He looks to Marx and the brothers. "Thank you for having us. We'll be out of here first thing." He nods before turning on his heel and walking out of the room.

"You regretting calling Ol Lady on his mom yet?" Rider says with a smirk, "That kid doesn't look like he's gonna take it easy on ya."

"He'll come around when he sees how much I care for his mother," I answer, shrugging at him. It's not him I have to worry about. It's his mother when she finds out that I've claimed her.

Pops claps his hands loudly. "I can not WAIT to see how this shit plays out."

Blanche

I twist my wrist to illuminate my smartwatch, checking both the time and my steps. I blew straight over my 10,000 step target today. With all that exercise, I definitely deserve a little treat later. It's been 12 and a half hours since I kissed my kids goodbye and left the relative safety of Rose Grove. A quick drive across state lines into this forgotten part of Louisiana and now I'm sitting in my car waiting for my contact. I had started my day tracking my dear old uncle, and then spending a little time around the perimeter of Eden's Keep looking for weak spots.

Using my intel, I had planned to rid the world of Royal Landry tonight, but instead, I got an SOS call to help.

I get the biggest urge to message Niko, to check in and make sure he got the kids to Tav, but I know my boy and he knows what he needs to do. Even if he leaned into that stubbornness he got from me; his sister would make sure he did as he was told. Get them all to Tav. To safety.

Sighing as my thighs clench instinctively at just the thought of Octavius Tombs, I think back to the first time I laid eyes on him. He thinks it was at the conference 9 months back. For me, it was perhaps two years ago. He stood up there on the stage with his brothers, listing the different security measures mere mortals can afford to install before getting to the good stuff. The stuff that private investigators like me need. The light shone down on his deep olive skin, black hair flopping over his brow, his beard impeccably trimmed and lined up. He was beautiful, and since then I've always zeroed in on his pretty face at trade shows and conferences.

Until 9 months ago, when my short, curvy mom body caught his attention, and I bedded him in a way that I had never done before. Aside from my very short-lived marriage and three one-night stands, it's been me and the kids. Team Landry.

My earpiece picks up rustling coming from somewhere deep in the copse of trees I'm parked next to. Pulling my night vision goggles into place, I look into the wood at two people walking toward me. I can tell by the shape of their clothing that they aren't a threat. It's hard to attack someone when you're wearing a full-length dress and carrying all your worldly possessions.

Sliding my goggles up onto my head, I open my door, step out from my car, and hustle my way toward them both. The fear on their faces subsides when they see it's me, and not someone from the compound sent to bring them back.

"Blanche?" A voice softly calls as they close the distance between us. I have two contacts within the Keep. Justice, my male contact, and Loyal. The irony behind her name never ceases to amuse me.

"I'm here," I call out, and I can see the nerves leave their footsteps as they pick up the pace.

Loyal and I share a quick embrace before I step back and look at the woman with her, her wide eyes staring at me. She looks young and like she's going to crap her pants at any moment. Even though I grew up in the same environment as her and have a gaggle of kids, I never was, nor never will be, gentle in my approach to anything.

"Hey, I'm Blanche. What's your name?"

She stares at me for a moment, her bottom lip quivering before she swallows. "L-lovely. Lovely Landry."

"Of course it is," I mumble to myself, although judging by her questioning look, I'm sure she heard me. "Which one of those fuckers is your father?"

She takes a step back, obviously not used to women swearing. Well, she better buckle up. We have a two-hour car ride to get through.

"Um," Her eyes dart to Loyal who jerks a nod in her direction. "The Prophet. Mercy Landry is my father."

"Is he dead yet?"

"Um, no. He's being so brave and hanging in there. God has blessed him with more time." I answer with a snort. If God existed, he wouldn't have chosen Mercy Landry to do shit for him. "If you don't mind me asking, who are you exactly?" Lovely asks in her quiet voice.

Letting out a deep breath, I square my shoulders and look at the woman I'm going to spirit away, taking her to a new life free from marrying old men whose saggy balls don't work.

"Luckily for you, I'm your big sister and I'm here to take you somewhere better. Somewhere gray pubes won't touch you."

"Um, thank you?" Lovely says while looking mighty nervous.

Loyal doesn't ease her fears either. She knows this is for the best. She just hands over a bag of stuff to me before looking at Lovely, giving her a quick squeeze, and leaving back the way she came.

Taking that as our cue to move, I heft up Lovely's things and lead the way out of the woods. Because Lovely has grown up with Mercy as her prophet, I know she won't speak again until she's spoken to. It's how girls are raised under his regime. It didn't work with me, obviously, but according to Mercy, that's the Devil's fault.

Growing up in Eden's Keep wasn't all that bad. I was from my father's first family, the youngest and only daughter, after three brothers. In the beginning, it was a place for like-minded people to congregate. My father was a God-fearing man. He read the scriptures and wanted to build an Eden on Earth, where people could live according to the Bible. Helping thy neighbor, working the land and living off its bounty. Then, my mother died. Whatever held my father together snapped. He started having "visions". Visions that God was speaking directly to him, wanting him to be his prophet, helping people to lead a good life, a godly life.

Obviously, that also meant becoming a bigamist and sexual predator. Between him and my uncle, Eden's Keep turned into what could only be called a cult. Gullible people looking for a place to belong soon came in their droves, thanks to my uncle Royal Landry's proselytizing. Next came the young wives and then came getting rid of my brothers. I mean, The Prophet can't have all the women if his young, virile sons are around, can he? They all got dumped on the streets to fend for themselves and I got married off.

The mewl of a baby drifts through my bitter thoughts, stopping me in my tracks.

"What was that?"

"What was what?" Lovely whispers back.

Mewling sounds out again, this time with snuffles and a little cry. Spinning to look at Lovely, I notice the pile of fabrics she is holding in her hands is moving.

"Lovely. Is that a baby?"

Tears pool in her eyes, and she sniffles. "Please, even if you don't take me with you, please take my baby. I - I can't have her there. I've got to save her."

Stepping closer, I peer into the swaddle Lovely is holding and stare down into wide eyes that mirror her mother's.

"Who is her father, Lovely?"

"R-royal Landry."

Looking closely at Lovely, I take in her features. She's not much taller than I am. Full curves, although that could be because she has recently had a baby. Black hair, heart-shaped face. Pretty in a severe type of way. And young. Exactly Royal's type. Lovely will be the fifth girl I've transported out of Eden's Keep with a baby belonging to Royal. Who knows how many are still in there, waiting for the kind of love they dreamed about as girls, only to find that Royal Landry is a monster. The baby snuffles again, putting my thoughts on the back burner for about the 50th time tonight, and drawing my attention back to the matter at hand.

"How old is she?" I ask, reaching out a finger to run it over the baby's soft cheek.

"Three days. Royal doesn't know she's been born yet. It's not his day to visit."

Well, that and he's been a little busy selling women.

"Come on, we better get you both strapped in and warm. We'll figure out what to do when we get home."

"Um, where is home?"

"Home for me is Rose Grove, a few hours from here. You're not going there though. It's too close to the Prophet and the rest of those assholes. I'm taking you to my brothers who will transport you further away from Eden's Keep and Royal Landry. Don't worry, you're safe with us."

Turning on my phone to see missed messages from the kids and Tav, I quickly reply to Niko to let him know I'm safe. I have a rescue with me and I'll be home as quick as I can. He replies that they're all safe and well and he'll get the kids off to school. That's not his job, it's mine. If I drive nonstop, I'll be back at first light and tell him so, but he says not to worry and then calls me an old lady. Little shit. Typing that he's a smart ass, I hit send and then lean back against the headrest, letting out a sigh.

"You two OK back there?" I turn to look over my shoulder, checking in on Lovely. She still looks fucking terrified, but her baby suckling at her seems to have calmed her nerves.

"Yes, we're OK. Little miss was just hungry," she gazes down at her daughter, a soft smile on her face.

"What's her name?" I ask, turning to face forward, starting the engine and turning the heater on to warm up.

"Um, I haven't named her yet. I was waiting for Royal, but I-I heard some bad things about him from the other wives.

How, he, um, he won't wait for you to heal before he takes his husbandly rights. I-I had a hard delivery, and I didn't think I would be able to, um, service him. I went to ask for help from one of the older women, but then I, um, I," She cuts off abruptly, tears in her eyes and her chest heaving, as if on the verge of a panic attack.

"Lovely! Name 5 things you can see," my voice stern with the command.

"You, the trees, my baby, my favorite embroidery, and your yellow handbag."

By the time she's finished rattling this off, her breathing is back to normal. Huh, that was fast. Maybe she's stronger than I gave her credit for?

"OK, Lovely, can you tell me what happened when you went to find an older woman for help?" I soften my voice as much as I can, but I have a feeling whatever she's going to say is going to piss me off.

She nods miserably. "I overheard her saying to another woman that Royal will be so happy with our new baby girl. He's been stressed because he has a buyer, but the other wives had given birth to boys. They, um, they said he's going to sell my daughter. I had to leave. I had to!"

That motherfucker. And all those motherfucking women, complicit in his schemes. I need them on my list.

"Lovely, when we get to my brothers, I need you to write the names of the women. I'll sort this all out."

Her eyes well up again as she whispers a thank you, looking back down at her baby. I jump when the phone in my hand vibrates, giving me such a fright that instead of screening the call, I answer it immediately.

Tav's smooth "Hey Pixie, you safe and sound?" drifts over

the speaker. Like magic, the tension I had been holding in my shoulders melts out of me at the sound of his voice.

He's been calling me that since we spent the last night of the conference wrapped around each other. Since that night, where I saw Heaven and little baby Jesus at the behest of Tav Tombs, he's been there. First, it started off with little messages here and there. Then lunch dates, until he graduated to meeting the kids and coming to dinner now and then. I guess you could call it dating, if dating was done in slow motion thanks to work and kid schedules. Whatever you want to call it, I liked it. Tav was more than a man I was seeing; in the months since we'd met he'd become my best friend. Then Mercy got sick and my plans to rid the world of Eden's Keep got bumped up the timeline a little. Meaning I had to pull the plug on what Tav and I had growing. I can't drag him into my plans, expose him to the darkness in me. I need to protect him.

"I'm safe and sound. The kids?"

"All tucked up in bed. You know I'd keep them safe."

Knowing that they're safe with Tav helps any residual tension I was holding dissipate. "Thank you, Tav."

"Pshh, think nothing of it, sweetheart. I told you I'm here for the good, the bad, and all the in-between. When you're ready."

Instead of answering him, I decide to change the subject. I have a mission.

"My job took a turn. Instead of reaching my target, I have two packages to deliver to my brothers, then I'll head home. I've told Niko -"

"Pixie, it's good. Niko has told me what's happening. You won't need to be home until just before school finishes. Take a nap at your brothers' and stay safe. We've got your back."

Chewing my bottom lip, I worry about leaving the kids at an MC, then remember that DRMC are the good guys. I've done my research. I know they're good men. Far better than most of the men I grew up with.

"You're sure?"

"I got this. Go do your thing and I'll see you tomorrow. Be safe, sweetheart."

"Be safe," I whisper back to him before ending the call.

"Wow, your husband sounds great," Lovely says gently, with a sad smile on her face.

"He's not my husband. He's just a friend."

"Well, you're lucky to have a man like that in your corner."

"Yeah, I am," I reply, almost as if to myself before letting out a sigh, putting the car into gear and checking my mirrors. "Right, let's get you and your baby somewhere safe."

Chapter 2

Tav

Wandering down the long hall towards the guest rooms the kids stayed in last night, I can't help but be impressed by what Marx and Rhodie's dad, Mad Dog, achieved here. The clubhouse from the outside looks little more than a massive warehouse, but the inside is just like home. Wooden floors run the whole way through the main common room which houses the bar, dining tables, and a lounge area. There's a pool table and dart boards, even a foosball table. All of which Pops has been banned from using. There's a solid wooden door that hints at our church and double wide doors indicating the mouth of the long hall where Marx's office and all our rooms are located.

I hadn't planned on moving in when I decided to prospect. Originally, I had asked Marx if I could live at home with my family, work at Tombs Security as usual, and then stay at the compound on the weekends to do prospect duty. However, as time has moved on, I've found myself in my room here more and more.

I love being surrounded by people, but with Dayz, Gus, and even Pops having significant others, it feels different at home. I can't just let myself into my siblings' houses anymore. Not since I walked in on Rhodie in the smallest onesie I've seen in my life. He threatened to kick my ass if I told anyone, but that didn't stop me from snapping a pic through the window. I'll keep that safe for the future. You never know when you might need to blackmail your future brother-in-law.

"They left already, Prospect," Rider's voice calls.

Turning to look at him, I see he has Whitney by the arm and is leading her to the common room. The other few bunnies that live here full-time follow behind.

Raising a brow in question at him, Rider smirks at me. "The bunnies need to learn where they fit in the hierarchy. Ol Ladies come first, always. After last night's brawl, none of them are allowed on the premises."

Whitney starts to whine and then snaps her jaw shut quickly when Rider shoots her the most chilling look. Huh. Looks like happy-go-lucky Rider may have a bit of a dark side. Shaking my head at the thought, I remember that all these men saw things on deployment. So much shit, in fact, that watching Dayz do her thing is probably a walk in the park for them. I watch Rider lead them all out, hopefully to somewhere they can make better life choices.

Looking into one room the kids used, I note the made beds and the open curtains. I should have expected that. They're good kids to their core, but then what else would you expect when they've been raised by a badass woman? The first time I met them had been nerve-wracking for Blanche, less so for me. It's no secret that I've dated a few women with children in the past. People give kids a bad rap, but if you treat them like people and not like cock blockers, you're fine. Kids can sense bullshit, which is why I always try to tell them the truth. Like last night when I claimed Blanche in front of the kids. Niko may be pissed now, but he'll come around.

"Prospect," Savage nods as he and his Ol Lady Nat pass me in the hall on their way to the common room.

"Savage." I give him a chin lift back before smiling at Nat. "Morning, Nat. How are you feeling today? Need anything?"

She smiles wide at me, and then rolls her eyes when Savage pulls her even closer to him. "I'm doing good thanks, Tav. Peanut seems to not be making me too sick," She smiles as she rubs her small belly, Savage then laying his hand on top of hers.

It's a good look on the man. That and the DRMC cut he now wears. The first time I met him we were trying to rescue his Ol Lady and other innocent women who were in the process of being sold. After that it's been shit show after shit show, which must have really been weighing on his shoulders. Since he, his VP and his enforcer patched over, you can see the weight lifted, meaning he can enjoy his Ol Lady and her pregnancy without the constant threat of violence. Well, maybe.

"I'm on duty around the clubhouse today, so if you need anything, let me know. I always keep a pack of saltines on hand for Ana, but she's about the same amount of pregnant as you, so I can double up if need be."

Savage holds out his fist to bump. "Thanks Prospect," I gently tap his fist and wave to Nat as they continue down the hall.

Breakfast is already done and dusted, what with the bulk of the brothers off to their day jobs at the various businesses DRMC own. Normally I'd be in the office, but I've been taking

Mondays off to help out the MC a little more, maybe even get my patch a little sooner. As a part owner of Tombs Security, being able to change my hours to suit is easy enough to do. Just run it by my pain in the ass family and voila! An extra day at the clubhouse spent cleaning up shit and running around after the brothers and I love it.

I snap out of my thoughts as my phone vibrates in my pocket, letting me know I have to meet Tank in the common room ASAP. Hustling my ass down the hall, I stop next to the huge man leaning on the bar.

"We got a run. Old Man Whitlock has run out of 'shine, so we gotta call by Old Man Henderson's and grab a case. We may as well check in and deliver to the others while we're out."

"I'll grab the keys to the SUV." I nod at him, feet already moving.

It may not be the type of run other MCs are doing. No guns, drugs, or women for us. We run moonshine back and forth to a small network of vets in the area. Henderson makes smooth stuff, still high enough proof to knock you on your ass and see Jesus, but it's safe. We do pickups whenever the men run low, deliver it, and spend a little time with them. They may not have wanted in on the MC lifestyle, but as the MC sees it, they are still brothers in arms and they deserve to be taken care of.

Signing out the keys from Wire and Remy, who I'm certain were in the middle of some type of geeky foreplay, judging by how red Remy's face was, I head out to meet up with Tank. But not before checking in with every brother I pass along the way. These guys are an extension of my family, and just like with my family, I like to ask how they all are, offer advice (not that I have any), and help them in any way I can.

Settling into the soft leather of the SUV I'll be driving today,

I wait for Tank to pull up alongside on his Harley. Instead, the door flings open, making me almost shit myself.

"I'm driving, kid. You're shotgun."

"Sorry, I thought you'd take your bike,"

"Nah. Figured I should do my sponsor duties." He smirks at me before grabbing my shirt and pulling me out of the driver's seat. Which would have worked better if I was the type of rebel to not buckle up. As it stands, I'm hanging out of the door like a goddamn puppet, trapped by the seatbelt. Tank lets out a huff, leaning over me to press the release button. Because of the odd angle, my head is now level with his groin, and he has a really fucking unfortunate hole in his jeans. I now know that Tank is a free balling type of guy. Well, either that or he wears bandaid colored boxers. Wanting out of the danger zone, I grab onto his pockets and try to wriggle back a little, using him as leverage.

"Why the fuck won't this unbuckle?" Tank grunts.

"It's the safety feature. It thinks I'm upside down or something," I grunt back, still trying to use my grip on Tank's jeans to lever myself back into the car seat.

"What the fuck are you two doing?" I let go of Tank and let my body go limp. I know that voice. That voice haunts my dreams. "Son, is Blanche your beard?"

"What the fuck, Pops?" I peer at Pops through Tank's legs before Tank moves slightly, grabs me under my arms, and shoves me back into the car, none too gently.

"Fix this," Tank says, poking his massive finger into my chest. Hard.

"Pops, Blanche is my Ol Lady, once I convince her. And I would never go there with Tank. I respect him too much." I shoot a grin at Tank, who is now in the passenger seat, having given up getting me out of the car.

He just runs his hand down his face and makes the motion to get on with it.

"Well, I'd be fine if you were with Tank. I mean, it'd take a bit to get used to, to know my grandkid was a catcher and all, but what you do with your ass is your business."

I gape at him for a moment before all his words register. "Wait, what do you mean I'd be the catcher?"

Pops looks at me, darts his eyes over my shoulder to look at Tank, before looking back at me. Then shaking his head and walking off.

Turning with indignation to face Tank and his smug smile, I decide to cut my losses.

"Just get us to Old Man Henderson's in one piece, Prospect."

"Aye aye Captain."

Blanche

Axl Rose gently whistling the opening bars of "Patience" drifts through my waking consciousness so I yank the covers even higher until they cover my face.

"You can't hide from Axel Rose, sis."

The music gets louder and louder until I have no choice but to fling back the covers, angrily kick them off my legs and launch myself at Vic, knocking him on his ass, both of us sprawled on the floor. Not that it stops that infernal song. When I hit Vic square on, it knocked the phone from his hand. Now Chris and Dom have taken over singing backup vocals.

"Um, I heard a ruckus. Are you all OK?"

Our heads snap to the doorway, Lovely chewing her lip, shuffling from side to side, her floor length blue dress with lace collar swishing as she moves. Chris stops GnR and Vic and I get up off the floor and act like we're normal people. Well, as normal as we all can be. Especially when I'm braless in a butt ugly oversized tee with my mom panties on. The big ones.

"Oh hey, sorry, when Blanche is here we like to wake her up with GnR's Patience," Chris grins at her.

Her eyes dart around a moment before she clears her throat. "Why?"

"Didn't she tell you?" A grin starts to grow on Vic's face, so I punch him in the shoulder, not even rocking the big jerk. "Her real name is Patience. Which is an absolute joke because she doesn't have any - hey!" Vic yells when I charlie horse him and then leap back onto the bed to escape retaliation.

"Oh. Um, yeah, Patience, doesn't really quite suit you I guess." Lovely realizes what she says and turns bright red.

"Got that right," Dom snorts. "Let's head down for breakfast and we can come up with a plan. What do you say, new little sis?"

Lovely's face brightens, and she beams at our brothers while I take in the scene. Jesus, our father's genes are strong. All of Mercy's offspring have thick black hair with not a kink to be found. All of us have his dark eyes and pointed chin. All of us are solidly built. Obviously, it looks better on the boys, who at around 6 ft pull it off. Unfortunately for Mercy's daughters, the tallest tops out at around 5'5, making us short and sturdy.

"Get eyes for Christmas, *Patience*?" Dom asks with a smirk and then runs out of the room, the other two following behind him, cackling like loons.

"You know, people outside of the Keep are not at all like I imagined," Lovely says, a smile playing on her lips before shaking her head wistfully before she too follows them downstairs.

Flopping back on my bed, I check my phone messages to make sure that everything is all good at home. Niko sends me a pic of the little kids dressed and ready for school and I blink my eyes to clear the tears. I know in my head I should be there with them, but in my heart I know what I do, saving people like Lovely, is important. My kids understand that sometimes mommy needs to help people, but sometimes mommy feels guilty about that.

A message from Niko vibrates the phone in my hand. I glance at it and then bark out a laugh.

We're fine. Stop being a pussy, suck it up, and get back to work.

Following my eldest's orders, I throw on some clothes and head downstairs to find Lovely holding her baby, staring as our brothers work together to make pancakes and bacon.

"You good?" I ask as I plop down at the table beside her.

"It's like watching three unicorns. I've never seen men in the kitchen before," she whispers back in awe.

"We kinda had to learn when Blanche refused to feed us anymore," Vic shrugs.

Lovely turns to me, wide-eyed. "Why would you refuse to feed them?"

The boys snort before Chris answers her. "When the Prophet banished us, we had nowhere to go, but we wrangled a ride from a car salesman relocating a vehicle. He dropped us off at the diner here, and the first person we met was a tough old lady named Blanche. After we found jobs, we ate all our meals at the diner."

"Until Blanche kicked us out, telling us she didn't want us to die of heart attacks in her diner. After that, we had to learn to feed ourselves," Dom finishes.

Lovely's eyes bounce around as the boys continue cooking and finishing each other's sentences.

"Um, why were you banished?" Lovely asks, then realizing she asked something that could be misconstrued as overly personal, she lowers her gaze, head down.

"Hey, you can ask us anything you like. We're family, remember?" Vic says gently, waiting for Lovely to raise her head and look at him before smiling at her.

"Lovely, have you ever noticed that the men with the largest number of wives are all old fuckers?" Dom asks as he scrambles the eggs in the pan he's manning.

Lovely's brows pinch before she nods. "That's because they're the council members, remember?"

"Or, stay with me sis, they are making up the rules. The men with the most power get the women, the others get what they are given, which don't get me wrong, a lovely, willing wife and children is what everyone should want. But for guys like us? From the family line, young, virile, handso- ow!" I cuff my brother round the head to get him back on track, "Harpy," he hisses at me. "As I was saying, we are a threat to the council. As Mercy's eldest sons, it would be natural for at least one of us to take the mantle when he's elderly, infirm or deceased. Hell, if we really wanted to, we could have challenged him to stand down. The threat was too great, so instead, he turned us out onto the streets, to fend for ourselves in a world we knew nothing about."

"That must have been very, very scary," Lovely whispers, her eyes welling up. I thank whoever is listening that Lovely managed to get out of there. This woman is exactly what her name means. Royal would have destroyed her if she had stayed.

"It was. That's why we do what we do. We take in the young men who are cast out of the Keep for nothing more than being of age and wanting a wife. Blanche goes in and collects women such as yourself, then she brings you to us and we take over." Chris answers, working in perfect rhythm with Dom and Vic as they plate up our breakfasts.

"When I left Eden's Keep I was lucky enough to have been in contact with our brothers. I knew I would never survive in the outside world, pregnant and alone. The boys came and got me, and taught me everything I would need to live out here. Blanche, the wonderful woman from the diner, she taught me to thrive." I say with a big grin, digging into my eggs. Vic always cooks them to perfection.

"Yup, Patience's first night as a free woman we introduced her to Blanche. The two grumpiest women in the world fell in love over bitching about us," Dom grumbles.

"Fell in love is right. Loved her so much I stole her name," I add, wiggling my brows at Lovely.

She looks down at the tiny bundle in her arms, running a finger over her little brow, and down her button nose. She straightens her shoulders and looks up at me.

"You asked me last night what her name was. I'd like to name her after the aunt that saved her."

"*Patience*? Look, it didn't work out the last time. Maybe think of another name, Lovely," Chris says, his eyes darting to me, probably waiting for a nut punch.

"Ew no, not Patience. I meant Blanche. Blanche is the name of a strong woman. I want my baby to be strong and tough and not put up with any poop," she says, chin tipped in defiance.

"Baby Blanche is it. But I'm gonna call her Bee because I

already have enough Blanches in my life." Vic says, smiling down at the baby as he places a glass of juice in front of Lovely.

"Is that OK with you?" Lovely asks me, her fork hovering over her breakfast.

I take in my new sister and her infant. She had enough guts to realize that Royal is a piece of shit and wanted a better life. Going so far as to beg me to take her girl if I couldn't take both of them. She's a lot stronger than she seems and she wants her baby to grow up with the name of two very rough, crotchety women. Who am I to stop her?

"It's OK with me. It's a tough name for a tough little girl." I nod, noticing all my brothers smiling softly at the exchange. In return, I flip the bird.

"Baby Blanche, Bee, you're going to grow up strong, and tough and kind," Lovely's eyes flick to mine, and she smiles.

"Not once, not even in the Keep, have I ever heard Blanche referred to as 'kind'," Chris says, almost inhaling his breakfast. That's what happens when you grow up with two older brothers.

All four of us are a year apart, and if my mother was still alive I would give her a medal. That poor woman would have been pregnant for five years straight. I shiver at the thought.

"If Blanche wasn't kind, she wouldn't have saved me. Us. If she wasn't kind, she would have left the Keep and never had a second thought about the people in there needing help. Instead, she is out at night meeting women like me, women who need help, saving, and she does it without complaint," she huffs.

"Well, looks like little sister might have some claws," Dom says with a smirk.

Vic nods his head in agreement, "Yup. I was wondering what would push a sweet girl like you to leave. I see it now. You're not that much different from our Blanche here."

"Stick with us, kid. You'll be a badass in no time," I tell her as our brothers groan about "another one".

Lovely drops her head to look at her daughter, and I can see a little smile playing on her lips.

"Well, I think later on to celebrate your arrival, Lovely, we should take you to the diner. Blanche passed away a few years back, but I'm sure there are other grumpy old women to name yourself after," Chris says, the rest of us nodding in agreement.

"Or you could keep your name," I suggest with a shrug. "I changed mine because Patience never suited me and I wanted nothing to remind me of that place. You, though, I think you suit your name."

A thoughtful look crosses her face before she looks around the table. "Did you all change your names?"

"Nah. We aren't that imaginative. Victory, Wisdom and Christian," Vic answers, pointing to himself and then our brothers.

Lovely bursts into giggles, a little snort escaping before a belly laugh rips out of her, jostling her baby.

"Give me that baby before you deafen her, sheesh!" Dom says, swooping in to take Bee from Lovely's arms, allowing her to hold her stomach as she laughs more.

She takes a moment to settle, taking deep breaths before looking up at us. "Sorry, I'm sorry. I just never really thought how silly our virtue names sounded until now." She wipes a tear from the corner of her eye.

"Well, get used to it little sister, a couple of days in the real world and you'll realize how nuts the Keep really is, and you'll vow never, ever to go back." I smile at her, knowing that this is the first day of the rest of her life. And if I have my way, it'll be one hell of a life.

Chapter 3

Tav

"**I** know you said we'd ride together so you could do your sponsor duty and all that, but does that include talking? Because it's been half an hour and you haven't said a thing," I side eye Tank to make sure he's awake. Maybe he fell asleep and I'm talking to myself.

Instead, he grunts in reply. "I'm working through my thoughts."

Whipping my head in his direction, I stare for a quick minute before getting my eyes back on the road. "You work through your thoughts? Like, you just don't say them as they come to you?"

"No."

"Why not?"

"Because my last name isn't Tombs," he says drily.

"Hmph."

"Just trying to figure out where you fit into the chaos. You're open, more outgoing –"

"– Ana says I'm a golden retriever."

Tank huffs out a breath before tipping his head side to side. "Actually, that's the perfect description for you. Just trying to figure out how that works."

Swallowing, I think about my family. He's not wrong, I'm not high strung like Gus, definitely more fucking normal than Jules, he's weird. And, well, Dayz is the baby and the only girl, so she's spoiled.

"I spent a lot of time with my mom growing up. Gus would do shit with our dad. Jules liked being alone, and Dayz and Pops are tight. Pops is my dad's dad. Mom was totally normal."

"That why you like the MILFs?"

I'm already shaking my head, knowing the question was coming. People always assume I like MILFs because I lost my mom when I was young. That's not it. I don't need to be mothered.

"My favorite childhood memories are of family. All of us together playing football or having a picnic. Going on holiday, whatever. I loved being a part of that. When Mom and Dad died, it became about survival, I guess. Just making it through the day. When I got out of college, I met a woman with a kid. Never thought I'd want to be with a mom, but well, she changed my thinking. Just because a woman has a child doesn't make her less desirable or whatever. She was hot as hell and sometimes we spent time with her little boy. I liked it. Being part of their little family." I shrug. "But I've dated women with kids, and women without kids. Women older than me or younger. It doesn't matter. Especially now I've found Blanche."

Tank looks at me thoughtfully for a moment. "You're gone for her, huh?"

"What's not to go for? She's beautiful and caring and thoughtful –"

"A stone cold killer on a mission to murder her uncle -"

"Yeah. Perfect."

He shakes his head and then indicates a dirt road that I would have missed if I wasn't looking for it. Following the twists and turns, driving further into a wooded area, we come to a stop at a cozy little log cabin. It's not cold out, but I can see puffs of smoke coming out of the chimney.

An older man with a face like a screwed up fist steps onto the porch. Dungarees without a top underneath, unlaced boots, and a shotgun pointed directly at us.

Tank winds his window down and holds his hands out, showing that we aren't armed. He brings one hand in to flick the door handle and then steps out slowly. As soon as the old man sees who it is a smile breaks out, changing the whole look of his face.

"Tank, you big bastard! What the hell are ya doing in that cage, huh? Your ass is too big for that little dinky car," He throws his head back and lets out a rusty laugh.

Tank indicates I get out of the vehicle, so I follow his lead and do exactly as he did.

"I've brought the prospect I've sponsored. He can do all the heavy lifting," Tank smiles at the old man who squints at me before shrugging and waving me closer.

"Henderson. Name and rank, son."

"Oh, no rank, I'm afraid." I firmly shake his old leathery hand and let my smile grow when he squints even harder at me.

"You look familiar. Have I kicked your ass in the past?"

My head tips back as I bark out a laugh. "No sir, I think I'd remember an ass kicking from you."

He grins and then waves at us to follow as he stomps along

the porch, heading for the back of the cabin.

"Here she is, boys, all packed up, ready to wet the whistles of the old and infirm." He waggles his bushy white eyebrows.

I briefly wonder if I should get a bottle for Pops and then very quickly stop wondering. That would be a terrible idea.

"Your face is pissing me off, kid. I know I know you from somewhere, but I can't put my finger on it. What did you say your name was?"

Tank's eyes dart between the two of us.

"Everyone calls me Tav, but my full name is Octavius Tombs."

"Huh! That's it!" He snaps his fingers and points finger guns at me. "Fucking knew you looked familiar. You're one of Sid's, huh?"

I chuckle at his enthusiasm. "Yeah, he's my Pops."

"That's right. I remember when that unfortunate business happened. How's he doing? Getting on well?"

I lift the side of the crate that Tank indicated and help him move it to the SUV, all while answering Henderson's questions.

"He's doing great. Found himself a lady he likes spending time with. He's also been hanging around the MC. He likes it."

"Well, I never pegged him for an MC type of guy," Henderson mutters, stubble rasping under his hand as he rubs his chin. "But if he's happy, then good for him."

Tank and I lift the case into the back of the SUV and slam the door shut. Henderson leads us back to his porch where some glasses and a pitcher of lemonade have been set up.

"Thanks, babe!" He yells through the open door before sitting and waving his hand at us to follow. "You know, I have never met a man who had as much shit thrown at him as Sid Tombs and come out the other side unscathed. He's a rare man, your pops. He still vicious?"

I choke on my lemonade as the mouthful goes down the wrong hole, spluttering for a moment while Tank sips his all dainty like.

"Sorry, sir, I was not expecting that question." I wheeze, trying to clear the tickle in the back of my throat. "But ah, yes, he is still vicious."

"That's the understatement of the century," Tank says under his breath before taking another pull of his lemonade.

"Ooh do tell. He was one of the best interrogators I'd ever seen. Ruthless, that man. Who's he been working on? They deserve it?" He leans forward, eyes glinting.

When I diligently read the MC bylaws, it clearly stated that we were abiding by Fight Club rules. You don't talk about it. This ole boy seems to want to break that rule and get us to spill. Frowning, I squint at Tank. Maybe this is a setup to fuck with me. Before I can figure out my next move, he answers for me.

"No names or anything, but we've had a human trafficking issue. And a rival MC issue. And falsely accused of murder issue."

"What Tank's saying is we got a lot of issues," I add, ignoring Tank's glare in my direction.

"All I can say is that Pops isn't the only one in the Tombs family capable of making a man spill his guts. Both figuratively and literally," Tank offers.

"Oh, is it you, kid? He teach you everything he knows?" There's a gleam in his eye as he looks at me and I really would like to please him, but I have to give Dayz props.

"Um, no. My sister."

His white brows pull low, and he looks confused before he brightens. "That little tiny thing? Lots of hair with the nose of a bloodhound?"

I try to stifle my laugh, but Tank's slips out. "Yes, sir. That's the one."

"Huh. I remember Sid bringing her to visit when she was a wee dot of a thing. Was obsessed with my pot still. Asked if a grown man could fit in it and how long it would take to boil skin and meat off the bones. Makes a shit ton more sense now." We all nod in unison at his statement because what more is there to say?

We chew the fat a little, finish up our refreshments, say our goodbyes, and hit the road to do our deliveries.

During the day, I meet Old Man Whitlock, who again knows Pops. Almost all the men we visit along the way home know Pops. It's quite touching that they all remember him fondly, even if his "techniques" made a couple of them vomit. Seems the grand-apple didn't fall too far from the tree after all.

Parking the SUV in the compound lot, I have to admit I have a little bounce in my step. The day went well. I learned Tank doesn't like spiders, and I met some very cool old boys who have requested I always do their run, so I feel like I'm nailing this shit.

"Prospect," Marx's muffled voice calls out from his office.

"Yeah, Pres?"

"Good work today. Tank said the old boys loved you. It'll be your run now."

I try to hide my smile. "Yes, sir."

"Good. Now go relieve Takoda on bar. After that, get to work making that scary little woman your Ol Lady. We need to find out where the fuck Hammer is hiding."

"Yes, Pres!"

Blanche

After talking with Lovely after breakfast, I need some space to think about my next moves. I slip out of the house and wander through the backyard, following the path through the trees to the back shed. I unlatch the door and step inside.

The outside looks like a piece of crap, the inside however has a set up wildlife places would kill to have. The inside is warm and damp. There are rocks dotted around, and a clear roof, allowing the gators to sunbathe and relax. A large lagoon pool area in the center flows out to the waterways behind the property. The boys have a large fenced outdoor area where visitors come to watch them with the gators between tours. The boys have always been industrious and hardworking. Even with their sheltered upbringing they've managed to carve out a life for themselves running swamp tours which doubles as a way to transport the women I pick up from the Keep. Eden's Keep doesn't care about the boys they discard, but the girls and women are a different story. They come looking.

"Hellooooo my baby!" I coo at the gator that is sunning himself.

He lazily turns his head before sliding off the rock he was on. He slowly walks toward me and stops at my feet so I can bend down and run a hand over his bumpy, rough flesh.

"Figured we'd find you out here while we did all the hard work tidying the kitchen," Chris says from behind me.

"Yeah, yeah, I was chatting to Lovely. I now have a list of names of the women complicit in Royal's bullshittery," I frown down at Smiley, my fingers running over the ridges on his skin, calming me slightly.

"I know you want to do this on your own sis, but we can help. We can do it just as well as you can," Dom says, leaning down to give Smiley a scritch before moving back.

"I know, but I want to see Mercy's face when he finds out it was me who brought the whole lot crashing down. Me."

My brother's nod and my attention is pulled away when I stumble slightly, Smiley bumping me with his large, rough head, upset that I'm not giving him my full attention. Squatting down, gently grasping under his chin, I give him a scritch on the smoother skin there.

"Aw Smiley baby, mommy missed you! Yes, she did! Yes, she did!"

"It's always fucking weird when they do that," Vic whispers in the background.

"Don't you listen to him Smiley, he's just jealous, yes he is!"

Smiley was another of my rescues. I happened across him as a baby, teeny tiny, and some fucker had pulled his teeth. Without them he wouldn't survive for long, so I brought him home and hand fed him. It was a wild time having two busy kids and a gator to look after, but we did it. Since then, my brothers have been taking care of him along with a small number of rescue gators.

"Now would be a good time to break it to her, brothers."

Spinning at Chris's comment, I stand to my full height, squinting at them. "Tell me what?"

"You're going to be a grandmomma!" they yell in unison.

"What!" I screech before getting down beside Smiley and giving him more love.

"Yeah, the sly old dog must have been spending time with Gretchen. The other males are too old or too young, so congrats, Granny," Dom smirks, and I flip the bird at him.

Making smoochy noises to my gator I give him one more scritch before letting him wander back to his rock.

"You do know that one day he'll eat your face off, right?"

"Don't be silly. He loves me. You guys, though, he'd totally eat yours." I snort as they roll their eyes and get to organizing food for the pack. "OK I have to get going, but first I've left an envelope for you with funds for Lovely," I hold my hand up to stop the bitching. "You need to take her shopping. She can't keep walking around in that hideous floor length dress and running shoes."

Chris lets out a sigh. "She has a point."

"Of course I damn well do. She and the baby will need normal people clothes. Is she going to stay here with ya'll?"

"We want to keep her with us, get to know her, but because Royal wants little Bee we're going to send her north. Not saying exactly where, the fewer people that know, the better." Vic says, a frown on his face. Of all my brothers, he's the one who struggles the most with what my father and his brother have created. Royal wanting to sell his own child is fucking with Vic big time. Last night I had to talk him down from going after Royal himself.

"North? Is Diligence Martin still the contact?"

"Yep. Still doing the Lord's work. Relocating people our father doesn't need or want in his flock any more. Fucker," Dom says kicking a rock into the pool.

I move closer to my brother, leaning my head on his shoulder. No words need to be spoken. The boys were 16, 17, and 18 when our father put them out. Old enough to know how to work hard, but so sheltered that I know that first year really messed with them. I was so freaking lucky that they knew how the world worked by the time I needed them. Being 19 and pregnant is hard enough. Being 19, pregnant and knowing nothing of the outside world was hell. Although I count my blessings. From what I've heard from some of the women we've rescued, the legal age ceased to mean anything within the Keep after I left. A year ago we helped a 13-year-old pregnant with my uncle's baby. At least Lovely made it to legal age before he sunk his hooks into her.

"We've got this squirt. We'll make sure our new sister and Baby Blanche find a good place to settle into their new lives. We'll keep in touch with her, but we need to keep her contact circle small until the threat is gone. In the meantime, you need to get back to your family." Dom turns his head and drops a kiss to the top of my head.

Turning, Chris and Vic pull me into a group hug, Dom joining us and they squeeze as hard as they can before someone puts their smelly pit in my face, turning our hug into a shoving match.

Breaking free, I wipe my face and give them all kisses.

"Be safe, sis. Call us if you need us."

"Promise."

Chapter 4

By the time I quickly freshen up after mine and Tank's very successful run and step into the common room, the Tombs have arrived. It's only been a matter of months that Chewy has been Rhodie's Ol Lady and yet I can't remember where the hell we hung out before we all became fixtures around the clubhouse. Shit, Pops is here all the time pissing people off and no one seems to mind. That's one reason I wanted to join, the ease with which these men accepted my family. I mean, shit, they're a lot.

"Hey man, I've got this. Go do what you gotta do, brother." I hold my fist out to Takoda and move up behind the bar, ignoring my family for the interim. I have a job to do and I know they'll step up to give me shit sooner or later, anyway.

"Thanks man," he says, bumping my fist with his before moving aside.

"Anything I need to know?"

"Yeah, there's a shit ton of ginger ale in the fridge for the pregnant women. Oh, and Pops has been barred from cornhole."

"What the fuck? It's only been here for two days! How the hell did he get banned so quickly?"

Takoda shrugs his broad shoulders. He's shorter than a lot of the brothers, but he's built like a brick shithouse. "I think he was hustling the brothers again. How the hell is he good at every game he plays?"

"The Devil is always good at everything he plays. It helps him steal souls," Judge says drily, stepping up to the bar.

Tank and Judge run the club's towing business, Devil's Big Tow. He's big and bald and even quieter than Tank.

"Hey! That's my grandpa you're talking about! He's not the devil. He's probably just a henchman or something,"

Judge smirks at my comeback and gives me a chin tip when I slide his beer to him. "Prospect," he says as before he wanders off.

"I'll leave you to it. I'm off to the gym to get kicked in the nuts by Remy," Takoda says with a wince before giving me a slap on the shoulder and heading off.

A few months back, Remy came to the clubhouse to learn how to hack from Wire and my sister. In the end she fell in love with her online best friend, became an Ol Lady, ditched her job as a librarian and now helps run self-defense classes at the Club's new gym. Dex, who left Death Riders with Savage, runs the gym. Us prospects have to do shifts there now and then. I like it; I like watching the kids who have it rough gain confidence in themselves.

I get to work cleaning the bartop and I can feel I'm being descended upon by my relatives. I know this. I have a sixth sense for this stuff. Being the youngest brother, you gain extra senses, especially the ones that tell you that your brothers are going to give you shit.

"Little brother, I never took you for a catcher," Jules' ugly face smirks at me as I glare at him.

"Pops!" I say in not quite a whiney voice. But it's borderline.

"Hey kid, you can't blame me. When you find out your grandson may have a very close relationship with his MC sponsor, you tell everyone. I can't keep that shit to myself," Pops says in the innocent voice he uses when he's causing shit.

"Well, I'll have you all know that I am not, nor have I ever been, homosexual. Even though there is absolutely nothing wrong with people being attracted to the same sex," I tell Jules and Pops, and then repeat myself when Gus, Ana, and Chewy join the group.

"Ah, cool, thanks for that, Tav. Now that that's out of the way, can you please ginger ale me and Nat?" Ana asks, smiling up at me.

"Of course I can, my very favorite family member," I answer her and get busy.

"I have no idea what he's on about. Does anyone else know?" Chewy asks no one in particular.

"I want to know why the hell you're all here and not at work. Tav, you're fine, but what about the rest of you fuckers? You know the office closes at 5pm, right?" Gus grumbles.

We all look at the Jim Beam themed clock behind the bar and see that it's not even 4pm.

"I came to collect Pops," Jules answers, quick off the mark.

"I came because I was horny," Dayz answers.

"Rhodie doesn't finish work til 5," Gus points out.

"Oh, and I had something I was working on in the Rev Room," she answers, her eyes huge, staring right at Gus, which means she is up to no good. It's Dayz's only tell when she has a secret. Instead of avoiding eye contact like a normal person, she maintains it.

"Tuesday, what are you up to?"

"Nothing,"

"I'll tell Marx," Gus goads.

"Tell Marx what?"

"Ah shit," Dayz mumbles under her breath, before turning to stare at Marx.

"Why the hell are you looking at me like that?"

"No reason, bestie," she answers in her slightly monotone voice, making the sustained eye contact even odder.

"Chewy, tell me right the fuck now what you're up to." He frowns down at her and again I marvel at how fucking oblivious she is to things. Any other person in the clubhouse would have shit themselves if they were the target of that look.

"I may have accidentally bought too much of something online. But I'm taking care of it," she says really quickly on a single breath, still staring up at Marx.

"What did you buy?"

"Yeah, kid, what did you buy? Something for the Rev Room? Have you had a new idea?" Pops asks, abandoning the beer I handed him and excitedly standing in front of his granddaughter, inserting himself between Dayz and Marx. The Pres moves him to the side so he can keep eyeballing my sister.

"Wellll, it wasn't originally for the Rev Room. I had a cool idea for little party favors for my friends cos the girl gang will throw baby showers for the preggos at some stage-"

"Did she just refer to me and Nat as preggos?" Ana asks, knowing full well Dayz did.

"- so I may have ordered some fun penis favors."

"Wait, why would you hand out penis favors at a baby

shower?" Rider asks out of nowhere. That's when I look up and, as usual, see the club brothers gathered for another Chewy Show.

"Well, the babies could have penises," Chewy answers, as if that makes sense. I mean, it kinda does. The babies could be born with dicks.

"OK, so you have penis favors. What's the issue?" Marx gruffly asks.

Chewy looks around the building, as if the framing is incredibly interesting.

"Chewy!" Marx barks.

"OK, OK, sheesh. Cool your jets, big guy, you'll give yourself a heart attack."

"What. Did. You. Do?"

"I accidentally ordered the wrong size and have been delivered 100 anatomically correct silicone dicks," she says with a completely straight face.

"That's a lot of party favors, girl," Nat says with a laugh.

"Wait, when you say anatomically correct..." Rider starts off,

"Yes, they are all average sized male dildos in every ethnicity you can think of. I have white dongs, black dongs - they're larger, of course, I have-"

"Enough! You need to get rid of them. I do not want, or need, 100 human-sized dicks all over my compound Chewy! Sort it out!" Marx says before taking a breath, closing his eyes and shaking his head. He opens his mouth, closes it, and then heads into his office.

"You know, I will never get used to how this place works," Dex says, before taking a swig of his beer.

"Me neither. Everyone looks so badass, and then the scary little lady orders 100 dildos," Flack, Remy's father, adds.

The Chewy Show always draws a crowd, especially with the brothers all returning home from work. The best part is no one teases her about it. They just accept that weird shit happens when Chewy is involved.

"Why the fuck is everyone crowded around my girl?" Rhodie barks as he pushes Fox and Nitro out of the way, trying to get to his Ol Lady.

"Rhodie!" she squeals before jumping up and kissing him like he's been away at war, essentially grossing everyone out. She pulls her lips off him, making a gross wet sound that makes me want to barf.

"My package arrived today, but it was incorrect. I have 100 dicks in the Rev Room. Want to help me with them?"

Rhodie pulls back, looking slightly concerned, "Will any of them go near my ass?"

"Fuck's sake, why are they like this?" I hear grumbled from somewhere in the crowd. I think it was Sniper.

"No! Of course not. I'll be sending most of them back. But I might keep a couple in the Rev Room for when we have guests," she says, wiggling her brows up and down.

"No guests, Chewy!" Marx's voice yells from his office. "This is a no torture, no murder zone til we get that Officer Martin fucker off our asses!"

"I really don't feel like rubber dongs are torture," Chewy grumbles under her breath.

"Depends how you use them. Some of them are quite heavy. I bet you could bludgeon someone with one of those things." Nat offers, everyone slowly turning to look at her. "What?" she asks, all innocent like.

"I like the way you think! Baby, put me down. One of you preggos go get Remy and meet me out in the Rev Room. We have girl shit to do." Chewy clicks her fingers and Rhodie lets her slide down his body while Ana and Nat roll their eyes and then waddle their way down the hall to get the other girl gang member.

"I remember when we didn't have any women in the club-house. Things were a lot simpler back then," Rider remarks sadly, shaking his head.

"What the hell are you on about? Before them, we had the club girls," Fox points out.

"They don't count. They did whatever we wanted them to do. These ones don't at all. If you ask them to do something, they go all wild on you and threaten your balls," Rider says with a shudder.

The brothers all grumble in agreement, dispersing to what-ever it was they were doing before Chewy announced her shipment of dicks. I see Pops edging his way to the cornhole board before Tank and Judge silently shake their heads at him. His shoulders slump a little before his head snaps up, and so do both middle fingers.

Laughing to myself, I go back to checking to make sure all the brothers' drinks are topped up, Savage indicating the need for a refill.

"I saw what your woman did to her cousin, you know," he says, taking a long draw of his beer.

"Yeah? What of it?" I answer in a measured voice. I know I'm meant to respect him, given I'm a prospect and all, but I won't have him talk bad about Blanche.

He studies my face a moment before smirking. "She'll fit in well with the rest of the girl gang. If you can convince her to be your girl, of course." The smug bastard winks at me before wandering off to join Sniper and Flack at the pool table.

After bar duty finishes, I step out into the parking lot stretching my arms overhead. Monday bar duty always finishes early, the brothers liking to turn in early for work the next day. We may be bikers, but we all have jobs and businesses that need to be run.

I'm too wired to turn in just yet. Tomorrow I need to see Blanche and break it to her that I claimed her. It's going to take all the negotiation skills I have to leave her place with my balls intact, so I'm going to need to come up with a plan. Which means I need some time to empty my mind.

Striding over to my bike, one I bought in the early days of Tombs Security, I straddle her and sink into the leather. She's a classic Harley softail, and I only got her because I had seen some guys riding in a group through downtown Rose Grove and thought they looked so fucking cool. As a witness on the sidewalk watching them all travel as one, it was awe-inspiring. Since I've been prospecting I've been on short runs with a brother or two, mainly doing business stuff, dropping off payroll, that sort of thing, but I know that Flack is organizing a Poker Run to raise funds for the local library so the whole club will ride as one, and I can't wait.

Starting my girl, I let the vibrations roll through my body before shaking out my arms, gripping my handles and rolling toward the main gates. Jimmy is on gate duty and I tip my chin at him as I get closer. The sound of the bike rumbling gets exponentially louder, and as I look to my left, Tank gives me a single nod before he roars out of the gates, me hot on his heels. All the worries of how I'm going to break it to Blanche that I claimed her melt away as the road stretches out before me.

Blanche

Dropping into a seat at the reasonably tidy dining table, I flip open the top of my laptop and wait for it to wake up. My quick trip to Louisiana put me a little behind, but seeing the boys and rescuing Lovely and Baby Blanche made it all worth it. Now to get back to my actual job, catching cheaters.

I have six active cases at the moment, all of them medium ugly men with varying degrees of hair loss and bellies. It will never cease to amaze me how married middle-aged men will jump into the first young, gold digging vagina that shows them any attention while their much hotter wives are working, looking after the home and the kids. Case in point, Wayne Cross; the supermarket manager who is unimaginatively having an affair with Louise, the much younger check out operator. Why? I have no idea, but I know it's not for his looks. I shudder to myself as I watch him on the home camera his wife Lacey asked me to set up.

Most cheaters book a seedy motel room. Not Wayne. He's cheap, so he brings her to the house he shares with his wife and bangs her in the walk-in closet. I watch as they make their way to the bedroom, and I swear I see the bored look on Louise's face as he mauls her neck.

The doorbell rings at the same time my phone vibrates with the incoming video. Glancing at the screen, my stomach flutters a little when I notice that my unannounced visitor is the man that has plagued my dreams for months now. Tav Tombs. Standing in my doorway. Judging by his outfit, he must have been in the office today. I know that some days he works at the MC compound. On those days he wears his leather cut. Not today, though. Sure, the camera distorts him a little, but there is no denying his broad shoulders in his t-shirt with the Tombs Security logo on the front. His slim waist tapering down the thick thighs encased in tactical pants. If I zoom in and squint, I can almost see the large bulge between those thick thighs.

The doorbell sounds again, snapping me out of my ogling. Get it together Blanche! Standing, I shake out my hands, arms and legs, and make my way to the door. Swinging it open, I'm met with Tav frowning at me.

"What's with the face?"

"Why did you open the door?"

What? Tipping my head at him, my brows pull down in a mirror of his own face. "You rang the bell. I opened the door. It's kinda how this thing works."

"You should have spoken to me through the camera. Make sure that it really was me."

"Why would I do that when I saw it was you?"

"But how could you be sure it was me?" He presses hands out as if trying to get me to see his point.

"Tav, I know what you look like. From all angles and in all positions."

A small smile grows on his lips and he runs his gaze up and down my body. My nipples pucker, and I know I'm in dangerous territory. It's the only territory I'm ever in when it comes to this man. The slight clenching in my underwear reminds me I'm not doing this right now. No men. I need to concentrate on my kids, my job and Eden's Keep.

"That you have, Pixie," he answers me, his voice husky before he coughs to clear it. "I'm not here for that. I just wanted to make sure you're all good."

So. Goddamn. Thoughtful. I may not want a man, but I enjoy

Tav's company, which is why I invite him in. His large body follows me down my hall into my open-plan kitchen dining.

"Take a seat and you can let me know how the kids went the other night. Oh, and don't touch Elio's stuff, he's teaching us to play a game he made up," I point where I want him to sit, away from the different Lego pieces Elio has in some type of grid pattern and away from my laptop and files. I need to keep client privilege and all that jazz. Once my investigation is over and his wife has taken him to the cleaners, I'll then yell it from the rooftops if anyone asks my opinion on Wayne Cross. But until then, it's a no-go zone.

"The kids were fine. The little ones were their usual selves. Niko and Sage were a little more wary, but that makes sense because of their age and what you do." He nods at me, not in the least concerned about what I do. "Niko, of course, was protective of you, and um, I don't think he's happy with me."

I suck in a breath and stare at Tav who is trying very hard to avoid eye contact. "What. Happened?" I don't want to come out and ask what he did, because I know my son, and no matter how responsible and grown up he can be, he's also 17 years old and can be a bit of an ass hat.

Before Tav can answer the door handle rattles and then little feet pound on the wooden floor until they hit where I'm sitting.

"Tav!" Cove yells as she launches herself into his arms, where he catches her. Of course.

Elio follows close behind, choosing to climb onto the lap that Cove isn't sitting on, quietly saying his hello.

"You know guys, Tav isn't a climbing frame," I say drily as I stand to get their afternoon snack prepared. If I don't feed them a little something now, they will absolutely riot later.

"They're fine, Pixie. We're old buddies, huh guys?"

They both nod enthusiastically and then talk over each other to tell him what they did at school today. I watch their interaction as I peel, core, and quarter apples for them. They've been like this with Tav from the very first moment they met him. There's just something ... easy about the man. I can't imagine anyone not liking him. Women included.

The number of women I'd overhear at the conference talking about how hot he was and how they had tried to get his number and he would rebuff them gently was in the tens. Which is loads for a security conference given most of the people there are of the male variety. Anyway, tens of beautiful women and to think he ended up with me that night is crazy. So crazy, in fact, that even before I set out on this journey to rid the earth of the Landry cult, I had tried to cut it off. Tav was not convinced. He's spent every day since that morning after our tryst wishing me a good morning and a good night. He brings me little things that he says reminds him of me and if I'm honest with myself, I was well on my way to getting rid of my "No relationships" rule. Then my father fell ill. I thought I had more time to put my plan into place. I want him to know that it's me dismantling his dream. I want him alive while I kill the evil, one by one, leaving him for last.

"Mom? Did you hear?" Cove's sweet voice asks, and I don't have the heart to tell her I wasn't really listening.

"What was that, baby?"

"Can Tav stay for dinner?" She pleads, her eyes huge in her face, her pigtails wonky from her day at kindergarten.

Looking at her brother, I notice he's still impeccably dressed. It's hard to believe they are the same age. Elio spends all day in the same kindergarten class as his sister and somehow gets nowhere near as messy.

"Baby, I haven't even decided what we're having," I stand at the counter, paring knife in hand as I try to think what we have in the fridge and pantry to whip up.

"Pixie, let me take care of this. You've had a busy 48 hours. I know that as soon as you got home from your trip, you got straight back into work and mom mode. Let me take care of you." He smiles gently at me, then the kids as they cheer in his arms.

Shit. Every time he does things like this, that little wall around my heart gets weaker and weaker.

He wraps one strong arm around both kids on his lap and leans slightly, pulling his phone from his pocket, scowling at it before sliding his thumb over the screen and putting it to his ear.

"Yo?....It's Tuesday. We don't eat dinner together on Tuesday." his eyes flick to mine before he rolls them. I wave my hands trying to get his attention, whispering that if he has dinner plans it's OK. "Well, I have people, so you better put out extra settings..........Yup, yup, you got it......Kbye,"

"Tav! You better not have pressured your family into having us at family dinner! I can order in perfectly fine you know. I don't need you coming in here bossing -"

"Pixie. It's OK. My family wants to meet you, and I want you to meet them. Meet the people that kept the kids safe. Well, some of them."

"You're sure?"

"Um, I think so." his dark brow furrows and his perfect white teeth bite down on his plump bottom lip.

"Taaaav?"

"OK. Maybe I didn't think it through. My family is nuts. Sometimes not in a good way, either."

"I like Chewy. She said it's OK to not like people," Elio says in his soft voice. I look at Tav in question.

"My sister is on the spectrum. So, she's special? Different?"

"Why are you asking me?"

"No clue. Let's just say she's unique. But lovable. And very excited to see Elio again." Tav smiles down at my youngest son before ruffling his hair.

Elio struggles with people, so knowing that two from the same family have him feeling comfortable and happy helps me make my decision.

"OK. I'll let the big kids know. Looks like we're going to dinner," Blowing out a breath, I roll my eyes as all three raise their hands in victory and cheer.

Chapter 5

Tav

"This is a bad idea," I mumble under my breath. I know it is because my ass is starting to feel sweaty. It could be from all the clenching it's doing. How the fuck did Gus walk in there with Ana for the first time? I should have asked him before I jumped in the deep end and got excited about Blanche meeting my people.

"Come on Tav! Let's go inside. I want to see your grandpa. I bet he's really, really old, because you're really old."

I tip my head to look down at Cove's wide eyes pleading up at me.

"I'm younger than your mom,"

The little stinker throws her head back and laughs in my face like I told the funniest joke, Blanche joining in with her.

"Don't look at me like that, Tav Tombs. This was your idea."

"Fine. Just, don't judge me based on their behavior, OK?" I look at the Landry's five pairs of dark eyes staring back, giving me varying degrees of comfort. The little ones are wide-eyed with excitement, Sage's with amusement, Blanche's look slightly nervous before she rolls her eyes and pulls her shoulders back. All while Niko glares at me.

Gripping the little kids' hands tighter, Cove on one side, Elio holding mine and his mom's hands, we step closer to Pops' farmhouse; mine and my siblings' cabins behind us.

"How much longer are you going to take Fuck Knuck - OW! I mean Fudge Knuckle?" Pops' gruff voice calls out as Niko bursts into laughter. Well, I'm glad something makes this kid happy. And also snaps me out of my anxiety as the familiarity wraps itself around me.

"Yeah, yeah, hold your horses! We're coming!"

Leading my new family into Pops' house, we cram in the doorway of the dining room as I make the introductions.

"Blanche, kids, this is my family. That boring looking man is my big brother Gus, and the lovely lady next to him is his wife, Ana. She works for the Bratva."

They both smile and wave politely, and I try to ignore the sharp intake of breath from Blanche and the shocked look on her face when I introduced Ana.

"It's not really the Bratva," Ana says, waving her hand at Blanche, obviously ignoring all the Tombs family heads that snapped in her direction when she said she doesn't work for the Bratva. "What? I'm the secretary," she shrugs and then stuffs a bread roll into her mouth.

"Tamayto, Tomahto Ana. Anyway, that big, mean looking man is-"

"Yes, yes, that's Jules, woo woo. I'm Tuesday. Or Dayz or you can call me by my Ol Lady name, which is Chewy. This is my man Rhodie. We're enforcers. Nice to meet you. Hi Elio!" Chewy punctuates that word vomit by waving at Elio and patting the empty chair next to her.

He looks to his mom who seems a little shocked before she nods her head at him. He drops our hands and beelines his way to Chewy.

"Whoa, I've never seen him do that before," Niko whispers to Sage who nods at him.

"And last but not least, the head of our family, Sid Tombs, and his lady, who is also Ana's mom, Debs."

"Just call me Pops. Pops and Debs. Now let's eat. I could die at any moment, you know."

"Is that because you're really old?" Cove's little voice asks, her brows pinched.

Blanche's eyes are glaring death lasers at Cove in horror, but she needn't as my whole family roars with laughter.

"I like you, wee thing. Why don't you come up and sit next to my old ass? You can keep an eye on me," Pops says, winking at Cove, who smiles widely and races to sit in between Pops and Debs.

It's then that I notice the seating arrangement. Because I've brought the Landry's, Pops has put in the extra table leaves, extending the table from the usual 10 seater to more like a 15 seater. And instead of everyone sitting in their usual places, which would make sense, they've spaced themselves around the table, meaning any extra seating is between them. Sage takes a seat next to Ana, Niko, fittingly next to Jules, Blanche sits on the other side of Elio near Chewy and I'm on the other side of Rhodie, next to Pops, Cove and Debs on the other side. It's weird as hell and now I'm getting paranoid that this is a setup.

Pops starts carving the meat and Debs passes around the side dishes, helping Cove dish up her mac and cheese. The plates make their rounds, and before long our own plates are full and everyone is digging in. Everyone except me. This all seems a little too normal. Chewy is chatting to Elio, Sage is in conversation with Ana and Gus, even Niko and Jules seem to be sharing grunts at each other.

Leaning towards Rhodie, I hiss around his head to catch Pops' attention.

"What's going on?"

HIs head slowly turns toward me, a glint in his eye as he slowly chews his mouthful. "Whatever do you mean, Octavius?"

My head snaps back, shocked he'd call me by my full name when I haven't done anything wrong. Recovering quickly, I lean back again. "You know what I damn -" my eyes flick down to Cove before looking back at Pops. "I mean, darn well mean. What's going on with all this, this, normalness?"

"Oh, thank fuck! I thought I was the only one who thought this was weird," Rhodie rasps under his breath.

"Listen kid, this is the first time your two families are meeting, so we are being our usual hospitable selves. Debs even made brownies," Pops says with pride, but I don't miss Blanche's eyes darting to mine when he mentioned my two families.

"Oh, we're just friends with Tav," Blanche says, staring at me before smiling at my bastard family members around the table.

I hang my head, taking cleansing breaths. I know that I'm going to be exposed at any moment now. The kids and my whole family know that I've claimed Blanche. Everyone at this table knows, except the woman in question.

Looking up, I find Niko staring at me. Not in the angry or suspicious way he normally does. No, this is worse, because this is the look of a kid who knows the shit is going to hit the fan at any moment and he's ready for it. His lips twitch a little and a snort escapes. Frowning, I realize the snort didn't come from him. No, it came from my asshole brother sitting next to him, with a damn near identical look on his ugly face.

"I hate you Julius Marion Tombs," I say to him through clenched teeth.

"Whoa! Your middle name is Marion?" Niko says incredulously.

"Shut it, kid,"

"Excuse me, did you just tell my kid to 'shut it'?" Blanche says calmly. A manner that belies the fire in her eyes and the fact she is now holding the carving knife.

"How the fuck did she get the carving knife when the meat is all the way over there?" Rhodie muses.

I expect Gus to say something, but he's too busy leaning back in his chair, eyes flicking between Jules and Blanche and their standoff.

"See, Elio? People are weird. They get butthurt about all sorts of things that don't matter," Chewy says to Elio matter-of-factly as he nods his dark head and shovels another spoon of mac and cheese into his mouth. That's when I notice his plate is full of mac and cheese and little else.

"Jules! Pull your head in! Yes, Marion is a pansy ass middle name, but it's yours so suck it up and stop enraging my future grandbaby-in-law," Pops growls across the table at him, causing Jules to mumble a not very heart felt "sorry," in Blanche's direction.

She nods at him, still scowling, and slowly puts the carving knife on the table before Pops' words sink in.

"Hold on, Sid. That's a nice sentiment and all but we aren't

Tav's future anything," she says gently.

Pops waves a leathery, wrinkled hand at her. "Psh, course you are. You're his Ol Lady. He claimed you at the club the other night."

Blanche

"You fucking what?!" My head whips around to look at Tav, not even caring that I just swore in front of my kids.

Actually, I admit it, they've heard worse out of me. I watch as Tav, the handsome bastard, swallows a couple of times, his eyes darting around the room, stopping for a moment to glare in Pops' direction before settling on me.

"Um, maybe we should take this somewhere private?"

"Hell no! You, Tav Tombs, are going to do this right now. What the hell did you do?" I know that I have the angry eyes on. That's what the kids call them. And I feel like it's warranted. A man has *claimed* me. As if the shit that I went through in Eden's Keep isn't bad enough, I get out for this shit to happen again. Oh, hell no. "Kids, finish up, we're leaving. Pops, Debs, everyone, thank you for a lovely and interesting evening." I go to stand and realize that my kids are still seated.

"Pixie, take a seat, and let me explain?" Tav says, his whiskey colored eyes pleading with me.

I dart my gaze to Sage and then Niko. They're the eldest. They know the shit I've been through. They know my background and where they came from. I have kept none of it from them.

It's for their safety that they know. My big boy looks around the table before meeting my eyes and giving me a small chin tip. Looking at Sage, she does the same. Looks like I'm staying.

I drop my weight back into my chair with a huff, and then cross my arms over my chest like a petulant teen. "You have 3 minutes to make your case."

He clears his throat, looking around. His slightly unusual sister grins broadly before giving him two thumbs up.

"You know how I feel about you. Shit, everyone knows how I feel about you. I know you have ...reservations. I also know that you have a goal that you wish to achieve. Let me help you. Let me have your back. That's all I want." He runs his hand down his face, rubbing at his jaw. "OK, look. In the Devil's Rose MC bylaws, it states that an Ol Lady is special. It's actually written into their bylaws."

"What does this have to do with you claiming me, Tav?" my voice hard.

"When the kids turned up, you'd been gone for 12 hours. We didn't know where you were or if you were OK. I claimed you so that I would have the whole MC at my back if I needed to ride in and get you. I didn't do it to stifle or own you, but to be your backup if you need it. With you as my Ol Lady, it offers you and your kids a higher level of safety than you or I alone can provide." And there goes another little piece of the wall I had tried so valiantly to put up so Tav wouldn't smash it down.

"I mean, as someone special to Tav you would have had us, anyway." Chewy says with a shrug, her siblings and sister-in-law nodding in agreement. "Although we're not that scary."

"I beg to differ," Ana says drily, Rhodie agreeing with her.

"Why the hell are you agreeing, Shit Stain? You're the fuc- I mean fudging enforcer for the MC. Unless you're agreeing that you aren't as scary as us, in which case, you would be correct. Pussy." Rhodie rolls his eyes at Pops' comment, a smile playing on his lips. "I swear, all I wanted was for my grandbaby to fall in love with one of those Bratva badasses. Now *they* know how to torture."

"You better take that back, old man," Rhodie growls out. "Or I'll swap your dick pills with sleeping pills."

"Jokes on you, asshole. I got the pecker of a teenager!" Pops crows.

"I don't think that's quite the brag you think it is, dear." Debs says, patting Pops' hand while Rhodie's eyes shine with glee.

Looking back at Tav, he holds my gaze, "What do you say, Blanche? Be my Ol Lady?" His face screws up and I know he thinks I'm going to shoot him down. I know I should shoot him down. I look at my littles, then my bigs, then the rest of the table, all waiting for my next move.

I clear my throat. "Do you mind if the kids and I have a quick meeting?" Tav's lips curl up a little and Debs rises, pushing her seat out from the table.

"Follow me," she smiles gently and tells Elio and Cove that we're just going for a quick family chat and when we get back she'll have dessert ready.

I follow her down the hall with my teens flanking me on either side and I realize that these two are almost adults.

"Here you go, make yourselves at home and I'll see you in a bit," Debs winks at the kids and moves to leave the room, not before laying her hand on my shoulder and giving it a squeeze. "Give him a chance, *e hoa*. He needs this as much as you do." She pats my shoulder and then leaves, pulling the door closed behind her.

"OK, listen up team. What do we think?" I ask the room. My two five-year-olds are sitting on the couch, feet sticking straight out.

"I like Chewy," this from Elio. "She likes playing my game with me. She's good."

Tipping my head, I look at the big kids. They both frown at their brother, then back to me, shrugging. Elio's game has been on our dining table for weeks. None of us can understand the rules or how it works, and he's getting so frustrated that we can't figure it out.

"Well, there's one upside to accepting, Mom," Sage puts forward. We all know how hard it is for Elio sometimes.

"I love Tav and Pops and Debs and Gus and Chewy and the growly man and the other growly man and the lady with the fat belly,"

"Ana isn't fat, she's having a baby, Cove," Niko says with a little smile at his baby sister.

"A baby? Whoa," she breathes out.

"Niko, Sage?"

Niko blows out a breath. "I don't like that he claimed you, but I think it means something different to what it means in... there."

"Yeah, Mom. This way someone has your back. I didn't like it when you didn't come home. I couldn't sleep. I need you to be safe and if you have to become a biker's Ol Lady to do that, then I want you to do it," Sage tells me, her voice wobbling a little.

Shit. I'm on this mission because it will make the world a better place, but I don't want my choice to ruin my kids' lives. I try to keep both sides of my life separate. This is the first time it hasn't worked out as planned.

"I hate to say this but, he seems like a good guy." Niko says with a grimace. I let out a snort because I know how hard that would have been for him.

Niko has been overprotective of me since he was a little boy. For the first few years of his life, we were on the run from Royal, using the networks my brothers put in place. Royal caught up to us three times, and all three times he tried to take Niko with him. The very last time there was a hell of a fight, Niko witnessed the whole thing and has never forgiven him. That was when I decided it was time to fight back. Eden's Keep hates anything to do with law enforcement. They want to draw as little attention as possible to themselves, so the restraining order I slapped on Royal, combined with my threat of going to the media, had him backing off. After that I moved to Rose Grove, joined my brothers' network and have been rescuing people ever since.

"Just, lay down the rules. You're your own woman. You don't take orders from men." Sage parrots the words I told her when she started dating.

"Well, looks like you lot are gonna see me on the back of a bike," I snort at the mental vision.

"Cringe, Mom."

I turn to open the door and find the surprised faces of Tav and his family, minus the in-laws, before they look everywhere but at me.

"So we're thinking of going with a light floral wallpaper for this hall," Pops says waving his arm around the hallway as the others "hmmmm" and "ahhhhh" and nod. Well, Tav and Gus play along. Jules stands like a statue and Chewy keeps asking what he's talking about.

Niko gives me a look that screams, "Are they for real?" before shaking his head. His shoulders shaking as he tries to hold in his laughter.

"Oh, you lot ready for dessert, then?" Gus says to my littles who whoop and run back into the dining room followed by the older kids.

Tav hangs back with me, his large hand brushing against mine until I grip his, giving it a comforting squeeze. The tension melts from his body and he gifts me with a brilliant smile.

"You won't regret this, Pixie."

Chapter 6

Tav

"Hey big Daddy," I greet my brother as I drop into the seat across from his ridiculously tidy, big wooden man desk. No sleek lines for Gus. Just well oiled wood and a big leather chair. So manly, so cliche.

"Will you stop calling me that? It's creepy in a weird sex way, and I don't want our employees to hear you."

I wave my hand at him, and he frowns back. First off, our employees know how we roll. Second, he exudes big daddy energy so I tell him so.

"Rhodie does too, you know,"

I jump a little, unaware that Chewy was behind me at the conference table. "Jesus, Dayz, you almost made me shit myself. Also, don't say shit like that about Rhodie again." I shiver at the thought of my sister doing anything remotely sexual or calling Rhodie daddy. Gross.

"Whatever."

Two knocks on the doorway and Jules walks into the office, giving me a shove before flopping down into the chair next to mine. This is how we always sit. Dayz at the conference table on the other side of the office, Gus in his manly seat, and me and Jules in the two chairs facing him. I don't know why it's this way, it just is.

"Ah, there is our little ray of sunshine," I cheesy grin at Jules while he gives me the stink eye. His usual setting.

"We have a few things to cover. Least of all is what the hell you are going to do with an Ol Lady and four kids, Tav. Have you even thought about where you're going to live?"

I knew this shit was going to come up. Gus is the ultimate worry wart and over planner. Well, he was until he got a wild hair and proposed to Ana in the middle of a security meeting. Although I can't begrudge him that, he now has a wife, a baby on the way, and is disgustingly happy. Has he become somewhat more relaxed? No. But does his wife like to bust his balls, therefore making her dear to our hearts? Yes, yes, she does.

"We've spoken about it, and for the meantime, we're just going to take things slow. Obviously they can't fit in my house, and with the little kids we don't want to confuse them with my moving in too soon. So I'll be spending evenings with them and see how it goes."

Gus nods absently before frowning again. "What about prospecting?"

I roll my eyes, "Got that covered. I'll stay weekends and Mondays at the clubhouse like I have been doing. It's going to be fine, Gus. As the kids say, it's all Gucci."

"Why do they say that?"

Turning to look at my sister, she has her inquisitive dog look on her face, brows pulled in, head tilted.

"I have no idea sis, all I know is that they use it, therefore so will I. I want the kids to know I'm cool,"

Jules snorts obnoxiously, but says nothing else. He doesn't need to because I can see Gus winding up.

"Do you really think you can handle this? A woman with four kids? What if their father wants back on the scene? What then? Can you be the bigger man and let him see his kids?"

"I don't imagine that will be a problem because he'll be dead soon," I mutter under my breath, but Dayz not only has the nose of a bloodhound but also the hearing of a bat.

"Why will he be dead?"

"Oh no reason," I smile at her, but she's not even looking in my direction, so it's a waste of time.

"That brings me to another point. The woman is a murderer, Tav!" Gus cries.

I stare at him. Then stare some more, hoping that he notices the irony in that statement. Nope.

"And?"

"So you're saying you're happy to tie yourself to a murderer?"

I go to answer, but Jules beats me to it. "Are you being serious?"

"Of course I'm being fucking serious! Our little brother has claimed a woman, a woman who has been giving him the runaround for months now. A woman who has four children, recently killed a man, her cousin no less, and her family work with Hammer. What if she's lying? What if she's a spy? What about this situation is no one understanding?"

"August, I love you. You acted like both mom and dad to us when they died, but you are not my father. You are my brother and I will not think twice about knocking you the fuck out if you keep talking about Blanche that way. You don't know her. You don't know where she comes from or what she's been through. I never once questioned when you married Ana, even though she's Bratva and we knew nothing about her. So I expect the same courtesy." My jaw clenches as I make sure my words are well measured, so he gets the point. Any big show of emotion will convince Gus that he's right and I can't handle what I've gotten myself into. I can handle it and so much more because she is worth it. Blanche is worth it.

Gus closes his eyes, does that counting thing he does, runs his hands through his hair and lets out a long breath. "OK. I'll back off. I just, I don't want to see you hurt, Tav."

"I know, big brother, I know."

"OK." He nods once, then looks down at his papers, effectively shutting down that conversation and moving on. "Jules, I will need a report on the house you kitted out recently. The mom was certain someone had been hanging around the yard. We have any leads on that?"

"Yeah, it was the ex husband wanting to catch glimpses of the kids. Police are involved."

Gus nods before moving on to the next item. "Dayz, how you getting on with building a profile on that Officer Martin? I don't like the way he manhandled Mama Debs. I want everything on him."

"Yeah, he's an interesting one. I've gathered a lot of good shit, but I think there's still more. I'll give a report at the clubhouse, so I'll fill you in then."

"Good. Tav, I'm not assigning you to anything personally at the moment," He raises his hand when I open my mouth, "Not saying you can't handle it, but you need to spend time with our new family members so I'm giving you that instead of coordinating our teams out of hours. Got it?"

I smile at my brother's serious face across the desk. He said "our new family" instead of "your new family". Whether or not he wants to admit it, he's given me his blessing.

"Yeah, I got it."

"Right. Our FBI contact has requested our help. Dayz will coordinate comms and I'll send out Alvez's team. Anyone got any issues with that?"

We all shake our heads. Alvez is solid and we trust him. Tombs Security is Gus's brainchild. After the death of our parents, he gave up his degree in architecture to switch to Security Management. He waited until Jules finished college then both came back to Rose Grove to set up Tombs Security. It slowly grew over time until Gus and Jules were working all the hours God gave them. Alvez was their first ever hire. After that came a few veterans looking for work and then me and Dayz joined the business when we finished college. Dayz before me because she's a friggin genius and I'm just me.

"Alvez's team is the best we've got," Jules agrees.

"Good, that's settled. Now get out of my office and go do shit."

Standing, I smirk at my brother, then tip over all his pen holders on his desk. I do this every meeting we have and you'd think he would have given up by now, but no. Gus likes things his way and this extends to his wanky pen holders and all.

"Tav?"

I raise my brow at my brother in question. "Yeah?"

"Proud of you, little brother. Blanche will make a good Ol Lady. If you can keep her," He smirks at me as he says this and then his face sobers. "But if she hurts you, there won't be any force in the world that will hold Tuesday back, least of all me."

Blanche

A knock at the door has me jumping as I had completely zoned out, staring at the pot bubbling on the stove. The pounding of little feet down the hall snaps me into motion.

"Hold up littles! I'm coming!"

I throw the tea towel on the counter as I rush past to answer the door.

"It's Tav mom! It's Tav!" Cove yells at the top of her lungs, pointing to the tablet on the hall table that shows who is at the door through our security camera.

I wipe my hands on my jeans, make sure my top doesn't have any stains, or new ones at least, and run a finger under each eye to catch any melting mascara. I mean, I don't do too much to my appearance. I'm too damn busy for that shit, but I equally don't want to look like a bog witch.

I grip the door handle, take a breath, and then berate myself for acting like a lovesick teen. I give myself a pep talk about being a badass bitch, a tiger mom, and all that stuff before swinging the door open.

"Hey Pixie," Tav's deep voice washes over me as his dark eyes hold mine, the heat palpable in them before his attention moves to the two dancing around my feet.

"Hey gang!" Tav says as he squats down, resting on his haunches. And what haunches they are.

"Hey Tav! Are you having dinner with us?" Cove asks as she hops in place while Elio just leans against Tav.

"Yup. Your mom asked me and I couldn't say no. She's the best cook I've ever met!"

Both kids frown up at him before they're off, telling him

about school and all sorts of important kid stuff.

Tav listens patiently as he herds them toward the kitchen. Not before leaning over and dropping a kiss on my cheek, his beard tickling my skin on the way past, causing goosebumps to break out. I know what that beard feels like on my body. I slam the door shut, take a few deep breaths and then get back to my station at the stove.

"OK Pixie, what do you need me to do?" Tav claps his hands together and looks around at the chaos that is my open-plan kitchen/dining/lounge.

Where I grew up, it was drummed into us girls that we had to keep a tidy house. Raise the children, obey our husbands, cook, clean, nurture, all that crap. I never cared for it then and I didn't care for it when Tav visited in the past, but now, being Tav's Ol Lady, someone he claimed and is hoping to see in his life in a long-term capacity, has me feeling a little weird about how sloppy my home looks. Looking around the open plan area, I try to see it through Tav's eyes. The little shoe half sticking out from under the couch. The sweaters that were taken off after school and thrown on a chair or on the floor. Not even the smallest kids' clothes. Niko's big man sized football cleats kicked into the corner are still there from last night, as is Sage's hair brush lying on the back of the couch.

"Hey, you with me?"

Turning my gaze to Tav, standing so close his chest almost flush with mine, his brows knitted together in concern. His eyes roam over my face before he turns to look around the room.

"Babe, I've been here before. There's nothing here that I don't love."

"Tav, dude, this place is a mess," I give him the "are you

kidding me?" mom stare I perfected early in my motherhood.

"You see a mess, I see a home with a family. A home full of love and chaos and noise and - "He waves his hand around, "- stuff. Stuff that makes up the family you built. I'm hoping that over time, if you'll let me, I'll be able to leave some of my things lying around too." His lips curl and I slap him on his hard chest with a snort.

"Well, seeing as you love our chaos so much, why don't you try to find where the hell the kids put the dishes after the last time they unpacked the dishwasher and set the table, yeah?"

"Aye aye captain!"

With a salute, he starts looking through drawers and cupboards, Cove and Elio being less than helpful, as it seems they can't remember where they put anything either.

I take everything off the stove, making sure to check the dumplings are cooked to perfection before I dish them and the chicken onto the blue plastic plate, the side plate, the dessert plate and the serving platter that Tav and the kids decided we'd be eating off today. I'd like to say that this is unusual and that I normally seek out the correct dishes, but I don't. I used to, but once the two little ones joined us it was whatever was going to be easiest. Tav carries our meals to the table, the kids point to the places they like to sit. Which today seems to be so close to Tav they're almost on top of him.

"What about Sage and Niko?" Tav asks, before putting a dumpling in his mouth, closing his eyes and groaning in appreciation. I appreciate it too, because that noise went straight to my clit.

"No, they'll dish up themselves when they get in, which should be soo-"

The front door bangs open, hitting the wall with a crash as

Sage yells out for me.

"MOM! Mom, Mom, they tried to take Niko!"

I drop everything and run to the hall at the same time Tav does. Standing in the doorway, Sage half carries her brother, his arm over her shoulder as he leans heavily on her. My feet are frozen to the floor, staring at my baby boy, blood coming from his forehead.

"Let's get you further inside. Sage, take your brother to the downstairs bathroom. Get him a cloth for his head, yeah?" Sage nods, a breath shuddering out of her before she follows Tav's instructions. "Pixie, you go comfort Sage and Niko. I'll get the little kids set up in the lounge with their dinner and a movie to keep them occupied. Go."

Tav's firm voice pulls me out of my daze and I rush down the hall to my eldest babies.

"Kids, fuck, shit! What the hell happened?"

Niko is sitting slumped on the closed toilet seat, his sister holding a cool washcloth to his forehead.

"We were coming home from school, and, and, HE came out of nowhere. He told me to leave, that he needed to speak to Niko alone. I refused. The man he was with grabbed me and tried to pull me away from Niko, but I fought back, Mom! Just like you taught me!" Sage's words come spilling out of her, "When the other man grabbed me Niko started fighting, too. The next thing I know someone hits Niko in the head with the butt of a gun and he's on the ground. I was so scared, Mom!"

Tav walks in just as Sage bursts into tears. I'm torn between settling Sage; Niko, who has been eerily quiet, and storming out and hunting down those fuckers. Tav gently removes the washcloth from Sage's hand and turns me toward Sage. I gather her in my arms and hold her tight, her sobs wracking her body.

I breathe in the scent of my eldest daughter, soothing her with little noises. The same noises I used to make when I first brought her home. Lifting my head, my eyes meet Tav's in the bathroom mirror. His large hand holding the washcloth to Niko's head, his other arm wrapped around my son's shoulders, Niko leaning on the man that claimed us as his.

Tav breaks eye contact with me, looking down at Niko as he brings the washcloth off of Niko's forehead.

"Shit, kid, they got you good. OK, can you tell me your date of birth, where you were born and how old you are?" Tav asks, squatting down next to Niko, eye to eye. He's turned on the torch on his cell phone and is currently shining the light in Niko's eyes.

"Umm, I was born... 8th of March, yeah, in 2007?" He closes one eye and squints the other at me. His speech slow and slurred. "After mom left Eden's Keep."

Tav frowns at that piece of information before giving me a puzzled look. No one outside of the Keep really knows it exists. As far as Tav knows, I was a member of a very strict church where the men treated women like shit. Sure, the MC may have tracked down Valor. Royal's eldest son had taken over his father's fervor for preaching to the worldlies, converting them to join their flock. But no one outside of the Keep knows how it works. Except those of us who have made it outside of its prison walls.

"Pixie, I think we should get him to the clubhouse. Switch is a doctor. He sometimes works at the hospital, so he's legit. We need Niko to be looked at, and I don't think taking him to the public hospital is safe. Whoever did this will think to look there." Shit, he's right. "Sage, how did you two get away from the men who attacked you?"

Sage lifts her head from where she had nestled into my neck. "We were maybe a block away from home. A really nice lady came out of the big house with all the flowers, you know the one, Mom? Anyway, she must have seen what had happened because she came out with a gun and her phone recording everything. She told the men to fuck off, and she was filming their every move. They got into a car and drove off. She loaded us into her car and dropped us off at the curb, then she drove off to 'find those assholes'." I try really hard not to laugh at that, but damn, I need to meet this woman who saved my babies. Once things settle down, I'm going straight to the big house with the flowers to thank her.

"Shit, I think we might need to turn up on her doorstep with a huge goodie basket or something to thank her. She sounds cool," Tav says with a little chuckle. "Right, Pixie, let's pack you and the kids up in your car and get Niko to the clubhouse. I'll ring ahead to let Switch know we're coming."

As much as I hate being bossed around, having Tav here has helped keep me calm. I also have to admit it's nice to face a crisis with someone at my side. I think back to all the nights I've had to deal with colic or vomiting bugs on my own and wonder what it would have been like to have someone there to help. Oh well, no use wondering, I've been there, done that and got the stained t-shirt. Even so, in this situation, having Tav take control has been surprisingly nice. Though I'll never admit it if you were to ask me.

"Come on, kid," Tav helps Niko up off the toilet and holds him steady for a moment. "You OK to walk on your own?"

Niko goes to nod his head, then grimaces.

"The answer is no. Here, lean on me and we'll get you situated."

Sage and I move out of the entrance of the bathroom and stand in the hall, watching Tav help Niko toward the internal garage.

"I know you're a major badass, but I'm really glad Tav is here, Mom."

"Me too, baby, me too."

Chapter 7

Tav

After depositing Niko in the front passenger seat of Pixie's car and making a quick call to Marx, I head back inside to gently let Pixie know that from this point forward, we'll be all staying at the clubhouse. I really fucking hope she takes the news well. Although a big part of me, the part of me that has a fine dick with a set of well-shaped balls attached, that part fears for their safety.

"Pixie?"

Her cute face pops around the corner of the doorway into the living area. "Niko, all settled? I didn't want to bring the kids out too soon. I figured if I told them where we were going in the car they'd squeal and cause Niko pain." She's so sweet, my woman. Always thinking of others.

"He's all good. But I need to talk to you. I spoke to my Pres. We're thinking that maybe it might be safer for you and the kids to pack a few things and stay at the clubhouse for a couple of days. I'll be there the whole time with you and all the guys are good guys. They're-"

"OK."

My mouth snaps shut as I stare at the woman in front of me. "Come again?"

"OK Tav. We'll go to the clubhouse. If he's here in town, and willing to try to fucking take my kid in BROAD DAYLIGHT, that means he's gotten desperate or grown some balls. We, I, need backup. For the kids." She tips her face up to mine and not for the first time. I see fear mixed with rage there. If I ever fucking find out who did this to her, to these kids, I'll end him in a way even Chewy will be impressed with.

A knock at the door breaks through my thoughts of torture, my gaze snapping to Blanche's.

"Are you expecting anyone?"

"Shit, no! You're the only person who ever comes here." She taps a few things on her phone to pull up the security feed, tipping her phone so I can see as well.

"That's Officer Martin. He's a dickhead"

Her eyes shoot to mine as she frowns. "How do you know him?"

"He was part of a raid at the clubhouse a little while back. Hammer had left a deceased girl on MC land. He came in and roughed up Mama Debs,"

Fire shoots from her eyes before she stomps her way to the front door, flinging it open.

"Can I help you?"

Office Dickhead takes a step back, before recovering himself quickly, his gaze running up Blanche's body, before his eyes widen when he sees me standing behind her.

"I got a call to say some kids were dropped off here. A -" he looks down at the notepad in his hand, "Niko and a Sage Landry."

"Yes, that's right, they live here," Blanche answers with a fake smile.

"That makes perfect sense, then. We had a call from a concerned member of the public that saw two children placed in the car of an African American woman and driven away. We had to make sure they weren't kidnapping victims. I'm sure you understand." He smiles tightly at her and there's no way I can shake the slimy feeling he gives off.

"Well, you see, Officer, they almost were the victims of kidnap. That lovely woman saved my kids from their father, who has no right to see them."

Officer Martin's eyes harden. He stands taller and looks down at Blanche. "Ma'am, children need their father."

"In all due respect, Officer, that man has no rights to my children. He isn't listed on the birth certificates, he hasn't even dropped a dime in child support, and the restraining order against him would suggest that my children don't need anything from that man. Now, if you'll excuse me, I have a family to take care of." With that, Blanche slams the door in his face and starts pacing the hall.

"Fuck, fuck, fuck. He's going to know where we live now." She stares up at me with her dark eyes.

"What makes you think that?"

"Because I recognize that officer. I've seen him with Royal."

Shit. This just got a little more complicated. "It's going to be OK, Pixie." She looks up at me, her eyes searching mine before she lets out a breath and pulls her shoulders back. "Good girl. Pack the kids' things and let's get going." I drop a kiss on her top of her head, pat her ass and head into the lounge to round up the rest of what I hope will become my family.

* * *

I usher the Landrys into the clubhouse and, as if she's always lived here, Cove skips ahead, coming to a stop in front of Rider.

"Hi Rider!" She waves at him before twirling and then plopping down next to him on the couch.

"Hey, Little Miss! How's it hanging today?" Rider asks, as he smiles down at her.

"To the left, Rider, to the left," Cove says in a somber voice, shaking her head, ignoring the roars of laughter coming from the men dotted around the room.

"Cove!" her mother hisses at her before closing her eyes and letting out a breath.

"Right, where's this kid?" Switch's voice booms out from down the hall as Niko's body flinches.

"Yeah, sorry, brother has the voice of a fucking fog horn," I whisper to the kid who still has his arm flung over my shoulder, helping keep him steady.

I walk him down the hall, his mother tight to his side, Sage holding her other hand. I'm glad this hallway is wide as hell, otherwise we'd be wedged in. We're almost in Switch's room when Blanche stops abruptly with a gasp, looking around.

"Where's Elio?" Her eyes are wild and it's then I realize she's more afraid than she's been letting on.

"Hey, Pixie, it's alright. My family are here. Chewy waved out to Elio on our way past. He'll be fine with her. But if you want, I can get her to bring him to you?"

Her body deflates slightly as she shakes her head. "No, it's good. I'm good. Just wanted to make sure they were all safe. Let's get Niko settled." And again I watch as she steels herself, her fear melting away once again.

This is part of the reason I fell for her all those months back. There's something vulnerable about her, but it's hidden so deep inside her that the small glimpses I get seem like it is all a part of my imagination. Then I got to know her more. I saw her ferocity in the love for her kids. I saw her single-mindedness in getting justice for the people she works for. I see it every day in her mission against the people who raised her. I may not have seen it when she killed her cousin, but I can damn well imagine how fucking fierce she would have looked. I see all of this and more. I see the softness of the woman underneath the hard exterior.

"On the bed, kid, let's see what we've got, huh?"

My head snaps towards Switch in shock. I have never heard him speak in anything less than a yell. Not even when Gus was his patient. What in the actual hell is happening?

"Let's look at you," he mumbles as he feels around Niko's head. "Good head of hair on you kid, good thing you got a bump to the front of your head, otherwise I'd be having to shave this all off for a better look," he says with a wink.

"Wow, he's really good at this," Blanche breathes out as she watches Switch shine the penlight in Niko's eyes before checking other parts of his body.

We watch him for a few moments while he hums and ahhs, then he takes some notes.

"Niko, I'm going to leave you here to rest for a moment. You can sleep if you need to. I know people say you shouldn't sleep with a concussion, but that's old news. Your brain needs to heal. I'll be back in to check on you. I just need to talk to your mom first."

Niko leans back on the bed, and his eyes close immediately.

Switch tips his head toward the door and Blanche and I follow him out, Sage choosing to sit next to her brother, scrolling on her phone.

"He's had one hell of a knock, but he'll be fine. He will need to relax, and take it really easy over the next week I'd say, give his brain time to really heal." Switch's normal voice is back and Blanche looks like a deer caught in the headlights. "Questions?"

"Um, yeah, how do you switch your bedside manner off so quickly?" Blanche asks, wide eyed.

A smile grows over Switch's face. "Why do you think they call me Switch?"

And with that, he steps back into his clinic room, shutting the door on us.

"That was.. rude," Blanche says with a chuckle before sobering and running a hand down her face..

"How you doing, Pixie?"

She tips her head side to side, as if weighing things up. "Well, I feel fucking angry. Scared, tired, fucking livid, worried, shaky and fucking murderous. In that order."

"I can help you with scared, tired, worried, and shaky, but I'm afraid we'll have to wait to murder people. Marx wants a word after you check on Cove and Elio."

She closes her eyes, takes a deep breath, lets it out, and then looks at me. "Lets go, Ol Man,"

Blanche

Tav leads me through to the common room, I guess you'd call it. There are people scattered around, some are playing pool, others are leaning on the bar talking. Cove is still yammering away at Rider, who, bless him, is paying attention, nodding now and then. My eyes dart around the room, looking for my little boy. This whole thing will be overwhelming for him. He enjoys routine, and he's not the biggest fan of people. My eyes land on his dark head, his hair as per usual tidily combed, slicked to the side how he likes it. He's sitting across from Chewy, a little frown on his face, his head bent over a collection of odds and ends that he's assembled on the table, much like his setup at home. Chewy is across from him with the same look on her face, intently watching Elio's next move. I edge closer to the pair, feeling Tav following behind. I watch Elio chew his lip before sliding the bottle top in Chewy's direction, taking a dime from her side. She huffs before hunkering down and looking closer at the jumble of things in front of them.

Unable to stand it any longer I break their silence. "Chewy, how do you know how to play Elio's game?"

She turns in my direction, eyes remaining on the table in front of her a moment longer before her gaze flits to mine, and then over my shoulder.

"Everyone know's how to play chess," she says, frowning, as if I've asked the dumbest question ever.

"Elio doesn't."

"Are you sure? Because that's what we've been playing this whole time."

What the hell? "Are you saying Elio is playing chess?" I wave my hand at the bottle tops and dimes and little packets of salt and pepper on the table.

"Of course he is. See? The bottle tops are the kings." She points to the bottle top, but I'm still not seeing it.

"But Elio doesn't know how to play chess."

She looks at Elio, then back in my direction. "Have you told him that? Because I'm pretty sure he would tell you, you're wrong. If you wait a moment, you'll see."

She swipes the screen on her phone, checks something and then holds her hand up above her head, holding up three fingers. She puts one down, then the next, then the last one before pointing at the door where, right on cue Rhodie walks through the door, making a beeline for his Ol Lady. He puts a package on the table, lifts Chewy, gives her a smacking kiss on the lips, then takes her seat, settling her in his lap.

Chewy snuggles closer and then pushes the package toward Elio. "There you go buddy, open that sucker and we can really get down to business."

A wide grin splits my little boy's face as he tears open the paper, his eyes going huge when he sees the contents.

"What is it, Elio?" Tav asks gently.

Without saying a word, Elio turns his package around to show us. A chess board. He hugs it to his chest reverently before opening it, taking out the pieces, and setting the board like he's been doing this for years.

"Holy shit, my baby boy has been playing chess and I never even knew." My hand comes to settle on my chest and I feel like a piece of crap. How could I miss that? My baby had been trying to show me, tell me, have me join in his game and I never once thought long enough or hard enough about it to figure it out myself. That, alongside what happened to Niko and Sage this afternoon has me feeling like a fucking failure. I've set my goal, and in doing so I've dropped the ball when it comes to my babies. Shit.

"Hey, Pixie, look at me," Tav says as he gently turns me. "I know where that pretty head of yours is going, and you're wrong. You are an amazing woman and mother. You're doing this alone. You work and you raise four cool as hell kids. No normal person would have figured out what Elio was playing. Chewy and Elio have genius brains that sort through information differently than ours. You haven't failed him. You've given him an aunt that understands him. Together, they'll rule the world. Which, come to think of it, could actually not be a good thing." Tav's brows pull in and my eyes roll automatically.

"Well, thank you for putting me at ease and now giving me the shits over what mischief those two will get into."

"More than you'll know," Tav says under his breath, but loud enough for me to have my head snapping in his direction.

"What?"

"Nothing. Let me introduce you to my brothers and then we can talk to Marx." Tav takes my hand and tugs me toward the bar.

There's a young man behind the bar, short, stocky and muscular. He's wearing a prospect cut like Tav, so I'm guessing he also has all the crappy jobs. Tav's told me a few of the things he's had to do, not in too much detail of course. That's secret man club stuff. Although from what I can gather, Tav seems to spend a lot of time cleaning things up.

"Takoda, this is my Ol Lady, Blanche. Pixie, this is Takoda. We get the shit jobs," He smiles broadly as Takoda gives me a two finger wave and then goes back to wiping down the bar.

"This big guy is Tank. He's my sponsor. He's like my biker mentor,"

Tank smiles and gives me a chin lift. Ooook. Looks like these are men of very few words. A squeal comes from the hallway and I spin to see who is making that sound.

"Look, Mags! There are kids here!"

A little girl around Cove's age with a dinosaur on her shirt runs out of the hall over to my daughter on the couch. "Hi! I'm Jovie. What's your name? Do you have a mommy or daddy here? Or did the good men save you?"

I tilt my head in question at Tav. He leans down, his lips brushing my ear, giving me shivers. "That's Jovie, Wire and Remy's adopted daughter. Remy saved her from being sold by Hammer and her father, and now she's their daughter. They live here in the clubhouse and she's been dying for some little friends."

Cove jumps off the couch and, using her outside voice inside, loudly tells Jovie that her brother was almost kidnapped by a bad man and he's seeing the doctor biker. I cringe, hiding my face in Tav's arms while he chuckles beside me.

Jovie gasps dramatically "Don't worry DRMC will help, they'll catch the bad man and make him pay."

"Oh, it's OK. My mommy is going to do that," Cove says, nodding seriously.

"Oh, my mommy gets bad guys, too! One day I'm going to be tough like my mommy and daddy and I'm going to wear a leather vest like Papa Flack and Uncle Marx and Uncle Rhodie and Uncle Rider and Uncle Tank and Uncle Judge and Uncle Sniper and Uncle Fox and Uncle Nitro and sometimes Uncle Switch. But I'll smell like pretty things and not armpits."

"Ew," Cove says, nodding in agreement while all the adults

in the room watching the exchange try hard not to laugh at these two little girls nattering away like old women.

"Wire, this is Blanche, my Ol Lady," Tav says, turning me toward a tall, incredibly good looking man, his dark skin shimmering in the light. "Look, I know he's pretty, but you're mine. And he's taken anyway," Tav grumbles.

"He is pretty, isn't he?" A sweet voice says, "Hi, I'm Remy. Wire's Ol Lady and Jovie's mom. She's over the moon to have another little girl to play with." She smiles at me, her bright blue eyes full of warmth, and I'm overcome with wanting to hug this woman. She just exudes gentle mom vibes. Which is usually not at all the type of person I want to hang out with, but I get good vibes from Remy.

A loud whistle pierces the air and we all turn to the mouth of the hall where Marx is standing. The last time I saw him he was demanding to know where Hammer, my uncle's business partner, was. At the time, I had no idea. I was more interested in getting rid of my cousin and making sure he wasn't going to pick up any more women to add to my uncle's stable of slaves. My disgust over what my cousin was doing overpowered the urge for me to bend to Marx's will. I may be full of piss and vinegar now, but my programming as a kid means that I have to consciously tell myself not to bow down to men in power. Like Marx. The only problem I have is that I'm in his territory, asking for protection from the very men he is looking for. I'm stuck between a rock and a very sucky hard place. On one hand, I need to finish the mission I set out to complete. On the other hand, my goddamned kids were assaulted today, my son almost kidnapped by the men I'm trying to end. I've accepted being Tav's Ol Lady for the security it will offer my family, however I know that's going to come with a trade. Shit. I weigh up my options. I can either take my kids home and go it alone, leaving them exposed and breaking Tav's trust. Or I trust in Tav, and the men he calls brothers and ask them for help. Which is really damned hard when you've been handling everything on your own for the past 37 years.

Looking at Tav's gentle whiskey-colored eyes, then looking to Marx, I know what I have to do.

Chapter 8

I watch as Pixie's head swings between Marx, me, and the kids. I know she is weighing up her options. She may not have wanted to be my Ol Lady, but she accepted she needed the extra security that brings. I can only hope that she accepts the help the MC can give her as well.

Marx's gaze lands on me, tipping his head toward his office. I let out a breath I didn't even know I was holding, take Blanche's hand and lead her down the hall. I'm glad he didn't want to do this in front of everyone. My pixie is a private person. It took me months to knock down her walls before she shared a sliver of information about her past, and I know that what she told me didn't even scratch the surface.

Pixie walks into Marx's office, head held high, and I shut the door behind us, effectively shutting out my MC brothers and nosey siblings.

"Take a seat. Would you like anything to drink?" Marx asks, holding up a bottle of whiskey.

Blanche nods once, then sits in the leather chair across from

Marx. I sit in the one next to her, resting my hand on her thick thigh. I'm not sure if the gesture is to calm her or myself. Blanche takes the whiskey from Marx, shoots it and gently puts the glass back down, her face screwed up as the amber liquid goes down.

"Ask me anything you like. I'm an open book," she says, looking Marx square in the eye.

"How's your boy?" Marx asks, leaning his large as hell frame back in his office chair.

I notice Blanche stiffen, then give me a quick glance. She didn't expect this from the Pres. She expected the head of the MC. The gruff, grumpy fucker that barks orders. She'll soon learn that Marx may be all those things, but he's also a man that is utterly dedicated to the family he has made here.

"Oh, he's OK. Thank you for asking. Thanks for letting us shelter here, too."

"It's what we would do for any of the Ol Ladies. We're a family here. Because you are Tav's Ol Lady that extends to your children. But make no mistake, just because Tav trusts you, doesn't mean I automatically do. I have a lot of people depending on me for their safety."

Blanche sits frozen in her chair, assessing Marx. She sits silently for what feels like an eternity, Pres staring straight back at her.

She nods once before addressing him. "I understand completely. That is why I am willing to make a deal with you." Marx's brow raises at this. "I will give you Hammer and some of the people involved in the trafficking ring."

Marx runs his hand over his beard, tugging when he gets to the end strands. "What do you want in return?"

"I want to personally end the men in the council and all the men in my family line."

Her thigh under my palm is tense, the only sign that she's nervous.

Marx grunts. "How many men?"

"Luckily for you, the bulk of the council is made up of my family. Six. I get all six Landrys and the other two council members."

"Why." Marx states. Not a question, a demand. This is where Blanche is going to have to trust us with her past, her secrets.

She chews her lip, brow furrowed before she blows out a breath and murmurs "Fuck it," under her breath.

"My father is Mercy Landry. He is the prophet of Eden's Keep. It's a compound hidden in a nondescript woodland about 3 hours from here, on the outskirts of Louisiana. It started off innocuously enough, like most cults. Then they got greedy. The ones with the power got all the wives, and the young fertile women. The boys got shunned, abandoned in their teens on the side of the road, left to fend for themselves. My brothers were some of the first. We communicated in secret until I was married off at 18 to Royal Landry."

My head snaps around to stare at Pixie. "Hold up, isn't he Mercy's brother? He's your uncle!"

"Yup. That doesn't matter in the Keep. The woman I rescued last Sunday, she's my half-sister. Also, married to our uncle."

"Fuck."

"Fuck is right," she says on a tired breath. "She needed outta there because Royal has a buyer for their three-day-old baby. That's why he has to die."

I curse under my breath, feeling anger and bile rising. Who the fuck forces their nieces, and I know it's forced because no one would willingly fuck their uncle, but who forces young women to have sex with them and then try to sell their babies? I look at Marx, who looks cool, calm and collected, but I can tell he sure the fuck isn't any of those things.

"OK, and why does he want your boy?" Marx asks after a moment, a frown marring his face.

"That I don't know. He has other sons, like Valor, who, until recently was on the council," she answers with a smirk. "He's come after us a few times before, and he only ever asks for Niko, never the others. Not even Elio."

Marx and I look at each other in confusion. "Wait, you told me you escaped to your brothers when you were pregnant at 19."

"I did." She turns to me, her large dark eyes darting between mine, trying to work out where I'm going with this.

"So why would he want Elio? Or the others, for that matter?"

"He's their father. Sage, Cove and Elio aren't my biological children. They're all rescues."

My jaw drops at her confession. This woman, this brave, fierce, amazing momma bear, not only saved these kids, but has raised them all. Looking at Marx I notice he has a look of respect on his face.

"Where are their mothers?"

"I'd like to hope they're safe in the Keep. But there's a chance they could all be dead."

Marx scowls and fists his hands. "Eight men, that's the number you need to kill?"

"Yes sir," my Pixie says, her lips curling up slightly.

"This will have to take place out of state. With the police breathing down our necks we're keeping our noses clean."

Blanche tips her head side to side, in an almost nod. "Looks like we have a deal."

"I'll call church."

Blanche

I follow Marx and Tav out of the office, my legs a little jellified, but nothing I can't handle. I know these men would never hurt me, but that interrogation, or negotiation or whatever you want to call it took me back to the years I spent in the council room, all those men looking down at me because I was "touched by the Devil", which is old fucker language for willful, independent, and not a fucking doormat.

Shaking it off, we come to a stop in the common room, everyone quieting down when Marx's large boots land heavily on the wooden flooring. I have to admit, this place is a hell of a lot nicer than what I was expecting. I expected nicotine stained wallpaper, gross carpet and furniture with god knows whose body fluids all over it. Instead, it's a clean, welcoming place, like the gruff men and women in it that have taken care of my kids when I couldn't.

"Blanche, I know you come from a place where women aren't in positions to speak for themselves, so I'm going to ask if you would like to address my men in church?"

I stare at the Pres, impressed that a man in a position of power would even think to ask.

"I would like to check in on and feed my kids. Can I ask that Tav represents me in church? He knows enough about my past to be of use. Between the two of you, I'm sure you can handle it without me." I try to keep a straight face but I feel my lips twitching the longer I stare at Marx.

"You're going to be a pain in my ass, I can feel it already," Marx says with a sigh before tipping his chin at Tav and bellowing "Church" so loud my ears ring.

"Thank you for trusting me with your past," Tav murmurs in my ear, sending a shiver down my spine straight to my vagina. "I'll see you in a bit, Pixie." He drops a kiss to the top of my head and joins the line of men filing into church after dropping their phones into a box by the door.

I wait for the heavy door to close behind them before I head down the long hall to Switch's clinic room. Pushing the door open gently, I see my two eldest babies, heads together, murmuring to each other.

"Hey bigs, everything OK in here?"

Sage nods her head, her brother's eyes still a little glazed, but he's noticeably less pale than earlier.

"Yeah Mom, we're fine. Just watching some crap on TikTok." Her eyes dart to her brother's, where they share a look.

"Spill it, Sagey, I know you two are up to something." I plop down into a chair next to Sage, arms crossed, giving them my meanest mom look.

"Are the DRMC going to help with Royal? Because if they're not, we've decided we are going to help you. He needs to die, Mom. He could have taken Elio and Cove straight off the street and I'm not sitting around waiting for that to happen. We end it now," my big girl says, her eyes full of fire, her attitude all piss and vinegar.

"There's no goddamn way I'm letting you two get involved! No -" I raise my hand to stop Sage from arguing, "This is my path, not yours. I can handle the weight of taking a life. You two, you are just starting your lives. I won't let this touch you." I lean over and drop a kiss on Sage's head before standing and leaning over my eldest, kissing him on his forehead, the anger rising when I see the small cut in his hairline. I sit back down with a sigh. "The DRMC are on board. They're going to help and we are going to trust them, OK? I need to know you are all safe. Tav and his brothers can provide that safety for you. It'll be over soon. I promise."

They share a look before Sage nods, and Niko raises his thumb.

"Good. Now, I need to feed you both. What do you feel like?"

"No need Mom, Mama Debs already fed us. She brought in dinner about an hour ago,"

"And dessert," Niko adds, his smile all goofy.

I roll my eyes. "That woman is going to seriously spoil you kids."

"Hells yeah she is! She said we're her grandbabies and she's so happy we're safe that she gave us extra ice cream," Sage laughs at this and I shake my head. "You should probably check to see what she gave the littles," she says with a sly grin and I give her my best mom glare before booking it down the hall to find my youngest two. If Cove's had ice cream she's going to be hell on wheels all night. I come to a stop at the mouth of the hall and look around the dining room, trying to spot the dark heads of my children.

"If you're looking for the kids Mama Debs has them. Cove seemed a little wired after dessert, so she's having a jump rope competition with Jovie out back. Elio is the judge," a beautiful brunette says. "I'm Nat. Savage is my Ol Man," she steps toward me, her belly bump prominent in the tight DRMC T-shirt she's wearing.

"Oh, Blanche."

"Yup, Tav's Ol Lady. We know," she smirks at me. "Wanna come join the girls while the kids are occupied?"

I follow her to the table where Ana, Chewy and Remy are sitting.

"Are those dildos?" I ask, pointing at the thing that looks very much like a dildo.

"Yup. Chewy's order of mini silicone penises for Ana and Nat's joint baby shower somehow got mixed up and she ended up with life-sized dildos," Remy shrugs.

"Wait, first off, why would you even need penises for a baby shower?"

Chewy looks at me as if I'm simple, "Because the baby could be a boy."

"OK. What if it's a girl?"

"Well, that's where I had an issue. It's very hard to find silicone vagina party favors. I was thinking maybe boobs will do," Chewy replies.

"Chewy, I love you like a sister, but my baby shower is not having fake tits in the goody bags."

"Without the boobs, the penises don't make sense," Chewy says, her brow furrowed.

"Yeah, because that's what doesn't make sense," Ana snorts.

"You had other questions?" Chewy says, turning toward me but not actually looking at me.

"So many," I say, not sure where to start.

Chewy gives me a funny look before brightening, "Actually, it's a good thing the girl gang is assembled. I need help with the dildos. With the men in church, we have about an hour."

Nat nods for a moment before her brows furrow slightly.

"Speaking of church, why are you out here with us and not in there? I thought you'd be all up in there, what with the shit that's going down," she gestures toward Chewy.

"Meh. Rhodie will tell me what they got up to. And no doubt Wire and the Computas will be given a task and I'll find out then," Chewy answers, holding up an average sized penis. The balls resting in her palm as she wiggles her hand around, making the whole dildo jiggle, the mushroom head whirling hypnotically.

"Why would you be in church? Isn't it for the patched members? The brothers?" Everything I've seen or read says it's a no woman zone.

"If it was for patched members, Tav wouldn't be in there," Chewy points out, her eyes on the knob in her hand.

She has a point there.

"Anyway, we don't have much time. I need you lot to help me come up with a plan for these dicks. Marx wants them out of the clubhouse but the company won't take them back, so I have 100 dildos that need to be repurposed,"

"100!? Holy shit, that's a lot of dildos," bursts out of me. Clearly, the other women knew this because no one seems overly bothered by this news at all.

"Yup," Chewy says, popping the 'P'. "Do you think that weird religious cult you were in might want some?"

"Wait, you were in a religious cult?" Nat asks.

"Pretty much. Eden's Keep started out as a small flock. Then it got larger and the main council got greedier and needed more and more wives. My father, the so called Prophet, has 13 wives,"

"Ew," someone says under their breath.

"Well, I'm glad you made it out, and with your babies, too,"

Remy says, smiling at me. My god, she is the nicest woman in the world.

"Yup, I'm glad you're out too, but again, do you think this place, Eden's Keep, might want some dildos? Get those ladies breaking free of their repressed backgrounds and all that?"

"Yes Chewy, everyone knows the best way for people to break free from the shackles of a religious cult is to do it with an anatomically correct, average sized penis." Ana says with a snort.

"Really?"

"No!" Ana, Nat and I all say in unison.

"Well, it would have worked on me, just saying," Chewy grumbles.

The back door opens and closes and we all look up to see if the kids are back, but it's just Pops wandering through.

"Ladies, what problems are we solving tonight?" He asks, plopping down in a seat next to Chewy, picking up a dark brown dildo and copying Chewy's exact movements, his large palm cupping the dark balls, eyes on the tip while he jiggles it.

"That is so wrong," Ana mumbles to no one in particular.

"We are trying to figure out a way to repurpose 100 dildos," Remy answers.

I jump when Pops slams his down on the table with a thump and then watch closely as he pokes it. It bends one way before bouncing back up again.

"There you go. They suck on to things," he says as if he discovered gravity.

"Ah, yup."

He looks around at our blank faces before picking up another dildo, grabbing a cap off the back of the couch on the way past. He steps up to the wall, pulling his arm back and thumping the dildo into the wall, causing it to suction on. Pops nods once in satisfaction and then hangs the cap on the end of the dildo.

"Taadaaa!" He waves his hands around like Vanna White.

"Well, it's not a terrible idea, I guess," I shrug and then join the rest of the ladies in creating a row of dicks ready for coats and hats to be hung on them.

Chapter 9

Tav

"Yo, listen up! As you probably know by now, Tav, Blanche and their family will stay with us for a while. That fucker Royal Landry tried to take her boy off the street today. Hit him in the head with a fucking gun. He's with Switch in his clinic quarters, so we need to keep the music to a minimum tonight boys,"

All the brother's nod their heads at Marx, and then, surprisingly, to me. "Don't worry brother, we got you," Tank says quietly from the seat next to me.

When I first filed into church after my brothers, I had a feeling of belonging come over me. It feels right, like this is where I'm supposed to be. In this room with these men, making the world a better place. I try to do it every day in my work with my siblings, but sometimes there are things we can't do, lines that we can't cross when we wear our Tombs Security hats. There, we are the good guys. Here, though, here we are the good guys who sometimes do bad things for the greater good.

"Royal, he's the one working with Hammer, right?" Dex asks.

"Yeah, brother to the Prophet and the one tipped to lead when he dies," Marx replies.

I raise my hand because as a prospect I don't feel right just blurting shit out. Marx runs his hand over his beard and I see him trying to hide a smirk before tipping his head at me to go ahead.

"Royal is also Niko's father."

"What the actual fuck? Isn't Blanche the Prophet's daughter?" Rhodie growls, the faces of the other brothers like thunder.

"She was forced to marry him when she was 18. Her brothers managed to get her outta there when she was pregnant with Niko. For the past almost 18 years, he's been trying to get the boy back. She doesn't know why he's so important. Royal has many sons older than Niko."

Wire frowns for a moment before speaking. "Remy and I have been looking into every angle to do with Royal, and we keep hitting dead ends. On paper, he's just a high-ranking member of Mercy Landry's flock. Everything we've found so far points to a legit church about 3 hours over the state border. There isn't even a record of a Blanche Landry."

I want to be irritated that they looked into my Pixie, but I know that in their shoes I would too.

"Try looking into Eden's Keep. From the little Blanche has told me, the church is a front for a larger commune type set up deep in the woods. Her father set it up before she was born. From the outside, it looks like a legit church, but it's actually a cult. The kind where old men get all the women and young men get kicked out as soon as they come of age. I'm sure you can all use your imaginations to figure out what it's like."

"What the fuck?" Judge mutters.

"So we need to decide how fucking far we want to go. Blanche will help us get to Hammer. In return, she wants to take out what she calls the council members. There are 8 of them," Marx looks around the room, gauging our reactions.

Fox lets out a low whistle. "That's a lot of lives to take. She up to it?"

"I'd say she's more than up to it after watching her jump out of the back of that truck where she'd taken out her own cousin," Savage says,

"Is anyone ever going to find a normal woman to lock down?" Fox asks, then dodges Wire's fist.

"My woman is normal!" he says through clenched teeth.

"Sorry to break it to you man, but she's not. No one is that goddamned nice," Sniper says, shaking his head.

Marx's lips curl up a little before banging his fist on the table. "Alright, you lot. Wire, you and your team will look into why Royal wants Niko. There has to be a reason. Anything you find might help us bring down Hammer. Remember that we still have that fucker Martin on our asses, too."

"Speaking of, we've clocked him with eyes on Devil's Big Tow," Judge growls.

"He's been seen at the garages, too," Nitro adds.

"Fuck," Marx growls, running a hand down his face. "I'll get on to Sergeant Davies. He needs to rein that pasty fuck in." He looks around the room, "From now on every time you see him note the date and time. I want evidence of his harassment, got it?"

"Are you sure we just can't make him disappear? I know someone who would love to get their old ass hands on him,"

Rhodie smirks.

"No murdering! Not yet, anyway." He waits until we all nod in agreement. "I want all men keeping their ears and eyes open for any trafficking activity - women going missing or dodgy shit going on. Wire, you and your team know what to do. Look into anything and everything. We'll use that information to fuck them all up, take Hammer out while we're at it. Blanche will have her revenge on the 8 council members, and collectively we shut down their entire operation."

"Well, when you put it like that Pres, it sounds easy," Savage says rolling his eyes.

"Bet you're glad you're not in that seat anymore, huh?" Dex teases his ex-pres.

"Oh, I am fucking overwhelmed with joy that I get to sit my ass right here and take all of Marx's well barked instructions," he grins while Marx flips the bird.

"Yeah, yeah. Get out of here fuckers," Marx brings down the gavel, or the meat tenderizer with a bang and everyone files out.

I hang around until it's me and Marx. "Pres, I just want to thank you for having my back. It means a lot to know that I have an MC family that can help protect Blanche and the kids,"

He stares at me for a moment. "You know that we would have had your back anyway, right? Doesn't matter that you're Chewy's brother. You and your family have had our backs since your crazy little sister broke into my compound. You've taken bullets and lives for us. We're family whether you wear a patch or not, Tav. Blanche and those kids are yours, which makes them ours." He looks thoughtful for a moment, his dark brows in a frown. "Did you join my MC to keep Blanche safe?"

I shake my head at him. "I've always been the youngest

brother. The one who hung around Mom and wanted to keep the peace. There's a reason my face is prettier than my brothers - no broken noses, see?" I point to my perfectly straight nose as Marx snorts. "Since Gus and Chewy and Pops, to an extent, found their people and fell in love, they -" I blow out a breath, "they don't really need me anymore." I look at my hands spread out on the large wooden table that sits in the center of church.

"You're a fixer, Tav, the diplomat. I've known it since the moment you parked your SUV in my compound asking to talk to your sister. Pops is the patriarch. The man who kept you all together when you needed it. Gus is the leader. Jules is calculating and Chewy is so fucking brilliant it's scary. But you, you keep things ticking over, you smooth the way so your family can work at their very best. I've seen you do it here with the brothers. I've seen you do it with that prickly ass woman you claimed. You genuinely care, and that's something that you can't fake." He stands to leave the room, dropping his huge hand on my shoulder and squeezing on his way out. "We're lucky to have you, kid. Now let's go tell Blanche and the girls what the plan is."

I stand and follow my Pres out. "You know that you're not that much older than me, right?"

"Shut up."

Blanche

The men all start filing out of church heading for the bar. Tav hasn't come out yet and I'm starting to get a little worried.

"Mommy! Mommy! Mama Debs asked if we can have a movie night with her and Jovie. Can we please? Please please please?" Cove asks, her little hands clasped under her chin. Elio stands beside Mama Debs, holding her hand.

Looking at the time, I notice it's still reasonably early. Well, later than I would normally let them start a film, but after what happened today I'd already decided to keep them all home from school tomorrow. I will continue to do that until the threat is neutralized. Remy was nice enough to offer to sit and help them with schoolwork if I can organize their schools to send it all through. That's on my to do list tonight once I put them to bed.

"Yes, you can. But no sugary snacks, OK, Mama Debs?"

"Of course not!" She says, and I'm pretty certain I can't trust her on that one because she has a glint in her eyes like she's already assembled a whole grazing platter of pure sugar for tonight's movie night.

"It's OK, Cove's mommy, we're only allowed popcorn for night time movies," Jovie says to me, her cute little face super serious.

"Thank you Jovie, that makes me feel a lot better." She grins and then takes off, following Mama Debs into the kitchen, her curly hair like a halo around her head.

My eyes follow them for a moment before swinging back around to the door to church, just in time to see Tav following behind Marx, a smile on his face. He's nowhere near as big as Marx, but Tav's broad shoulders and lean swimmer's build get my heart racing every time. That and the whiskey-colored eyes that search for me in the room. He finally meets my gaze and his face lights up. He's so fucking beautiful and gentle, and again I regret pulling him into my world. I've killed someone and I plan on killing more people. Darkness, filth like that shouldn't touch this man, and yet it will. I know it will.

"Wire, Remy, Chewy –"

"Sir, yes sir!" Tav's sister yells as she jumps to her feet. Marx stares at her for a moment, then ignores the outburst.

"Your team is on Royal intel. He's never tried taking the other kids, only Niko. Find out what makes him so special. It may help us unravel their operation."

"Do you have anything that will help us with that?" Remy says in her sweet voice. "No offense, but I tried looking into your past earlier to get a head start on Niko's father, but, well, Landry is such a common name in Louisiana and I couldn't find any records that matched you or Niko anywhere." Remy wrings her hands and I really want to pull her into a hug, even if I'm annoyed she tried looking into my past. But if this is going to work, and these people are going to trust me, I have to trust them in return.

"Look under Patience Surette Landry. That's my birth name and the name I registered when I had Niko. His birth name is Nicholas Surette Landry." I hesitate for a moment and then remember I'm doing this for my kids. "Royal is his father, but he's not named on the birth certificate. I know it's fucked up, and it wasn't, um, consensual, but it is what it is and he's a great kid."

Remy clasps her hands in front of her large bust and looks at me with her giant blue eyes shimmering with tears. "You are one brave momma and I know you don't know us that well just yet, but we'll do whatever we can to help your kiddos. Trust me."

Fuck. What a sweetheart, I mumble to myself, but not quiet enough.

"I know, right? She's the best of us. Then there's the rest of us," Nat says with a grin as she indicates herself, Ana, and Chewy.

"Hey! Speak for yourself! I'm bloody delightful," Ana mutters.

"Anyway," Wire says, shutting down the women bickering, "Remy will get a start on looking into Royal. What have you got in terms of Hammer?"

Blowing out a breath, I think for a moment. "I know that there's a shipment going out soon. My sister's 3-day-old baby is meant to be on it."

A chorus of "What the fuck?" is thrown around by almost every man in the room and my nerves settle, knowing I'm in the right place.

"It's OK, she's safe!" Tav yells out. "Pixie got her out the night the kids stayed with us."

The grumbling settles as the men find their places again.

"I'll call my brothers, see if our sister knows anything more. It may take a while to get in touch with her, she's been transported up north in secret so Royal can't get to her."

Marx nods his head at this information.

"Tonight we let Wire and the team find out as much as they can with Blanche's help. We need to know exactly who and what the fuck we're dealing with. We're still being watched by the fucking Rose Grove PD, so we need to keep our noses clean. No murdering. That's directed at you, Chewy." He glares at

Tav's sister while I stare in shock. Surely he can't mean actual murder, right?

Looking around at everyone in the room with amused looks on their faces I have to wonder. I get these guys are an MC, however from my research, they aren't a 1% club, meaning they're more weekend riders, people who do it because they love bikes, right? Clearly, the MC brothers would have taken lives. They're all ex-military, but Tav and his family are in laws to the club. They run a security company. They must be joking about Tav's sister murdering people.

"I repeat, no murder. Or torture for that matter, at least not until we get the pigs off our backs. Especially that fucker, Officer Martin," Marx grumbles.

"I know that greasy turd," I voice out loud, all heads snapping toward me.

"How do you know him?" Tav's eldest brother Gus asks. He looks concerned. And constipated. He arrived to pick up Ana when we were in the middle of redecorating the clubhouse with rubber dongs.

"He came to my house acting like the concerned PD officer, wanting to make sure my kids were OK. I recognized the slimy bastard from Eden's Keep. He's been meeting with Royal."

"Well, I think we now know why the hell this Martin guy has a hard-on for us. If he's working with Royal and Hammer, then we have a dirty cop problem," Savage offers.

"Also explains why the hell DRMC and the Bratva were both hit with murder investigations. It's easy enough to do when the person framing you works for the PD," agrees Dex.

"Hmm, it does make sense, but how the hell did Hammer, Officer Martin, and Royal all cross paths? Hammer has never lived in Rose Grove, Martin grew up in the same trailer park that Wire spent weekends, and Royal is Louisiana based." This time Gus. He's always wanting to cross all the T's and dot all the i's.

Marx knocks twice on the table in front of him. "Wire, add that to your list. The more intel we have, the easier it will be to take them all down."

"Ah, guys, I've managed to hack Officer Martin's cruiser. Aside from showing a scary amount of time outside DRMC buildings, it says here that he took a little trip to Louisiana four days ago." Chewy has her hand up to get everyone's attention, but there's no need. As soon as she starts talking, everyone listens. It's a nice change from where I grew up.

I'm momentarily distracted until Tav turns his whiskey colored eyes to me. "That was the day you rescued your sister and her baby," he snaps his head toward his sister, "around what time or times was he there, Dayz?"

Her fingers fly over the keys, the tapping loud in the quiet common room. Her brows pull down, and she purses her lips for a moment. "It says here he was there at around 9pm. The next day he headed further up north, before turning around and coming back. I wonder what was so important up north?"

Fuck.

"Where up north?" I ask, pulling my phone from my pocket, pulling up Vic's number.

"Last stop was Sunny Hill before he turned around,"

"Shit. Hold up." I raise a finger to ask Chewy to wait a moment, then I dial my brother. It rings twice before he picks up.

"Well, well, well, if it isn't our horrible sister. How's it going, squirt?" Vic's voice booms out on speaker.

"Hey Vic, you're on speaker with the Devil's Rose MC," I try to keep the smile out of my voice because I know he'll be all pissy I didn't warn him. Given that we didn't grow up with a lot of technology, Vic finds phones uncomfortable and his biggest pet peeve is being on speaker. Which means I have him on speaker every time I call him.

"Oh heyyyyy everybody. I hate you, Patience," he hisses after the pleasant greeting, causing the MC to laugh.

"OK, I'll stop messing with you. Where did you drop Lovely and Bee?"

"Why?"

"We think a Rose Grove police officer may have followed you. I've seen him meeting with Royal when I was running surveillance and Tav's sister tracked his cruiser. He was in Louisiana heading north not long after the rescue." and then I decide to tell them the rest, really quickly, like ripping off a bandaid. "Oh, and Royal tried to take Niko tonight, BUT he's fine and we are all safe at the DRMC clubhouse," I say quickly and loudly to stop Vic from having a complete meltdown.

"What the fuck did she just say?" I hear Dom and Chris in the background and Vic telling them exactly what I just said.

"Fuck, sis, are you all safe? Do you need us to come down there?" Vic says evenly while Dom and Chris talk over him to let me know they're coming. God I love them.

"No, I'm fine. I just need you to tell me where you took Lovely. I need to know that she's safe."

"We took the waterways, passed them off around an hour from home. Diligence then took them and handed them off again. As far as we know, her and Bee are safe and well. They check in once a day."

"Oh, thank God. That baby girl is too little and too precious to have all the evil in the world after her."

"We've got this. You take care of our nieces and nephews. You need anything you call us. We can be there in 3 hours."

"Will do. Love you all," I hang up and look around the room, the men and women all smiling softly at me. "Well, there you have it. Whoever Martin was meeting, it thankfully wasn't my sister or her baby."

"So, I'm guessing, judging by that conversation, you and your family run a sort of underground railroad type thing for people leaving Eden's Keep?" Chewy says, not even taking her eyes off the keyboard she's typing on.

"Oh, um, yeah. To begin with, we'd settle women and their children in the same small town as my brothers, but time and time again Royal would come looking for them and then using his bullshit mind control techniques, he'd use their fear of God to guilt them into going back. After that, we set up a series of contacts. Past members and their families now step in and help them get as far away as possible. We offer new clothing, names and ID if needed, that sort of thing." Looking up I notice Tav's eyes shining, he's puffed out with pride and the thought that someone like him can be proud of what we've achieved makes my chest feel warm.

"Using the waterways is genius," Rider mentions.

"Well, it's easy and accessible. My brothers run a swamp tour and gator business,"

"A WHAT!?" Chewy screeches, her eyes wild with excitement. I can honestly say this is the first time the woman has looked me in the eye.

"A swamp tour and gator business,"

"So they have gators?" she waves her hands as if to tell me to hurry the hell up with the information.

"Well, yeah. They rehabilitate injured gators, orphaned

babies, that sort of thing. My gater Smiley lives with them,"

"YOU. HAVE. A GATOR??!! Tav, you better fucking marry this woman!"

I try hard to cover my chuckle, but I don't think I did a very good job. Not that it matters, because she's now turned her attention to Marx.

"Marx, we need-"

"Don't say a fucking word! Not one Chewy!" Marx barks. He then rummages in his cut pocket. Are those antacids?

She huffs as she sits down on Rhodie's conveniently placed knee.

"Let's get to work. Everyone know's what they're looking for."

"I think we should get Officer Martin out of the way first. Who wants to come pick him up with me?" Pops offers.

"No murdering!" Marx roars.

Pops drops his head, huffing out a large breath and I try hard not to snort as he looks just like Niko used to as a toddler when I told him no.

"Yes Pres," He grumbles, then raises his head to look at me and give me a wink. I try to stifle my giggle while everyone talks amongst themselves, organizing who's on what, who is reporting where, and so on.

Chewy is right in the middle with the MC brothers and I'm intrigued. I learned all I know about MC's from Sons of Anarchy and a bunch of MC romance books and I always thought that Ol Lady's had no say; it being a man's world and all that. But these huge scary men are listening to what Chewy is saying, taking on board her ideas. Same with Remy and, in fact, all the women here.

"Not quite what you expected huh?" Nat says, snuggled into

the side of a tall, dark-haired man that I'm guessing is her Ol Man Savage. Jeez Louise, these two make a stunning couple.

"Not at all. I knew enough about the MC to know that my kids would be safe here if I had to send them to Tav. I knew they were good men. But they were men, a group of them, and in my past a group of men, no matter how morally upstanding they are, can be chauvinistic as hell. Which is why I was pissed when I found out Tav claimed me. I'm my own woman. I don't need anyone, especially not a man, to tell me what to do." She smirks at me as if knowing full well what I'm going to say next. "But since I've been here, it's been anything but that. I mean, look at how closely they're listening to Chewy," I gesture toward the group.

"Her brain connects the dots faster than anyone I've ever met. I mean, yeah, she's a bit wacky, but she's damn good at her job."

"Security?" I ask.

A big grin stretches Nat's face. "Nah, enforcing,"

Chapter 10

Tav

Once everyone agrees on the best course of action, which is pretty much Wire and his team doing a deep dive into all things Eden's Keep while the rest of us keep an eye out for Officer Dickwad, I have enough time to drop a kiss to the top of Blanche's head before she heads off with my sister to supply them with whatever information might help.

"Well, Tav, I can see why your girl was cagey all this time," Gus says as he drops into a seat next to me at one of the long tables.

"Yup. I still can't be too sure that she won't take off on me after all this is done, but the plan is to get her to fall so madly in love with me that running away won't even enter her mind." I let him in on my cunning plan.

Ana flops down on Gus's lap, his big hand coming up to rest on her belly, pressing against her shiny blouse. "Tav, trust me, as a reformed runner from relationships, that woman has strong feelings for you. It's just that her fear and anger are stronger. I think once she's dealt with that, she'll be all yours."

She smiles at me before pressing a kiss to Gus's stubbly cheek. I watch as my brother melts and send up a prayer for it to be my turn soon.

"Tav, do you know where Blanche is? The kids are getting sleepy and I think they want their mama," Mama Debs calls from the hall entrance.

Pushing myself up from my seat, I head in her direction. "Pixie is busy helping the Computas at the moment. I'll grab them and get them sorted. Thanks Mama," I drop a kiss to the top of her curly gray head, patting her on the shoulder. "Go find that grumpy old man you like so much," she snorts, her eyes twinkling before she cups my cheek, rubbing her thumb on my beard and smiling.

"Love you, Tav,"

Her words hit me straight in the gut and remind me that people don't have to be related to you by blood for them to be your family. "Love you too, Mama,"

I blink a few times and then make my way down the long hall. Last time the kids stayed here we had the girls in one room, the boys in another. I notice that both Cove and Elio are in the same room this time, their toys already neatly stacked in the corner. Elio is sitting cross-legged at the foot of his bed, looking at a book. Cove is lying on her tummy on top of her bed coloring and Jovie is on the floor between the two of them, spouting out random dinosaur facts.

"OK kids, it's time for bed."

Jovie gets up immediately, going first to Elio. "Night, night Elio, I'll see you in the morning," she puckers up and drops a kiss to the top of his head. "Night, night Cove, you can sit next to me at breakfast tomorrow," she wanders over to Cove, puckers up and drops a kiss on her head too. She is such a little sweetheart.

"Night Jovie! Thanks for playing with us. I'll sit next to you and we can eat pancakes together!," Cove says in her overly loud voice. I wonder if I should introduce her to Switch?

Jovie walks up to me, raising her arms, so I pick her up then pull her in for a hug, "Thank you for looking after my friends today, Jovie. Night, night, sweet girl."

She pulls back and drops a kiss on my cheek, "Love you, Uncle Tav,"

I place her back on the ground and she skips off down the hall, with far too much energy for this time of the night.

"OK, Littles," I say, using their mom's nickname for them, "Let's get cleaned up and into PJs. Your mom is a little busy at the moment."

"She helping catch the bad men?" Cove asks excitedly.

"Yup. She sure is. So let's surprise her by doing our nightly routine and getting ready for bed, huh?"

Both kids get up and talk at the same time, telling me what usually happens. This is where my well-laid plans all seem to fall apart. Cove only likes having baths, but the clubhouse doesn't have a bathtub. Which I inform her and am then met with tears. And not quiet, resigned tears, but huge fat tears coupled with heaving breaths and an explanation I can barely understand. I look to Elio for help and he gifts me with wide eyes and a shrug. Looks like me and little dude are both at a loss.

My inability to control this situation gets worse when Rider stops by. "Whoa, what's going on?"

I turn my wide eyes to Rider, I'm sure he can see the plea and panic in them because he takes a backward step towards the door. "Cove only takes baths before bed, she can't have a shower because then she won't be able to get to sleep? I think that's what she said."

"Oh, little buddy, we don't have a bathtub here. But we have a bucket I'm sure you can fit in?" Rider offers. Cove stops crying, looks at him wide eyed, before opening her mouth and roaring hard enough to scare a meep sound out of Rider. He looks at me and says something like "You're on your own brother" before booking it out of the room.

"Fuck, I mean, oh fudge!" I mutter to myself. Come on, man! You've dealt with spoiled rich guys in body guarding situations that have worse tantrums than this. This little girl is just over tired and feeling sensitive.

Before I can open my mouth Tank comes in, his bulk making the space feel cramped. "Hey little one, why all the tears?" He goes to one knee and waits patiently for Cove to answer.

"I - I- I-, I always have a bath before I go to bed. I can't sleep without my bath and bubbles," she stutters. Good to know the word I couldn't understand was bubbles. For a moment there I thought she said dog's balls.

"Well, showers don't have bubbles, but I have something that you might like. I have a special thing called a shower bomb –"

"Ah, brother, is that a good idea?" I whisper at Tank, who frowns back at me before turning to Cove.

"It's a special fizzy thing that you put in the bottom of the shower and when the hot water hits it it fizzes up and smells nice. What do you think? Do you think it'll do?" By the time Tank finishes explaining shower bombs, Cove is nodding her head and jumping in place. Even Elio has moved closer to his sister and is looking intrigued. "I'll come back with a bomb for each of you." With that, Tank stands, turns toward me and moves to leave.

Just before he reaches the door, he turns to look at me with a stink eye that could rival Jules. "Not a word to anyone about my shower bombs, prospect. Not. One. Word."

I mime zipping my lips, locking them and throwing away the key with a smirk on my lips.

I get the kids organized and into separate showers with the bombs gifted by Tank, and I have to admit they are pretty fucking luxurious. In no time, I'm tucking Cove into one bed smelling like "Unicorn Splash", while Elio chose the "Dino Bubble Blast" scent. I make a note to order some for the kids. And maybe some for Tank for Christmas. I'm sure he'll enjoy that little gift from Secret Santa.

"Mommy always reads to us before we go to sleep. Can you please read to us, Tav?"

"Of course I can, sweetheart. What story would you like?"

"It's Elio's turn to choose,"

I turn to look at Elio, his hair still in its usual style, nicely combed, even for bed. He smiles at me and holds out a book with two cute penguins on the front. I settle on the floor between the two beds, and get to reading. By the time I'm nearing the end of the story, both kids are out and Blanche is leaning against the door jamb smiling down at me.

"Hey Pixie."

"Hey Tav," she whispers back.

"I can't leave yet. I want to see what happens to Roy and Silo."

She grins at me, walking into the room. She takes the book from my hands, gazes down at me with soft eyes, before sitting her plump ass down between my legs. She takes one of my hands and pulls it across her front, my other arm coming up on the other side so I'm holding her to me.

She lifts the book, looks at what page I'm on and the chuckles softly.

"What? I think that zookeeper is going to help them out. They've been sitting on rocks, Blanche!" I whisper yell at her to get my point across.

She rolls her eyes and starts reading in a hushed voice. I lean my head back, close my eyes and let the feeling of having her and the kids here with me wash over me. This! This is what I've been wanting for a long time. Some people might think I'm soft, or a pussy, but I think there's strength in knowing that you have family around you. That you have people you would die for and people who would have your back anytime, anywhere.

Blanche's soft voice fills the room until Roy and Silo get the happy ever after I wanted to hear. Now? Now it's my turn.

Blanche

"Tav."

"Yeah Pixie?"

"Take me to bed, babe."

I feel Tav's smile from where my head is leaning against his cheek. "Of course, Pixie."

I rise, then move to kiss my babies on their foreheads, Elio first, then Cove. Tav stands, and does the same thing, then tugs their blankets up a little more to make sure they stay warm all night. I thought I may have been in trouble back when we met, when he wheedled his way past all of my well built defenses. Then I really thought I was in trouble when he took care of my kids while I was out rescuing Lovely. It got worse when he took control when Niko was attacked and now, now I know I'm in trouble.

After giving Wire, Chewy and Remy any and all information on Niko so they can find out why the hell Royal may want him, I went to see my boy myself. Sage had already gone to the room the MC had assigned her, she was on her phone chatting to her friends when I kissed her good night. Niko was still a little vague and out of it, but Switch assured me he would monitor him through the night and that there would be no lasting effects on Niko's brain, which was a huge relief for me. I wanted so much to go after Royal myself, but I know that I've made a deal with Marx and I am a woman of my word. For now, anyway.

Walking down the hall to check on my Littles, the smooth sound of Tav's voice drew me in. Watching as he sat sentinel between my two youngest, his quiet murmur as he read to them had the final walls around my heart breaking down. This man is everything. As he sat there misty eyed over gay penguins, I made a vow to make sure none of my filth, my past, touches his pure soul.

Gently, he takes my hand and leads me down the hall to what I assume is his room. He unlocks the door and lets it swing open. I was expecting his room to be all biker, smelly and manly or something. Messy clothes lying around, change on top of the dresser, that sort of thing. This? This is not quite what I was expecting.

"Tav, do you have something to tell me?" I take a step inside and turn a full circle. It's somewhat simple, with plain walls and gray carpet. And that's where the simplicity ends. A queen bed sits in the middle of the room and he even has a headboard. A single man with a headboard. There are bedside tables with matching lamps and a dresser that matches the side tables. There is a small loveseat at the foot of the bed with a throw rug draped over the arm. On the wall opposite the bed sits a small desk and chair with his laptop and another lamp. Everything matches, and he even has cushions on his bed, where he has not one, but four fluffy pillows. I complete my circle and my gaze lands on Tav. He's standing near the bed, looking sheepish, rubbing the back of his neck with his big hand.

"Um, I kinda got obsessed with home shows after my parents died. It got so bad Pops got me a therapist. She said it was a way for my young brain to switch off and not think about what happened when my parents died."

Oh, my poor Tav. He's told me before what happened to his parents. If I had crossed paths with the person who did it, I would have made them pay for taking this sweet man's parents. I said something along those lines to him once, and he gave me an odd response about his sister Tuesday. She's a mystery, that one.

"Well, I love your taste in decor, but now I feel even worse that you've been hanging out in my terribly decorated home. Oh my god! I've even let you sit on my stained couch with mismatched cushions!"

I'm horrified by this thought, but it's stolen away the moment Tav growls, closes the space between us and kisses the living daylights out of me.

"I love your house. Say another word about it and I'll spank that ass," His eyes glitter at his threat and even though my initial reaction is to shove him off and yell that he'll never put his hands on my ass, my lower stomach clenches at the thought. The hussy.

"I'd like to see you try," I smirk up at him

"Challenge accepted baby,"

He places his hands on both sides of my face, then smashes his lips to mine again, his tongue running along my bottom lip, seeking entrance. I open for him, letting his tongue glide along mine before I suck it gently, drawing a deep moan out of the man I can't get enough of.

I think I vaguely hear his door slam shut, but I'm too busy trying to get my hands up his shirt. I want to feel his smooth skin on my hands. He breaks the kiss, removes his cut, draping it over the arm of the loveseat, before grabbing his shirt behind his neck and pulling it over his head. Why the hell is that so hot?

"Get naked Pixie. I want that sweet pussy of yours."

I don't need to be told twice. I tear off my clothes as fast as I can, only taking my time when I get to my jeans. Taking my mom panties off with the denim, I fold them over in a pile so Tav can't see them. If he even got a glimpse of my bamboo cotton, high waisted, muffin top control underwear in a very sexy old lady purple, his manhood, which is pointing directly at me, would shrivel up into his body, taking those nice balls with it.

He steps toward me, giving me a gentle swat on my ass that has me spinning to glare at him.

"On the bed, Pixie, I'm dying to feel you wrapped around me. Please. I need you baby."

Well, when he puts it that way. I place one knee on the bed, then deliberately, slowly, add my other knee. I crawl toward the middle of the bed achingly slowly, wanting to tease Tav as much as I can before the lust takes us both over. It turns out he has other plans. His large hands grip my ass cheeks, then he spreads them apart, groaning at the sight.

His warm breath tickles my core and in a quick movement his tongue licks me from clit to asshole, taking my ability to think and hold myself up on my hands.

"Hmmm, just like that baby, chest to the bed ass up is how I want you." His fingers swipe through my folds, gently grazing my sensitive nub, drawing a whimper from my lips. "Fuck baby, so wet for me, so perfect." and with that, he feasts on me like a starving man.

Sounds coming from both of us are obscene and I can't find it in me to care. Tav slides a thick finger into me, his thumb strumming my clit while his mouth and tongue work on my lower lips. My hands fist the covers on his bed, holding on for dear life, but it's no use. In a few short moments I can feel the tremble of my legs working its way up to my core, which explodes, sending a shock of pleasure through my body, my tightly clenched eyes seeing stars. My body shudders with violent aftershocks as my legs give way and I end up lying on my stomach, legs clenched tight as my orgasm keeps hitting me like little electric shocks.

Tav isn't done yet. I remember this from our first time together, the man is insatiable. He climbs onto the bed, his strong hands rest either side of my head as he straddles my legs, his precum dripping onto my ass cheeks.

"Come on, baby, open up for me. Let me into that perfect pussy I've been dreaming about."

He rubs his hard rod up and down my ass before angling himself down, his cock poking at my folds through my closed legs, drawing a moan from me.

"Fuck baby, your pussy is so wet for me,"

"Tav! Stop teasing me!" I pant breathlessly, clawing at the bedding.

His cock nudges me exactly where I want him, so I angle my ass up slightly, letting Tav slide home in one thrust, both of us moaning in unison.

His name is a mantra on my lips as I lose the ability to say anything other than Tav.

"Fuck baby, that's it, take me, take me all the way, you feel so perfect, I love the way you take me, just like that," he moans over and over, praising me, making love to me, his body draped over mine, touching me from head to toe. He's everywhere.

My moans almost drown out his commentary, his praise.

"God Pixie, I can't last, you feel too good, too right, I need you to come baby, work those hips, that's it, good girl, grind against me baby, work it, yeah, just like that."

"Tav, please!"

His moves get faster and deeper until I can't feel where he ends and where I begin. It's all consuming and I can feel the moment his hips move slightly, hitting that spot inside of me I never even knew I had until I met Octavius Tombs.

"Yeah, that's it, just like that. Take a breath baby and then grind, yes, grind on me, hit that spot, that's it! Good girl, do it again."

I follow his exact instructions, arching my ass up even more and grind on him every time he thrusts deep. I can feel it, the pressure builds in my lower stomach so I grind harder, faster, my breaths coming in pants, the bedding fisted tightly in my hands to ground myself as I feel my orgasm bearing down on me like a wave about to break.

"Tav, I can't last, please, please!" I beg, plead with him to send me crashing over the edge.

"Once more, baby, one more. Deep. Thrust." His words are punctuated with pants and thrusts, "Now COME!" he demands and the dam breaks.

A wave of pleasure hits me, stealing my breath. I tremble as the sheer force of my orgasm overtakes all logical thought until all I hear and feel is Tav's cock as his length pulsates inside of me. I'm unsure if we used protection or not, my mind too fuzzy from the screaming orgasms that Tav gave me before fucking me into oblivion.

"Thank you, sweet Pixie," he whispers in my ear, before kissing me on the shoulder.

I feel his fingers between my thighs, gripping the end of his cock as he pulls out of me. Turning my head, I watch as he removes the condom he had on, and I find myself a little disappointed to not have a part of him still inside me. Which is fucking crazy, given that I already have four children.

"Come on, babe, let's get cleaned up. I don't know about you, but I'm starving,"

My stomach chooses that exact moment to growl, which makes Tav laugh, and I marvel at the light, carefree sound of it that always takes me by surprise. He's such a big man, but he has such an infectious giggle.

"I'll get cleaned up and fed, as long as you dirty me up again later," I cheekily say and then sprint to the attached bathroom after slapping his tight ass.

Chapter 11

Tav

"He sounds like he's dying," whispers a little voice. I'm pretty certain it's Cove.

"He could be dying." whispers another voice. This time Jovie.

"Do you think we should do that mouth-to-mouth thing?"

"Ew, no way! His mouth stinks!"

"Shhhh! We don't want to wake him up," Cove's voice says, so close to my face that I feel her hot breath on me. "Ew gross,"

"See? I told you he stinks in the morning," What the fuck? Is that Rider?

I'm not sure whether to argue that my morning breath isn't that bad or pretend I can't hear them and wait for them to get bored of watching me. I contemplate this while the two little voices and one big voice dare each other to get close to my mouth. Making a show of rolling closer to the edge of the bed on the side they're standing on, I open wide and huff a big, pretend yawn in their direction, hitting them with the breath that they think is so toxic.

Three kid voices squeal, so I'm guessing Elio has been here the whole time, too. Opening my eyes, I'm greeted with them all holding their noses.

"Aw come on, it's not that bad!" Immediately after I say that I have to think back to make sure I brushed my teeth before bed. I do not want these kids smelling what I did to their mother last night.

"Tav, it's very, very bad," Elio says, with a serious look on his face.

"It's fu– ah fudging bad dude. You should get that looked at." Rider catches himself before dropping the f-bomb.

"Oh! Maybe you should see Mr. Switch! He's a doctor. We met him this morning when we went to see Niko," Cove says, eyes wide. Looks like Switch has made a friend.

"There's nothing wrong with me, kids. I'm as healthy as an ox. But I need breakfast." I turn to Pixie and see that she's not in bed. Huh, she must have gotten up early to check on the kids. "Have you guys eaten yet?"

"No, that's why we're here. They didn't want to eat without you," Rider says with a shrug.

"How did you end up hanging out with the kids?"

"Blanche brought her two out into the dining room early this morning, then got called into some business with Wire and the girls. Jovie's been hanging with us, waiting for you to wake up before we all get some grub."

"You have so many nose hairs," Elio whispers, staring up at Rider, his head tipped right back.

Cove tips her head to look at him for a moment. "You look like Shrek. But when he's a man."

Jovie also looks up and then nods in agreement. Tipping my head, I can kind of see it. Square jaw, longish hair.

Rider splutters, "The ogre?"

"Yeah! He lives in a swamp!" Cove says, clapping her hands.

Rider gapes at them, their smiling faces looking up at him like he's the best ogre they've ever seen. My snorting has him glaring at me.

"Let me get up and I'll get you lot some breakfast. Shrek, do you mind walking them out to the common room while I get sorted?"

Rider squints at me before ushering the kids out of the room while I laugh. I wait for the last of them to leave before throwing the covers off, sitting on the side of the bed, scrubbing my hands up and down my face, trying to remove the perma-smile on my face from last night. I've waited months for Pixie to get on the same page, and I think we are there. She's accepted that she's my Ol Lady and I'm her Ol Man. But that's just the beginning. I want it all.

I go to my chest of drawers, pull out some jeans and a tee, throw them on, and then add my cut over the top. I'm working from the clubhouse until I know that the threat to Blanche and the kids has been neutralized. I pick up the few things lying around, put them in my hamper, tidy, and make the bed, and then make my way out. Hopefully, the kids are still giving Rider shit.

Walking into the common room I see all three kids are sitting at the table, however, they are leaning so far over it while they talk to Rider sitting on the other side, that they are pretty much on top of the table. Judging by the excitement on their faces, and the scowl on his, I guess they're still trying to convince him of this Shrekness.

Looking around the room I find Sage sitting with Switch deep in conversation, Niko sitting quietly next to her on the couch.

"You know, a month ago I would never have imagined that we would have one kid here, let alone this many," Wire says, coming to stand shoulder-to-shoulder with me.

The three younger kids have ditched Rider and started a conversation with Fox and Nitro. This continues for a beat before they all turn their heads creepily slow to look in Rider's direction.

"Um, why are you looking at me?" He points to his chest and then runs his hand through his loose hair.

The kids, Fox and Nitro all look at each other and burst into laughter.

"He *does* look like man-Shrek!" Fox laughs, pointing at Rider, who looks none too impressed.

Standing in a huff, he stomps past the kids and their contin-ued laughter until he's standing toe to toe with me and Wire.

"Sort your kids out. Words hurt you know!" he hisses and then heads down the hall to sulk.

"Come on kids, let's get you fed, yeah? Your mom will be back once she's finished doing important stuff with Remy and Chewy." I swivel to look in Sage and Niko's direction, tipping my head to the kitchen to indicate breakfast, the big kids both giving me thumbs up. Taking that as a sign that they'll be up soon, I usher the Littles to the countertop where Mama Debs is serving, Wire following with Jovie in his arms.

That's their morning routine. Wire has breakfast with his little girl every morning. Watching them gives me a warm feeling in my chest as I join them.

"Hello my little *pepi*, what are you all in the mood for this fine morning?" Mama Debs coos as she leans over the bench, looking at Cove and Elio, Wire already carrying Jovie's pancakes to her place at the table.

"You say funny words, Mama Debs," Cove giggles.

"*Ae*, that's because I'm from very far away and we say different words sometimes. *Pepi* means babies," Debs replies with a soft smile.

The kids coo over her food and all decide to have whatever Jovie is having. Ushering them back to the table, Cove sits next to me with Elio on the other side.

"Little people," Chewy greets as she and my Pixie walk into the dining room.

Usually she would say "little person," in greeting to Jovie, but seeing as there's more of them, she's adjusted her wording. My sister may be all in with Rhodie, but I don't think she will ever go down the route with a dog and 2.5 kids. She doesn't dislike children, she just doesn't like them enough to be adding to the population anytime soon.

Pixie drops a kiss to the kids' heads, then mine as she walks down the line before heading to grab breakfast for herself. The older kids are down the other end of the table with the prospects.

"Niko looks better today," I mention to Pixie as she sits down next to me.

"Hmm, I think he's feeling a little too good. He's been grilling Takoda and Jimmy about prospecting," she grumbles before shoving a bite of pancake in her mouth, closing her eyes and groaning. "Holy shit, these are divine," she whispers almost to herself.

She takes another bite and I have to adjust myself under the table because those moans are hitting me square in the dick.

"Those are mommy's happy noises! That's the sound she was making last night when Tav was giving her a back rub," Cove loudly announces to everyone before chewing on another mouthful of pancake, oblivious to the fact that her mother is choking on her pancakes and I've spat my coffee all over the table in front of me.

"Is that right, brother?" Marx's voice says before his laughter rumbles out of him.

"Yeah, I, ah, had a bit of a sore back," Pixie says with a blush rising on her cheeks. I wrap my arm around her and pull her into my side, kissing her on the temple as she tries to hide her face, before she gets over it and remembers she's my Pixie, sitting bolt upright and flipping everyone the bird.

The door swings open, bouncing off the wall. All our heads snap toward the doorway, alert and ready for anything. Until Pops comes wandering through the door chatting to ... Officer Martin. What the fuck?

"As you can see, *Officer*, it's time for breakfast. Is there anything I can get you? Pancakes, waffles," Pops lowers his voice, "A bullet?"

"A what now?" Officer Dickwad's head snaps towards Pops who is smiling maniacally at him.

"A coffee, officer. What did you think I said?" Pops answers, looking about as innocent as Dayz when she does that stare-y eyed thing.

"Yes, fine. Coffee would be great." His beady eyes look around the room as if noticing us all for the first time. He's full of confidence and I have no clue what the hell Pops is playing at.

"Marx, I'm sure you don't mind that I invited Officer Martin in for breakfast. With the weather getting colder I thought I would give him a nice reprieve from sitting in his car watching us," Pops says with a smirk on his face, "You know, this could be a great time for us to get to know each other."

Marx raises a brow at Pops and then must buy into Pops's nutso plan because he nods his head. "Well, DRMC, let's welcome Officer Martin to breakfast."

Pixie whispers to Cove and Elio, who stand, taking their plates into the kitchen. Sage and Niko flank them and Jovie as they head in to Mama Debs.

"Take a seat, son! They ain't gonna bite!" Pops chuckles, placing his hand on Officer Dickwad's shoulder and shoving him into a seat at the table. He shuffles into the kitchen and gets busy making a coffee while the rest of us stare at our guest.

"Here you are, sir. I guessed how you'd take it." Pops says on his way out of the kitchen, before plopping a coffee cup down next to Officer Dickwad, a little of it sloshing over the side.

Dickwad takes a sip, grimaces, and places it down, jerking slightly when his gaze raises and he's met with my sister staring at him across the table.

"Hi."

"You're the security woman."

"Maybe."

He narrows his eyes for a moment, as if wondering whether or not he should double down. From the few interactions we've had with him, I know that he's not going to let my sister have the last word or look cleverer than him.

"You're Tuesday Tombs. Owner of Tombs Security, with your brothers, August, Jules, and Tav,"

Chewy smiles her most disarming smile. As a child, our mom worked hard using facial expression flashcards, books, and movies to help her learn how to interact with people socially. For the most part, Chewy is happy with how she is, but when she wants to, she masks her autism. I remember a time when Chewy started middle school and us boys being creeped out by her non-Chewy behavior. So much so that Mom had to sit us down and explain that the things that come naturally to us - interacting, reading non-verbal signs, fitting in - were things that Chewy had to learn by rote. It takes a lot out of her to mask all the time, which is why as she got older she just stopped trying to come across as "normal". Although when she wants to, she can tap into her prior training and become the most charming person you'll ever meet. Throw in the fact she's small with the same tanned skin as the rest of us, giant whisky-colored eyes, and pretty, well, it means that chubby, balding pink men like Officer Martin will be eating out of her hand in no time. Well played Pops. Well played.

"Oh OK, you got me! Wow, you are fantastic at research," she beams across the table at him, clapping her hands in front of her before leaning forward and resting her chin in her hand. "What else ya got?"

He takes another sip of his coffee before leaning back in his chair with a smug look on his face.

"I know your pops is a Vietnam vet, highly decorated."

"Officer Martin, have you been looking into us?" Chewy says all flirty-like and then caps it off with a little giggle.

From the corner of my eye, I notice Fox and Nitro both mouthing "What the fuck?" to each other. A laugh bubbles up, so I bring Pixie's hand to my lips, dropping a kiss on the soft skin to hide my smirk.

"I had to run background checks when all that business with your grandfather went down," he answers, taking a long pull of his coffee and then placing it down on the table with a thump, Pops taking a keen interest in his movements.

"Oh, of course, Officer. I'm so glad we have men like you helping keep Rose Grove safe. I bet Sergeant Davies loves having you on the team," she beams up at him, and I know the moment she sees his face darken slightly after the mention of Davies. It's clear the sergeant is a thorn in this man's side. "So, did you grow up around these parts? Is that why you take such an interest in keeping all the residents safe?

Chewy starts running her finger along the tabletop, veering close to where Officer Dickwad's hand sits. She looks at him through her lashes and he leers back at her. Looking around the room, I can see my brothers are all dumbstruck by what's happening in front of them. Not the least that Chewy is behaving like a club girl, all flirty and interested, but that Pops invited the cop that's been watching us to breakfast.

Dickwad stares at my sister before his eyes drift down her body, stopping for far too long on her boobs. I mustn't have been the only person who noticed because Rhodie lets out a growl over my shoulder. Chewy turns to look behind her, her friendly flirty smile dropping back to the usual impassive face we're used to. She rolls her eyes before giving Rhodie a wink and plastering the smile back on her face, then turning back to Dickwad.

She tips her head to the side. "Officer Martin?"

"Sorry, what were you saying?"

Pixie's inhale of breath is the first thing to alert me that something isn't right. Well, another thing in this whole weird scene.

"I was asking if you grew up here," Chewy smiles encouragingly.

He shakes his head as if trying to clear his mind, "Oh, um, yeah. Fuck, was there something in this coffee?" He frowns down at his cup.

There's a grumbling noise but this time it isn't coming from

Rhodie, it's coming from his big brother who is trying to hide the pissed look on his face.

"What's wrong, Officer? Is the coffee not agreeing with you? Maybe you have a sensitive stomach? I tested it myself and it was fine." Pops picks up the cup and takes a big gulp before slamming it on the table with a big "ahhhh."

Dickwad looks at his cup for a moment before his eyes roll back and he flops forward, face planting into the table with a thud.

"That worked a lot quicker than I thought it would," Chewy muses, "How much did you put in?"

"A double dose. I didn't know how long everyone would act normally for," Pops answers her, shoving Officer Dickwad's shoulder. We watch as he melts off the table onto the floor.

"What in the fuck do you two think you're doing? What about 'no torture and no murder' do you not understand?" Marx roars, hands on hips, towering over my grandfather and sister.

"Look kid, I'm off that fucker. I keep seeing his ugly ass face all over the place and I'm over it." Pops takes another swig of Dickwad's coffee, swishing it around his mouth a little.

"Ah, Pops, should you be drinking that?" Judge asks, looking concerned.

"Nah, it's fine. I'm used to this stuff. It won't knock me out, but it will definitely give me a chill vibe as the youth say." He winks as if he hasn't just told us that somehow he's immune to being roofied.

Pixie's eyes have been darting back and forth, taking in the scene. She leans into me, her lips brushing against my ear. "Marx wasn't joking, was he?"

I pull back, my brows pinched, trying to figure out what she means, "Joking about what?"

Her big, dark eyes bore into mine. "About the torture and murder. Chewy and Pops aren't, um, 'normal', are they?"

A laugh bursts out of me at her wording. "No Pixie, not at all."

Blanche

I watch as the brothers all talk amongst themselves, probably waiting for Marx's orders. He's pinching the bridge of his nose and I'm pretty sure he's doing the same breathing exercises I've noticed Tav's brother doing. Before Marx can even find the words, the door opens again. "Shit, what now?" he grumbles, turning to the doorway.

My head swings in the same direction, waiting for the next whackadoo thing to happen. When Pops led Officer Martin into the common room I almost died.

"Just us!" Ana coos, holding hands with Gus, "And look who we found!"

A beautiful older black woman walks in behind them, her hair in intricate braids piled on top of her head. She's in a power suit type thing, but instead of black, it's a lovely purple color.

"Hello my favorite- oh hell no! What about 'stay out of trouble' do you all not understand? Why the hell is there an unconscious officer on the floor of your clubhouse, Marx!" she says, with all the sass of a pissed-off mother.

"Hey Momma," Wire says, walking to the beautiful woman and dropping a kiss on her cheek.

"Hey baby," she replies, before hitting Marx with the death

stare.

Chewy holds her hand up like she's in class. "It wasn't him, it was me and Pops."

The woman's head snaps toward Pops. If the feeling of your balls shriveling up into your body had a human form, it would look a lot like Pops right now.

"Sidney Tombs! What did I tell you?"

"To stay out of trouble," Pops mumbles.

"So what's this?" She indicates toward one of Rose Grove's finest, out cold on the floor.

"That's not trouble. He just drank the wrong coffee. Besides, the guy is an utter asshole AND we're pretty sure he's connected to the trafficking, so I was just going to ask him a few little questions. Nothing more, nothing less." Pops shrugs, looking as if he's gained a little confidence in that spiel.

"You do know that accusing an officer of the law of being part of a criminal enterprise is pretty bloody damning, right? And incredibly hard to prove. Are you sure? Do you have any evidence?" She looks toward Marx, who weighs up his options.

"There is a high likelihood he's involved. We have evidence that he's currently working with Hammer." Marx's eyes flick to me and I give him the barest of nods. "We also have reliable intel that a baby is to be sold in the next week. She's safe for now, but we need to shut this down," he answers truthfully.

Wire's mom pushes her lips out, squints her eyes, and huffs a breath. She stands in the middle of the room, hands on hips, looking very formidable. "If I ignore whatever this is," she waves toward Pops, Chewy, and Officer Martin, "will you guarantee that you'll put a stop to this nonsense? Taking babies is hitting too close to home. Hell, I helped out two scared kids yesterday who were almost plucked right off the street!"

"Hold up!" I yell out, "A boy and a girl, the boy had been pistol whipped?"

Her head snaps in my direction. "You know them?"

"They're my babies! Thank you so much!" I rush up to the woman, wrap my arms around her, and squeeze her tight. "Thank you, from one momma to another," I whisper to her.

"Anytime, Mama, anytime."

We pull apart and Wire pulls his momma into his arms. "Thanks, Momma, those kids are Tav's family."

"Psh, I would have done it anytime, anywhere. I tried chasing those assholes down, but lost them when they hit the outskirts of town."

Wire forcefully pushes his mother back from him, staring at her. "What do you mean you chased them down? They were armed! You could have been killed"! Wire carries on berating his momma while she rolls her eyes at us.

He keeps ranting until Remy steps forward and loops her hands around him, resting them on his stomach, leaning her forehead into the middle of his back.

Wire's momma smiles at Remy before turning to Marx. "I mean it, Marx. You need to get onto these assholes who think they can come into our town and take our babies. But try to do it in a way that won't blow back on you all. I'm an old woman and don't have the time to be bailing a clubhouse full of grown men out of jail,"

Marx huffs a laugh, "Yeah, got you Momma,"

She spins toward Pops who snaps to attention, "Sidney, is this plan of yours going to result in another arrest?"

His eyes dart toward Chewy before his shoulders slump. "No ma'am. We'll be sending him on his way unharmed and in one piece after he wakes from his little nap."

Her eyes narrow as she assesses the old man, chewing the inside of her lip. When she comes to a decision, she nods once. "Good. Now where's my grandbaby?"

"Come with me Gigi, I'll take you to her," Remy's dad Flack answers, indicating down the hall. I met the suave older biker earlier this morning when he popped in to say good morning to his daughter.

I have to admit, I find this place more and more surprising. There is definitely more of a family vibe than I was expecting. There were things I knew about the MC. I wouldn't be worth my PI license if I didn't run background checks on the members, even if they aren't nearly as in depth as what the Tombs family can do. I knew that Marx and Rhodie were blood brothers and Rhodie and Rider had been best friends since childhood, as their fathers were original MC members. Almost all the members are vets. Wire was in Rhodie's unit, Judge and Tank were both stationed at the same place at the same time. Fox and Nitro have been best friends since childhood and served with Switch, and Remy's people all patched over just recently after disbanding their MC.

"So, am I right in believing that there will be no torturing or murdering of this guy then?" Rider asks, indicating Martin.

"Unfortunately not, BUT we have a plan. We're going CIA style," Chewy says, rubbing her hands together. "Boys, to the Rev Room!"

I lean in to Tav, "Do they have an S&M room here?"

He chuckles, his face lighting up. "Hell no! But it's Chewy's play on words for her and Rhodie's interrogation room,"

"Wait, so it's true? She is an enforcer?" I've heard her refer to herself as an enforcer, and Nat mentioned it as well, but I never thought it would be true. She's a woman and not a patched MC member. Would they really make her an enforcer? And if so, does that mean that she hurts, maims, and kills people too? Could Tav and his family, this family, actually be comfortable with this? Does that mean that maybe, just maybe, Tav won't be turned off by my hate, my anger, and my willingness to take multiple lives?

Shaking my head along with the thoughts bouncing around in my mind, I follow behind everyone as Tav and Tank lift Officer Martin and carry him out to a shed at the back of the compound, settled away from the clubhouse and the garages. Switch holds the door open for me and gifts me with a wink and a sly smile, as if to say "buckle up,".

Stepping into the remarkably clean and cheery room, I'm taken aback slightly. I really have to stop expecting MC club stereotypes because this is not the type of enforcer chamber I was expecting. The walls are a soft, relaxing color. There's a comfy looking couch along one wall, complete with cushions. There's even a coffee table and is that a platter of snacks?

"Ooh Mama Debs dropped off snacks!" Rider says with delight, swooping in to grab a brownie off the platter and plopping down on the couch.

The coziness of the room is in stark contrast to the shadow board of terrifying tools lined up on the walls. The brothers and Ol Ladies have all crammed into the room, some leaning against walls, others lounging on the couch. I move toward Tav and then come to a stop as he pulls on a hazmat suit, much like Pops and Chewy.

"Chewy, no fucking around. What's the plan? We cannot, I repeat, we cannot torture or kill him." Marx barks out around a mouthful of shortcake.

"Psh. Making someone bleed isn't the only way to get

information out of someone," Chewy waves him off. "We're going retro thanks to my friend who was happy to share some of this with me," she smiles a creepy grin and Pops claps his hands, rubbing them with glee.

"You all good, little Pixie?" Tav smiles down at me, as gentle as ever.

"Yeah, just a little confused. What's going to happen?"

He takes in the scene; the brothers looking relaxed, Pops and Chewy whispering to each other, Rhodie attaching Officer Martin to a St. Andrews Cross.

"It's hard to say. Given that we can't beat, maim, or kill him, this is new territory. But don't worry, I'm sure the team has something up their sleeves."

"Rhodie, soundtrack please, babe," Chewy asks sweetly before Rhodie drops a kiss on her lips and a pat on the ass.

The brothers all groan, and in no time music is being piped into the room.

"Is it getting hot in here?" Pops asks, with a twinkle in his eye as the opening beats of Nelly's song start pumping.

"Everyone, keep your fucking clothes on!" Marx bellows over the snickers.

"Good gracious ass is bodacious," Chewy sings under her breath while she opens Officer Martin's mouth and squirts something inside. Forcing his mouth shut, she rubs his lips all around. "Just gotta get all the Midazolam soaking in."

"Oh shit," Switch curses.

"What? What's shit? Can one of you fuckers explain to the rest of the room?" Marx grumbles, giving death glares to Chewy, and then Switch.

"Midazolam is one of the drugs the CIA was banned from using." Switch answers in his booming voice.

Marx does that thing where only one brow raises. "Why?"

"Because it's unethical to use truth serums on prisoners," Pops says with glee. "Lucky for us, we aren't the CIA."

Chewy takes the top off a tiny bottle and holds it under Martin's nose until he comes awake with a jerk. Instead of cursing and yelling and struggling, though, he seems dazed and confused.

"Well, there you are! How are you feeling, buddy?" Pops croons.

"I feel funny. Fuzzy. Tired. My mouth is so dry and I'm a little worried."

"Bingo," Chewy whispers, fist bumping Pops and turning to look at our prisoner. "Officer Martin, do you know who I am?"

"Yes, you're the youngest of the Tombs family. You were diagnosed as being on the autism spectrum when you were 8 years old. You graduated high school and college early. I think you're behind the disappearance of some of the major players in the trafficking game, but I can't find any proof."

There are a lot of raised eyebrows around the room, and the tension at how much he knows about Chewy is uncomfortable. He's been doing his research. Chewy, however, doesn't even blink an eye. In fact, she looks downright giddy that he knows so much about her.

Clapping her hands together and rubbing them with glee, she smiles, wide eyes twinkling.

"Let's get this party started, shall we?"

Chapter 12

"You're positive that he isn't going to come back here and fucking arrest everyone?" Tank asks as Pops releases Officer Dickwad from the St. Andrews cross where he spilled his guts. Both literally and figuratively.

I already have the cleaning supplies out of the closet and am ready to put Chewy's room back to rights as soon as we see the loose lipped officer from the premises.

"Yup," Pops replies, popping the 'p'. "He's out of it enough to not remember a thing, but I'll hit him with another dose of Midazolam before we send him on his way. Oh, and a little something to flush the Rohypnol from his system. That way, he'll just feel a little dazed, rather than dazed and feeling like shit."

Pres turns to look at Switch for confirmation. "Hate to agree with the old coot, but he's right. Midazolam calms the brain and impairs memory. Hit him with enough and he won't even remember this all happened."

"Exactly!" Pops finger guns Switch, "We'll give him a little more, then put him back in his cruiser. He'll wake up in about three hours feeling like he had the best goddamned nap of his life,"

Judge and Tank step forward and half carry, half drag blabbermouth out of the shed, presumably to his vehicle.

"Right, thanks to two people who don't fucking listen," Marx grumbles, giving Chewy and Pops the stink eye to end all stink eyes, "we know Officer Martin purposely led the murder investigation of Jovie's mom in our direction to take the heat off Hammer and Royal, at Royal's orders, and there have been two additional auctions we didn't know about."

"Yeah. But we didn't really get a good read on whether he's had a hand in the actual trafficking business. We also don't know if he's the only dirty cop in Rose Grove," Chewy points out.

"What's your read on Sergeant Davies?" Rhodic asks his brother.

"He's as straight as they come, and the only fucker in that department I would trust. We need more evidence that Martin is dirty. Once we get that, I'll hand it all over to Moss." Marx says, his brother nodding at his plan.

Hands on hips, Pres stares at my sister and grandfather, squinting at them. They stare straight back.

"I mean it you two. No torture, no murder, and I'm adding no drugging or kidnapping. At least until after we get the pigs off our backs. Fuck sake." He scrubs his hand down his face.

With that, he storms out, the brothers slowly following behind. The gentle warmth of my Ol Lady leans against my side. "You good Pixie?"

She squints those gorgeous dark eyes before tipping her head side to side, as if weighing up whether she's good or not.

"Talk to me babe," I balance the mop in my hand against the wall, before turning to take her hand and leading her to the couch. All of my family, both biological and MC, have gone their separate ways, leaving me and my Pixie in Chewy's brightly colored room, complete with floor drain and the distinct smell of vomit where Officer Dickwad barfed everywhere.

"I feel, I feel fucking ashamed, Tav." Her dark head drops as she stares at her hands, fiddling in her lap. I expected pissed, but not ashamed.

"Why would you feel ashamed? What they are doing, your uncle, cousins, Hammer, all of them, that's on them, not on you." I reach over and lay my much larger hand over the top of both of hers.

"There are women, girls stolen off the streets, being sold to god knows who. FUCK!" she jumps up from the couch, storming toward my cleaning bucket and kicking it across the room. "Not two fucking weeks ago, Tav, I put a bullet in Valor because I wanted to stop him from selling people. I beat DRMC there and I took my revenge against my father and the Keep. But I was shortsighted. If I had let him live, then you all would have enough to shut down the operation. Because of me, Tav, ME!" She thumps her chest with her fist, eyes blazing, "There are more women and children being sold. What have I done?" With that, she crumples to the ground, sobs wracking her compact frame.

My heart breaks for her, as she blames herself. This isn't on her and for the first time ever I see another facet of Blanche, my woman. I see the broken girl who has been fighting hard, so hard to right the wrongs of men who should know better.

I scoop her up in my arms and carry her back to the couch, cradling her gently, rocking her as I rest my lips against the short hair at her temple.

"Shhh, it's OK baby, we're going to shut them all down. All of them, and we'll find those girls and return them back to their families. Trust me Pixie, this is what we do. We find the lost and we bring them home." I continue rocking her, breathing in her spicy scent, the one that clings to my sheets, the one that makes me rock hard. But this isn't about that, this is about comforting my strong, fierce woman when she needs it.

"Thank you, Tav. For everything." She snuggles closer, her face in the space between my collar and jaw, her small hand rubbing the stubble on my face.

We sit in quietly, taking comfort from each other, before Pixie breaks the silence. "What the hell does Officer Martin eat? That barf stinks,"

A chuckle bursts free before I'm laughing with wild abandon, my head thrown back, my body shaking with laughter, bouncing my little Pixie.

"Want to help me clean up?" I gaze down at her sparkling eyes and then chuckle more when she screws up her nose.

"Ew, hell no! You're on your own!" She moves to stand, a thoughtful look on her face, "When you said you're usually on cleanup duty, is this what you mean?"

Looking around the room, I think about how many times I've been out here cleaning up after my sister and grandfather. "This isn't actually too bad. At least this is just vomit. Usually its body parts," I shrug.

"Wait a minute, so you're not bothered at all by what happens out here?"

Frowning, I try to understand what she's asking me. "Why would I? I mean, it's definitely unorthodox, and my sister takes more pleasure out of this than she should, but it's for the greater good." I stand so close to her that my chest brushes against those perfect tits of hers. "Pixie, I like to think we're good people that sometimes do bad things for the greater good. Are you going to be OK with that?"

She tips her head back to look at me, her eyes darting between mine as if looking for something. "Tav, I'm on a mission to kill 8 men for the greater good. I'm sure I'll be just fine with whatever it is you need to do."

"We're totally a badass couple. Probably even more badass than Chewy and Rhodie," I murmur to her.

"I wouldn't go that far, big guy, but we're definitely in the running." She moves to her tiptoes and presses a kiss to the underside of my jaw. "I'm going to go yell at my kids for a bit. I'll see you after clean up duty."

I give her an affectionate pat on the ass and move to pick up my favorite bucket she kicked across the room.

"Why are you going to yell at the kids?"

"Not sure yet, but chances are they've been up to no good since I've been gone," she winks and sashays out and I can't help but grin at how lucky I am.

Blanche

What a goddamned rollercoaster that was. I knew Royal and Co were fucking evil, but not this evil. I'd like to blame the drugs and things on Hammer, but I know deep down that Royal is sadistic enough to come up with that on his own. I'm willing to bet that Hammer is Royal's puppet, not the other way round.

"Mommy! Look what we've been doing!" Cove calls out, holding up a drawing. Well, I think it is. It's hard to tell because she's waving it around in the air.

"Wow, baby, that looks amazing!"

Elio looks up for a moment, giving me a little smile before turning back to his chess set. He's moving the pieces one side at a time, effectively playing himself. Shitting hell, what am I going to do with a chess genius?

"Just breathe, Mom, he has years before we'll have to spend weekends traveling to chess competitions," Niko says with a snort.

"How are you feeling? Still headachey?" I place my hand on his forehead, but he leans away from it.

"Mom, I'm fine. Still a little sleepy, but not bad. So, what was all that stuff with that police officer?"

I side eye my eldest for a moment, then the second eldest sidles up looking just as interested.

"He's involved in the whole Royal people auction thing."

They both suck in a breath. "What are we going to do?" Sage asks, snuggling into my side.

"We –" I wave my finger at her and her brother, "aren't going to do anything. Marx is coming up with a plan. DRMC will shut it all down."

Sage stares wide eyed at me. "They're not going to go to the police, are they?"

"No Sagey, they're not."

"Good."

I try to hide my smile at my girl's vehemence but instead decide to share it with her. She may only know about the Keep and the people there from my stories, but she knows from the times we've had to run or hide how dangerous they are.

"Just so you know, I'm not sending any of you back to school until Royal's taken care of." I hold my hand up to stop any protest. "I know it sucks, but I think it's best. I've already contacted your teachers and they'll be sending your work through. Same for the Littles." I give them my stern mom eye, only to be met with little resistance.

"It's OK Mom, we talked about it last night. We'd feel safer not going back and sticking close to the Littles until this is done." Niko pulls me in for a hug. "Love you Mom."

"Love you too, Son."

I pull back and see Sage side eye her brother. They're scheming something.

"Because we're so worried about safety and all that, we've asked Takoda to teach us to use weapons safely and responsibly," Sage says all in one breath.

She must see the look on my face because her eyes dart to her brother, who backs her up. "Mom, we would feel better if we could protect ourselves. We're not going to go on a rampage or anything. It'd just make me and Sage feel better if we knew how to use them. Just think about it, yeah?"

They smile their very best smiles and back away slowly, before turning and hustling their cheeky asses down the hall. I keep my frowny, angry mom eyes glaring at their backs until I can't see them any longer.

"Come on, *kotiro*, help me in the kitchen and we'll solve all the ills in the world, yeah?" Debs gently loops her arm through mine and none too gently walks me into the kitchen. From the serving hatch I can see Cove and Jovie coloring and chatting to their heart's content, Elio with his chess and Takoda watching over them. After years of doing this mom thing all alone, it feels weird to have all these people happy to help keep an eye on my kids.

"So, tell me all about what has your angry mum eyes on," Debs asks, bent over with her head inside a cupboard. "We're making brownies, so maybe you can tell me while you get the ingredients for me."

I get the butter out of the fridge, then start rummaging in the cupboards for the cocoa and the flour. "The kids asked if Takoda could teach them how to use a gun," I sigh.

"That sounds reasonable. I mean, I'm sure you know this, but you're American. I thought everyone knew how to use a gun," Debs says, concentrating on getting the oven preheated.

I try not to smile. "Well, yeah, I mean, a lot of us know how to use guns and open carry. But they're my babies," I pout.

Deb's rich laugh washes over me. "They'll always be your babies. But at some stage those babies grow up. I never once thought that my daughter would grow up to work for the Bratva. I mean, a little girl from the other side of the world in the Russian Mafia? That's crazy!"

I mean, yeah, it is kinda crazy, so I nod in agreement with Debs.

"You want to know the thing that made me feel better about her job?" She raises her brows at me, waiting for my nod. "What made me feel better is knowing that as a little girl she learned to hunt and fish with my husband. Ana knows how to use guns safely. That made me feel better. That as a parent we had provided her with the education and the knowledge. Even if she never grew up to wield a gun, at least I knew she was safe."

I know I'm frowning back at Deb's smiling face, but when I think, my whole face collapses into a frown. "I never thought about it like that,"

Debs shrugs, still with a smile on her face. "If guns are a step too far I'd be more than happy to teach them how to use a bow."

"What?" I splutter. I know I shouldn't, because I know you can't judge a book by its cover and all that, but surely this mild mannered, lovely little brown woman with a halo of curls is joking, right?

"You're looking at a bow hunting champion, *e hine*. I've been bow hunting since I was a girl."

"Made her a sharp shot with a gun as well," Sniper says quietly as he enters the kitchen. He drops a kiss to Debs' cheek, who then bustles into the pantry to pull out a small container. They must be special treats the way they look furtively around, Debs passing it off as if it's contraband.

I don't know too much about Sniper. He's one of the quieter brothers, sticks mainly to himself, which I guess makes sense seeing as his actual job in the military was as a sniper.

"Shooting arrows at moving targets trains you to shoot anything, really."

I think about her offer for all of 30 more seconds. "Alright, Debs, I would love it if you could teach Sage and Niko how to shoot a bow."

Whooping and hollering sound out and I lean through the hatch to see my two teens on the other side, backs against the wall. Spinning back to Debs, I glare at her.

"Was this a setup?" I ask, my eyes narrowed.

"No way! I'm offended you even thought I'd do something like that," she says, hand on her chest as if clutching at pearls. I almost believe her until I see the little wink she gives the kids.

I shake my head to myself, but I can't help the little smile playing on my lips.

"You raised good kids, Blanche. Just think what you would have done at their age," Debs says, pointing at the chocolate she wants me to hand her.

At Sage's age, 16, going on 17, I was living my life in the Keep. Going to prayer in the morning and then heading to my work placement. All girls over the age of 12 have work placements. Most of us work in either the kitchen preparing all meals for the Keep members, while others get laundry duty. We work these jobs until we're married, because obviously we'll be too pregnant to do anything else. If a girl is really lucky, and unmarried over the age of 18, they get to graduate to teaching the younger kids in the school on site. Obviously the curriculum leans more towards what Mercy thinks is important, rather than what's in the American education system.

At Niko's age, a few months shy of 18, I was preparing to marry my uncle. This is where my hatred for the Eden's Keep Council comes from. Eight older men, all chosen by Mercy, sit you in a room with other young women on the cusp of marriage. There we were made to watch pornography, video after video of women being used by men; vaginally, anally and orally. All to teach us how to please our husbands. If you didn't learn from the videos, or were unable to please your husband, there were special group evenings you could attend with your husband. Royal dragged me to two such evenings because he said I was frigid. On those nights, men would bring their wives to a small room off the side of the main hall. There were mattresses on the floor and we'd be encouraged to relax. From there Mercy himself would talk everyone through fucking, using one of his young wives as his assistant. We'd all be encouraged to join in. It was at one of these such events that I learned to zone out. Blank my mind to everything that was happening to my body.

Here I'd plan my escape from Royal, from my father, from the Keep.

Looking at my babies, on the cusp of the age I was during my last year or so at the Keep, I realize Debs is right. At their age I wouldn't have asked my mother if I could learn to use a weapon. If I had access to one I would have taught myself and then killed them all then and there.

"You're right, Debs, I wouldn't have asked. But I'm glad they did, and I'm glad they have you and everyone else to guide them. Thank you for offering to teach my babies."

Her gentle eyes take in my face, softening when we share a look that only mothers understand. Shaking the flour off her hands, she rubs them on the front of her ever present apron, then she pulls me into a hug, her surprisingly strong arms wrapping me up.

"I'm proud of you Blanche, you're a good girl," she pulls back, stroking my cheek and I tear up a little. It's been a long time since I had a mom in my life. "Now pull yourself together. How are the kids and men going to fear you if you're in here blubbering?" Her lips twitch as she gives me a wink and gets back to her baking.

I huff out a laugh and clean my face. To distract from my emotions I take a deep breath, then exhale, looking out the window. Before I can even finish my exhale, the rest of the breath is stolen by a laugh that bubbles up at the sight.

"What's so funny?" Debs comes to stand at the window with me, then bursts into laughter as well.

"What the hell are you two laughing at?" Niko's voice says, but he sounds distant as Debs and I hold on to each other, laughing like a pack of hyenas. "Wait, are those dicks on that police cruiser's lights?"

Roaring comes from the common room and I'm guessing the rest of the brothers have spotted what we have, Officer Martin driving off in his cruiser, his light bar decorated with 10 wobbling dildos.

Chapter 13

I'm sitting at the table in the common room trying to sort through paperwork from Tombs Security. It's nice that my brother has told me not to return to work until Pixie and the kids are all safe, but I don't want my siblings picking up too much slack if there are things I can work on.

It's been almost a week since my Pixie and the kids came to the clubhouse, and we still haven't nailed down a decent plan of attack. Royal, Hammer, Officer Martin and Eden's Keep are moving pieces which complicates things. We just don't have enough information for a coordinated strike. We can take out one or two, but not before alerting the others. We want to take out the whole operation, not leave survivors that will just start up again from a different base.

"Hey, um, Tav, are you busy?"

Niko stands awkwardly on the other side of the table. I tip my head at the seat across from me and shut my laptop. If Niko wants to talk, then I'm all ears.

"Yeah, man. Have a seat. You OK?"

He frowns over my shoulder, and I give him the time he needs. He's so much like his mother sometimes. Prickly to begin with, but I've noticed over the past few days, since they've been here, that he's started to soften up. I get it though. They've lived through Royal coming after them and who knows what else. He's right to be wary of men. I just hope that one day he'll accept my relationship with Pixie.

His eyes flick to mine, and he takes a deep breath before exhaling, his shoulders drooping. "I need you to promise me you'll look after my mom."

My brows pinch together as my head tips. I'm a little confused by his request. My role in this life, the one I'm trying to have with my Pixie and her family, is to look after her, to be there for her.

"Of course I'll look after your mom," I almost tell Niko that I love her, but those words are for her to hear first. My words don't seem to have any effect on him, as he's still tense as hell. "Is there something worrying you, Niko?"

"I'm worried that she'll get impatient and try to go after Royal herself. I need her to not do that. I want her to leave it to you guys. I mean, look at you! You all look like you'd be able to take them all out without breaking a sweat." Now that he's started talking it seems hard for him to stop. "Like, she doesn't need to go out there and put herself in danger. I need you to get her to just wait for you guys to take care of it, keep her here or something. Please? She's my mom and I know she's capable, but she doesn't have to do it by herself anymore. I, we, really need her." His dark eyes implore mine and I see the scared boy behind all the teen bluster and bravado.

Niko turns 18 in a couple of weeks. Essentially a grown man, not much younger than Gus and Jules when we lost our parents, and I still see the effect it has on my brothers every day. No kid deserves that and I know that it'll be over my dead body that these kids experience what we went through.

"Niko, your mom is my Ol Lady. It's my job to look after her and protect her and make sure she and you guys are happy, healthy and safe. But-" I hold my hand up when he opens his mouth to interrupt, "she's her own woman. She has her mission, just like DRMC has ours. We are working with your mom to end this. She deserves to slay her dragons and I will stand by her side as she does. In terms of her going off on her own, you and I will work together to make sure that doesn't happen, OK? I'm sure between the two of us we can make sure she's distracted enough to wait for Marx to come up with a solid plan."

He huffs before smiling at me. "Deal." He holds his fist out to bump, so I gently tap him. "Thanks, Tav."

"Anytime, Niko," I smile at him as he stands and heads toward his sister Sage.

"Nice work there, kid," Tank's smooth voice says as he kicks the chair Niko was sitting in out further so he can ease his much larger body into it.

"Why do you all call me that? I'm not that much younger than you guys," I grumble slightly. And not whiney.

"It's probably less to do with your age, and more your personality,"

I raise a brow at him.

He sighs, then looks around the room. The brothers have started filing in, as most of our businesses would have closed up for the day. "What do you think of Sniper?" He points at our brother sitting in the farthest corner of the bar, back to the wall.

Frowning, as I'm not sure where he is going with this, I decide to answer him. He's my sponsor and as his prospect I should do as I'm told. "He's a cool guy. He's seen some shit. I can see it in the way he holds himself. He spends a lot of time in his head and I think he's lost someone close to him. He's measured and thoughtful. He's a good man." I nod at my assessment as Tank tips his head at my words.

"Switch. Tell me about him." He tips his chin to Switch, having a loud conversation with Cove.

"He's a solid brother with a great sense of humor. I know he trained in the army and he's seen some nasty shit, but he still treats everyone with care and kindness. He's empathetic, and he cares about everyone in this clubhouse."

Tank's lips twitch as my description. "OK, what about Pops?"

"Pops?" My brows pull down, but I answer anyway. "Well, he's Pops. He may be a little weird, but he's protective and caring. He has so much love to give. He'd do anything for any of us, including the DRMC."

Tank's smile grows. "That's why we call you Kid. You have a childlike ability to see the absolute best in everyone and everything. You've just told me the three most damaged, unhinged men we know are thoughtful, kind, and loving. They are, in their own way, under the surface, but you see it clear as day. It's what makes you a good brother, and what'll make you a good father." He slides his chair back with a screech, stands and walks to the bar.

My chest fills with pride at his words. One day I hope I can be as good a father to my kids as my dad was to me. I'm really hoping that Pixie, Niko, Sage, Cove and Elio will allow me to be a part of their family. That would be the perfect cherry on top of the sundae. After killing all the people on our list, of course.

"He's right, you know," I jump a little when my brother speaks a little too close to my ear.

I spin to look at Jules, expecting a frown. Instead, he has his unreadable face on.

"You got all the empathy and sunshine that I missed out on. It's what makes you a good guy, Tav."

"Jules, you're a good guy. You're one of the best I know."

He gives me the lopsided smile that he very rarely gives and then heads toward the bar as well. I'm not on bar duty tonight and with my laptop closed for the evening, I'm gonna check on the kids and my girl.

I stand, grab my things, and head toward my room. It's funny, I still have my cabin next to Pops and my siblings, but these past few days my room here has felt like home. Every night I get to make love to my woman, and then fall asleep wrapped around her. Just thinking of her in my arms has my cock thickening, so I quicken my pace, unlock my room door and come face to face with my girl, pacing like a caged animal.

Kicking the door closed, I place my laptop on the little desk and hold my hands up in front of me, stepping into her path.

"Pixie, baby, talk to me. What's going on?"

She tips her head back to look at me, her brows pulled in, mouth a tight line. She grits her teeth before letting out a frustrated scream.

"I can't handle this anymore! It's been days and Marx still doesn't have a plan. The Computas are working around the clock and are struggling to find anything on why the fuck that man keeps coming after my son. My brothers aren't answering at the moment and I just feel like I- I- I don't know! I feel useless." She deflates now that she's put a voice to her feelings. "I just feel like going out there and putting an end to it now!"

"Pixie," I warn, "That is not a good idea. You made a deal with the Pres of DRMC. Marx will not storm into a place where we are severely outnumbered without knowing all the details. You need to stand down and wait."

Her eyes narrow and her jaw tenses. "Are you telling me what to do, Octavius?"

"Blanche," I sigh. "I'm all in with you. You're my Ol Lady. That means I have your back and I stand by your side. If you want to go out right now and take out Royal, then I'm there with you. But we have to be smart. There are so many moving pieces and things we still don't know."

Her little body deflates, shoulders drooping, her head tipping forward as if all the fight has left her. I don't want this Pixie. I want the one I fell for. The one with guts and fire and fight.

I run my finger along her cheek, under her chin, tipping it up to look at me.

"It'll be your time soon, just not now. But when it is? You will burn Eden's Keep to the ground and I'll be there to dance on its ashes with you."

Her eyes dart between both of mine, searching for something. She must find what she's looking for because she smiles softly at me. Moving up onto her toes, she kisses me, her plump lips brushing mine gently.

She pulls back with a sigh, slowly opening her eyes to gaze at me. "I love you, Tav."

My insides light up from within, and it's as if all my insecurities and fears are washed away in that one little sentence. I crash my lips down on hers, my hands cupping her face, angling her head as I control the kiss, my tongue dueling with hers, lapping at her mouth, tasting, delving, wanting deeper and deeper. Wanting everything.

Her hands move across my chest, pushing my cut off my shoulders, letting it slide down my arms until I catch it in my hand, gently tossing it over the desk behind me. I need to be closer, so I grip her ass in my hands, her legs wrapping around my waist, Pixie's heat rubbing against my hard length.

"Tav, I need you now," she breaks the kiss long enough to whine, her hands scratching at my shirt, trying to get to my skin.

I toss her small form on the bed and start stripping off my clothes. Pixie doesn't need to be told twice because she stands on the bed, stripping in double time, her clothes flying everywhere. I'll tidy those up later.

Once we're both sufficiently naked she throws herself in my arms, wrapping her legs around me once more as I stand at the foot of the bed.

"Get in me now, Tav," she demands before nipping at me, biting down on my lower lip until it hurts so good.

Gripping my hard cock at the base, I rub the mushroom head through her pussy lips, covering myself in her cream. I ease into her wet heat, my head tipping back on a groan.

She kisses my neck, sucking hard before licking a stripe to my earlobe, nipping it in her teeth before demanding "Fuck me."

Blanche

Tav's hands grip my ass cheeks and he lifts me slightly then drops me down on his cock at the same time he powers up into me, pulling a "fuck!" out of me from the depths of my stomach. Holy shit, this man will be the death of me.

He spins us toward the door, pressing me up against it, the cold surface shocking the breath out of me, but I have no time to think about that as Tav powers in and out, pushing me higher and higher up the door. In no time at all I feel the pull low in my belly, his cock hitting that special spot inside me that sends me flying.

"That's it baby, give it to me, cum all over my cock," he growls.

My body convulses and tightens, my orgasm pulsing through me, draining me of my stress, frustration and anger. As my body softens, so does the look in Tav's eyes, the man that somehow stole my heart. I'm still scared as hell, scared that he'll see the real me and reject me. Scared that he'll want to control me, scared of the depth of my own feelings, but I push that all aside and try to trust my heart.

His hands slide from my ass to behind my back, pulling me into him, holding me against his warm chest, his dark hair rasping against my still sensitive nipples, his short beard rubbing against the short hair at my temple. His cock is still hard, deep inside me as he gathers me in his arms and moves me to the bed, laying me down gently, almost reverently. Once I'm on the warm comforter, my head on the pillow, his strong arms bracketing me, he starts to slide out of me, slowly, and then somehow, even slower, he pushes back in.

He moves within me, dropping gentle kisses on my eyelids, my nose, my cheeks, my jaw. He presses his lips to mine and whispers "I love you," gazing into my eyes, my soul.

We make love.

For the very first time in my life, I learn what making love is, what it means, how it feels. We both go over the edge with tears in our eyes.

* * *

"Babe, babe, your phone," Tav's thick voice rasps in my ear.

Holy crap! We must have fallen asleep after that amazing moment. What started off with Tav fucking the stress out of me, ended with me feeling something I've read about in books and never thought I'd ever experience.

"Shit! The kids!" I hiss at Tav while searching for my phone.

"They're fine, Rider and Wire are teaching the Littles how to play chess with Elio, and Mama Debs has the big kids out the back with her hunting bow," he says, rolling over, propping his hands behind his head, his lips curling up as he watches me, ass bent over wrestling my phone out of my jeans pocket.

"Finally!" I yell triumphantly before sliding the answer button. "Vic! I've been trying to call-"

"Someone tried to take Lovely. Her and Bee are fine, they're with us now, any chance we can hide Lovely with you?"

"Shit shit shit fuck shit!"

Tav sits up immediately, worry on his face. Without even knowing what's going on he gets up, finds my clothing and lays it on the bed so I can get dressed. Flicking my brother to speaker, I throw my phone on the bed and roughly pull on my clothes.

"Who the hell tried to take her?" I try not to screech, but my voice is definitely a few octaves higher.

"Don't know sis. Some guy pretending to be police," Chris answers instead of Vic.

"Where are you now?" Tav asks, leaning over me to speak, his beard grazing my cheek.

"On our way back to ours to switch out vehicles," Vic replies. He's the planner of the three.

"Let me talk to my Pres, get shit sorted. Give us 10 minutes."

"Stay safe!" I yell to my brother before closing down the call.

Tav and I share a look before we both head for the door. The shit just hit the fan. Tav links his fingers with mine as we walk down the long main hall, stopping briefly to look into Marx's office. Seeing he isn't in there, we continue on through to the common room. Spying his bulk sitting at the bar with Tav's brothers, we head that way.

"Pres! We need to talk. A police officer found Pixie's sister and tried to abduct her," Tav says loudly, the bustle in the room dying down as everyone turns to listen. The room is full as it's almost dinnertime.

"Officer Martin?" Marx barks..

"We don't know, but my brothers have her and the baby. They need a safe space to take them."

My thigh muscles are tight with tension, shoulders up by my ears. I know that the clubhouse isn't a hotel, and they only have so much space and resources, but I really need my sister and niece to be safe.

"We'll set up a room. Can you call your brothers, please?" Marx asks, then nodding toward Nat and Chewy who head off down the hall, presumably to get things ready. Thank God this place is huge with room to spare.

I pull up Vic's number and hit the call button. It rings once before he answers and I switch him to speaker. "You're on speaker, Vic."

"Vic? My name is Marx. I'm the Pres of Devil's Rose MC. My people are sending through a picture. Can you confirm if this is the man that tried to take your sister?" Marx nods at Wire who leans over to check the number Pixie has called, then taps on his keyboard.

"Should be with them now, Pres," he says, eyes never leaving his screen.

There's some rustling on the line and then Lovely answers, "Yes that's the man! He said my sister sent him, but he wasn't in uniform. The woman I was staying with asked him to leave and he- he hit her! I picked up Bee and ran to the neighbors who called my brothers. I hid in their basement until they came and got me."

"Mother fucker! How far out are you?" Marx seethes. I've heard he has a soft spot for women and children.

The phone rustles again and Vic answers, "We're on the road now. I'd say another two hours."

"Let us know if you need an escort. We have MC friendlies up your way. We'll ready your rooms."

"Thank you, Marx. We'll keep in touch."

"Wire, Chewy, Remy, one of you, get me everything you have on Office Martin's whereabouts the past two days. I'm sure you placed trackers on more than just his work cruiser, Chewy."

"I wouldn't dream of such a thing," she says, staring at him with giant eyes.

Marx raises a thick brow, then rolls his eyes. "I need to know everything. If we want to bring all these fuckers down we need to know when they eat, when they sleep, when they shit."

"Aye, aye Captain."

Chapter 14

Tav

We all eat in relative silence. The Computas tapping away, their plates next to them on the table. Marx has been coming in and out. He even escorted Sergeant Davies into his office. The man didn't look too pleased when he came out half an hour later.

We're all tense as hell, waiting for Pixie's family to arrive. I'm fucking hoping they may be able to help us connect the dots, because we have been floundering for too long, fighting on three different fronts - Hammer, Royal and Officer Martin.

"Babe, it's getting late. Why don't you get the Littles ready for bed, yeah? Give them attention and hold them tight. We'll be mobilizing soon enough," I murmur to her. She presses her head into the side of my arm so I cup her face with my other hand, grazing her soft cheek with my thumb.

She turns her face to kiss my palm before sitting upright. "Come on Littles, time to get washed up and ready for bed. Uncle Tank had something special delivered for you," Pixie teases the kids.

Cove jumps up with a fist pump then races to stand next to Tank, "Thank you, Uncle Tank" she yells at the top of her lungs before throwing herself into the big man's arms. Elio offering a soft "Thank you," from behind his sister.

"Anytime Squirts, see you in the morning," Tank affectionately pats them both on the head, a smile playing on his lips.

"You ever thought of having kids?" I ask, knowing that Tank would make an amazing husband and father.

He lets out a sigh, "I had hoped when I was younger. Now? I'll be pushing 40 in a few years and no sign of my lady. But you can bet your ass as soon as I find her I'll be locking her down and having a passel of little Tanks," he ends with a grin.

"Let's hope she's a big woman then to carry around your giant offspring," Savage says around a mouthful of Mama Debs' dessert.

"You should have looked for a bigger woman," Nat says, frowning at Savage, "I'm stuck not only having to carry around your giant baby, but somehow push your giant baby's head out of my hoohaa,"

"I'm sorry baby," Savage says, kissing her on the top of her head. Nat softens, her glare replaced with a soft smile. "I'll still love your hoohaa no matter what shape it's in afterwards," Nat sits bolt upright and before Savage can move, she stabs him in the hand with a fork. "OW!"

"Serves you right you giant asshole! Do you think I want my hoohaa traumatized? Do you think I want to be ripped open from asshole to breakfast for someone that probably looks exactly like a mini version of you to scream in my face and demand my tits in its mouth every hour? Do you?!"

The sound of gagging has everyone's heads whipping in the opposite direction of Savage and his baby momma. Rider is positively green, and the gagging doesn't seem to be slowing down.

Unfortunately for him, Nat doesn't seem to be slowing down either. Quite the opposite. She's on a roll as she describes, in detail, exactly what's going to happen to her body. Savage is pale and looks like he's going to cry at any moment. Dex is filming this whole debacle. Some brothers have already hightailed it out of the room and still it doesn't stop. Gus is sitting frozen with his arm around Ana, who is beaming up at him, knowing that he has all this shit on top of his usual anxieties to worry about now.

"You men are all pussies, you know that?" Pops butts in before putting a forkful of food in his mouth. "Your woman has sacrificed her body to grow your child. She's going through some big changes. Her body will never be the same, but that's a good thing. All those marks and changes you see will remind you of what she gave you."

Both Nat and Ana smile softly at Pops, the men all pulling themselves back from the brink. Well, apart from Rider who's had to rush to the bathroom.

"Thank you, Pops," Nat says, standing, moving to Pops' side and dropping a kiss on his cheek.

"You're welcome, girl." Pops then turns to Savage. "I delivered my son, you know. Proudest moment of my life when I held that goopy screaming bundle in my hands. Your woman's down belows don't matter in that moment. Or any moment after that for at least six weeks because once that kid comes out? You'll be too scared shitless that you're going to fail them to go anywhere near your Ol Lady's hoohaa." Pops then shovels another bite into his mouth while chuckling.

"That's exactly what it's like," Flack agrees.

"Well, thank you all for ruining the beautiful act that is childbirth. I'll be adopting my children fully grown," Rider says, striding to his seat looking a hell of a lot better.

"You know, I have a way to help with your little problem," Pops says thoughtfully, looking at Rider.

"I don't have a problem, old man," Rider says with a look that could rival Jules' Resting Bitch Face.

"Sure you do. Every time periods and lady plumbing get mentioned you go all wobbly. Whatcha gonna do when you have an Ol Lady and she's got the painters in? Spend 3 to 5 days blowing chunks?"

Rider's frown grows even deeper, but I can tell he's taken the bait. Hell, all of us here can tell. "What do you have in mind?"

"Well, son, you could start dating men. No icky periods for you to deal with," he carries on when Rider growls at him. "Or, you can undergo exposure therapy," Pops offers.

"He's right, exposure therapy is a good way for you to overcome your fear," Switch booms.

"I'm not scared!"

"Sure you are. So, what do you say? We still got a couple of hours until Blanche's family arrives. That's more than enough time for me to work my magic," Pops says, rubbing his hands together.

"Fuck it, let's do it," Rider says.

"Rev Room?" Rhodie asks, Chewy's head popping up at the sound of her favorite place being mentioned.

"Rev Room."

Blanche

I gently stroke Cove's dark hair back from her face, pressing my lips to her forehead before checking to make sure she's tucked in. It won't matter in a few hours as she'll kick those blankets off and starfish on the bed, but as long as she's tucked in when I leave, my mom conscience is clear. I lean over my clever little boy and do the same thing, smoothing his hair to the side, how he likes it.

"Love you, my babies,"

Turning, Sage and Niko hover in the doorway with pillows and blankets in their arms.

"We're going to bunk in here tonight. We know the Uncles are coming and things have been tense, so we'll stay in here," Niko whispers softly,

"But not on the floor," Mama Debs says, coming out of nowhere, with Takoda following carrying two camp beds. "No grandkids of mine sleep on the hard floor," she cups both my big kids' cheeks before bustling off somewhere else, probably granting wishes and turning pumpkins into carriages.

"Thanks, Takoda," Sage says softly as he sets up a bed next to Cove for her.

"You're welcome, Sage," his impossibly deep voice answers and I can't help but notice my girl turning pink. Interesting.

Niko sets up the other camp bed at the end of Elio's bed. It's a little cramped, but they both assure me they're fine. They'll probably both be on their phones anyway, so I guess they don't need that much space.

"You can give our rooms to whoever needs it, brother," Niko tells Takoda, whose lips curl a little.

"Thanks, man, it's appreciated," the prospect answers before quietly leaving the room.

My raised brow has Niko mirroring my exact expression, "What? I'm thinking of prospecting. This is a good place, Mom, and we all know I'm not college material."

"But you're MC material?"

He shrugs. "I don't know about that just yet. But I know I'm hardworking, good with my hands and I want to help people."

I can't argue with that, as what he says is true. I just never thought my son's future was in an MC. Hell, I didn't think my future was either, but I guess things change. "We'll put a pin in this for now, but we are definitely coming back to this conversation, got it?"

"Yeah I got it," Niko says, making his bed and then laying down, his sister snickering at him.

"Don't think I didn't notice that blush on your cheeks either, Missy!" Sage's jaw drops before she slams her mouth shut so quickly her teeth clatter.

"What did I get myself and you kids into?" I mutter under my breath.

"You got us into an MC family, Mom, and it's pretty sweet," Niko answers, giving me a small smile then putting his ear pods in and lying down.

"Yeah, I guess I did." I drop kisses onto the tops of their heads before turning and making my way to the almost empty common room, the Computas the only people in there. "Where is everyone?" I say to myself under my breath.

"Oh, they're in the Rev Room," Debs' voice sounds out from the kitchen. Shit, that woman has good hearing.

"Have they got a guest?"

"No, they've got Rider,"

What the hell? I make my way to Chewy's happy place, letting myself in the door and then coming to a complete and utter stop.

Rider is cable tied to a bright yellow chair in the middle of the room facing a big screen. His thighs are spread and a metal bucket has been secured between them. He's wriggling and begging, but Judge stands behind him holding his head steady. Turning my gaze back to the big screen I watch as a woman in white pants rollerblades on a boardwalk.

"What in the actual fuck is happening in here?" I whisper quietly.

"Oh hey babe, you made it." Tav beams at me, comes forward to drop a quick kiss to my lips and then moves behind me, wrapping his arms around my waist, pulling me into his hard chest.

The image changes to Amy Schumer talking about Tampax and Rider damn near levitates out of the chair. "Fuck no! It's too much!"

Tilting my head sideways, I whisper to Tav, "What's happening?"

He leans down, his warm breath ticking the shell of my ear and causing my sex to clench. "Pops said he could desensitize Rider to periods and women's problems. It's not going too badly. He's only thrown up four times."

"It's mesmerizing," I whisper back as the images change again and again. I don't know if this is a weird playlist of period videos Pops has found or if it's something that Pops made up himself for this very purpose. Whatever it is, it's very informative. And effective. Rider seems to have calmed right down and is even bobbing his head along to the music.

"What in the fuck are you all doing?" Marx's voice booms out in the middle of a catchy tune about bleeding monthly, complete with dancing tampons. Gus stands behind him with Ana looking like she's going to burst into laughter at any moment with another dark-haired man who looks vaguely familiar. He also looks like you wouldn't trust him as far as you could throw him.

"Helping Rider with his little problem," Pops answers completely seriously. "Hey Roman,"

"Pops, good to see you've been keeping busy even with the murder ban," the Roman guy answers.

Marx rummages in his pocket looking for something and coming up short. Gus reaches into his own pocket, then holds out a pack of antacids to Marx who nods once, then takes what's offered.

"Tidy this shit up and meet us back in the common room, we have things to discuss." With that, he leaves, Gus and the other man leaving behind them.

"Well, son, you did good." Pops saying, slapping a hand on Rider's shoulder. "Oh, might wanna clean up before our guests get here. You stink." With that, he leaves the building.

Judge cuts the cable ties, and the brothers start handing over cash.

"What in the...?"

"They took bets on how many times Rider would barf," Tav says, chuckling as he leads me out of the shed.

"I tell ya, I love this place," Flack says as he smells the wad of cash in his hand.

I chuckle to myself, shaking my head, because I wholeheartedly agree with him.

Chapter 15

We all trickle into the common room, finding seats or places to lean. Chewy sits on Rhodie's knee, leaning her head close to listen as he whispers to her. Ana is standing leaning against Gus, his large hand on her belly. Debs is on the couch with her head resting on Pops' shoulder, and Pixie is on my lap. It's a nice feeling watching my family grow into an even bigger, rowdier family. I glance at Jules across the room, leaning on the bar, and I cannot wait to see who tames him. He deserves happiness and all the love in the world, even if he doesn't think so.

"We haven't met yet. I'm Roman Bartashev. Head of the Bartashev Bratva."

"And my best friend!" Ana pipes up with a huge smile on her face.

"Yes, and Ana's bestie," Roman says, rolling his eyes as he offers a hand to Pixie.

She squints up at him for a beat before holding her hand out. "Blanche."

"Oh, I know who you are. I was in the warehouse the day you dispatched your cousin. I admired your work,"

"Oh, thank you. I think?" She gives me a look, her eyes huge as if to ask, "What the fuck?" I try not to chuckle. She'll soon learn that in this lifestyle we may mix with mafia and men who could take you out as soon as look at you, but we all do it for a good reason. Well, most of the time.

The door opens and Jimmy leads in three big ass versions, and one taller curvier version of my Ol Lady. Pixie rushes toward them and they all hug, talking a mile a minute.

"Holy shit the genes are strong in that family," Rider mumbles, watching with wide eyes.

"Is that how families are meant to behave when they see each other?" Chewy asks, her head tilted to the side.

"Sometimes, baby. Depends on how close you are. I hugged Marx when I got home from deployment," Rhodie mumbles, dropping a kiss on Chewy's head. She frowns a moment before nodding. Probably storing that chestnut away for a later date. Jules catches my eye and gives me a little smirk. We all know that's how she'll greet us next time one of us has a trip away.

"Oh, um DRMC, these are my siblings. From oldest to youngest, Vic," she points to the widest of them all. Her brothers are around the same height as me and my brothers, but hers are heavier set. "Dom, and Chris. And this is our little sister Lovely and her baby, Bee," Lovely looks like she's ready to shit her pants at any moment now. She's curled into herself, her arms wrapped around her baby tightly. Her eyes dart up to look around the room, widening a little when she sees how many of us there are.

"It's OK, sweetheart, you and your baby will be safe here," Marx says softly, stepping closer to the group, but softening his stance so as not to scare her.

Her dark eyes, so much like Pixie's stare at Marx, darting over his face before a shy smile plays on her lips. She turns her eyes from Marx to the rest of the room. Taking a deep breath, then letting it out, her head comes up and her shoulders square.

"T-thank you very much for having us. Bee and I are very grateful for your kindness." Her head drops as she looks down at the bundle in her arms, and she smiles down at her baby. "We're gonna be safe little Bee," she whispers before kissing her baby on the head.

Dom wraps his arm around Lovely, and she leans into him, looking around the room.

"Thanks so much for helping us out, man," Vic says. "It was touch and go for a minute there,"

Marx stares at Lovely a beat longer before shaking himself. "Blanche is family. By extension, so are you. Besides, we all have a common enemy," Vic nods in agreement. "Mama Debs has food for you and rooms made up. While you eat, we'll hash out a plan."

The Landrys move toward the table and Pixie starts madly waving me over. "You summoned me my love," I murmur before kissing her on the neck.

"Yes. Boys, this is Tav. My Ol Man," she beams up at me and my heart stutters over her claiming me as I claimed her.

Vic stands to his full height, straightening out his shoulders, so he's looking wide as fuck. Chris stands shoulder to shoulder with him, his arms crossed over his broad chest. Dom flanks Vic's other side, a scowl on his face. I should be intimidated, but I'm not. I mean, I may not be as big, but I also grew up with brothers, so I know all about fighting dirty. I'm not worried about these guys because I have Gus standing on my left and

Jules on my right, both staring down the Landrys along with me.

"Are we doing one of those dick measuring contests?" Chewy says, standing right in front of me, head tipped back, staring at Vic.

Vic's eyes flick down and widen, surprised at Chewy. "And who are you, sweetheart?" he asks.

"Your worst nightmare," Chewy answers in her monotone voice. If that didn't shock him enough, then the large black silicone dick she's waving around in the air like a blunt instrument does.

"Wait, is that a dildo?" Chris asks, uncrossing his arms and looking at Chewy like she's nuts.

"Yup and there's plenty more where that came from," she says, punctuating that by poking Chris in the chest with it.

"Sorry, she's mine. Lemme just take her over here with me," Rhodie grunts, picking up my sister and carrying her and her dildo across the room.

Vic, Chris and Dom all share a look before they burst out laughing, "Yeah OK, Blanche fits in perfectly here. Take care of her, yeah?" Dom says, slapping me on the back and shaking his head. He looks over at Chewy and then bursts out laughing again.

"I don't understand anything that just happened," Lovely says, watching with wide eyes.

"Don't worry, we don't either," Tank answers drily.

She smiles up at him and makes her way to the table, taking a seat between her brothers. Pixie loops her arm in mine and rests her head on my shoulder. "That went better than I thought."

"Really? Because I have to admit, I didn't know where Chewy

was going with that dildo."

Pixie snorts and then leads me to an empty seat, pushing me down to sit and then placing herself in my lap. The Landrys are all at the table, Mama Debs having placed their plates in front of them. The looks on the Landrys' faces are downright comical, and I get it, the plates are piled high.

"There's plenty more where that came from, and I have dessert too," Mama Debs says, patting Lovely on the shoulder and getting a beaming smile back.

"Listen up! We've got shit to go over tonight," Marx barks out. "First off, as you can see Roman has joined us, and as usual, he comes bearing shitty news." Marx tips his head toward Roman and I'm pretty sure we all brace ourselves. It's never good news if Roman is here.

"I wouldn't say shitty news. Just not favorable." Marx grunts at him while Roman smiles broadly, "As you all know it is my stolen merchandise that is being trafficked with these women. Lexi has had reports of my product being cut with a cheaper product and circulated in parts of Moscow. I do not ship there, which means the buyers for the girls and drugs are as far afield as Europe." He looks around at the dark faces before continuing, "My people got a hit on them. Hammer and his friends are using the Cordoza Cartel to move people and drugs."

"Fuck!" Sniper spits out, running both hands through his hair. That's interesting, the man is usually very calm.

"It's OK brother," Marx says, dropping a hand on Sniper's shoulder. Sniper quietens down, but you can see the tension in his body.

"If it makes you feel better, I am in talks with Diego Cordoza," Roman offers.

"Somehow that makes me feel worse," Marx replies, Roman snorting at his remark.

"I do not agree with the sale of women, and there isn't enough room in the market for both my product and theirs, so one of us has to find alternative employment. I can guarantee it will not be me." Roman nods with a cold look on his face.

"It's creepy how he goes from normal to stabby like that," Pixie whispers in my ear. Her warm breath has me picturing what it'll feel like on my cock.

Grumbling can be heard in the common room, no one happy with the new information the Bratva is bringing.

"It's a genius plan really," Chewy says, stroking her imaginary beard.

"How so?" Savage asks, taking the bait.

"Think about it. Hammer's MC is done since we killed them all. Now he doesn't have the numbers to be on the streets taking the women he needs for his supply. Somehow he crosses paths with Royal and his cult. Royal hits a town, converts people with the promise to save their souls, asking them to move to Louisiana to join his church. These people willingly follow him, giving Royal and Hammer the women and children they need. They then sell them and Roman's stolen drugs to the Cordoza cartel. Did I miss anything?"

Marx nods, running a hand down his beard, nodding, "It's a fucking marriage made in fucked up heaven for Hammer."

"OK, then how the hell does Niko fit into the whole thing?" Pixie asks. "With all the trafficking, it makes no sense that Royal would split his attention between that and trying to get my son. Wire? Chewy?"

"The only thing we could find was your will, Blanche, that you lodged with your lawyer, leaving all your possessions to your children. That and an alternative will that leaves your inheritance to Niko solely," Wire answers.

"I only have one will, the first one you mentioned." Pixie says, her brows furrowed in confusion.

"Nope. There was another one lodged by Carterton, Munson and Associates," Chewy states.

"Who the fuck is that?"

"I-I might be able to answer that." All heads snap toward Lovely. She almost reminds me of Remy when she first arrived. Before Remy went all badass. Still sweet, but she won't hesitate to kick a man in the balls.

"We would love to hear what you have to say, Lovely. Any information you have will be super helpful," Remy says, gifting her with a gentle smile that Lovely returns in kind.

"Well, when that policeman found us he said that both me and Bee had to go with him. He said that Blanche told him she'd made a mistake taking us and that I needed to go back to the Keep and hand over my inheritance to Royal. That paying him was going to be the only way to keep him off our backs. I told him to have Blanche call me so I could hear it from her own mouth. That's when he went mad and Pleasant Dupree stepped in and told him to leave."

"What inheritance? You didn't give it to him did you?" Pixie asks, frowning at her sister.

"I can't. It's not mine to give,"

"That doesn't make any sense," Chewy asks, staring at Lovely, head tilted. "Also, what does that have to do with Niko?"

"My mother was Celine Surette." Lovely says softly.

"Hold up, she's related to my mom?" Pixie asks Lovely, staring into the face that looks so much like my Ol Lady.

"My mom went to Eden's Keep looking for her big sister. She found Mercy Landry instead."

"I remember her! She married him just before we were kicked out," Pixie's brother says. I think this one is Dom. His brow is furrowed, as if he's trying to remember more about her.

"Wait, how come I don't remember her?" Pixie asks her brothers.

"You always steered clear of Mercy's wives. You spent your time with Loyal and her mom," Chris answers, Pixie nodding in agreement.

"She was wife number 12." Lovely carries on. "She died two years ago. Mercy had caught a nasty cold, and I was caring for him when the lawyer came to read her last will and testament. If your mom's will is the same as mine, it would stipulate that her husband would inherit an annual stipend for every year they were married. The rest of her belongings would be split between their children equally."

"We were so young when mom died. I don't think I even knew she had a will let alone what was in it," Dom frowns.

"It's not unusual for Eden's Keep to keep things secret, either," Pixie adds bitterly.

"Let me see if I can get access to Adeline and Celine Surette's last will and testaments," Chewy says under her breath. She types away on her laptop, Wire and Remy doing the same as if it's a race to see who can hit the jackpot first.

"Ooooohhhhh," Remy breathes out, obviously the winner.

"Care to share with the class?" Marx asks drily.

"Your moms were cunning. Their lawyers have the wills and inheritances tied up so tight that in the event of your deaths, your money bypasses your spouses and goes to your children.

Although that doesn't really make sense, given that you have three other children and Royal only wants one," Remy says, looking to Pixie for an answer.

"Does the will stipulate biological children?" Pixie asks.

She reads her screen before looking up at Pixie, nodding.

My woman blows out a breath before looking at everyone in the room with a hard look on her face. "Sage, Cove and Elio are not my biological children, but they're mine all the same."

I hold her tight to me, watching the respect for my woman grow on my brother's faces.

"So if Royal wants your money, he needs Niko to access it." Marx says, putting all the pieces together.

"Yup,"

Blanche

"Wait, if that's the case, and it's all about my sisters' money, because he's married to both of them, and Royal needs the kids to access it, why the hell would he sell Bee?" Chris asks, leaning over to rub his finger along our niece's chubby cheek.

"Son of a bitch," I whisper when it hits me, "That mother-fucker! It's the men in Eden's Keep who register the births," I spit out.

"That asshole!" Chewy joins in, obviously following my train of thought. "If he doesn't register Bee's birth, then she never existed. Meaning he can sell her and there will be no paper trail at all."

Lovely nods sadly, "Then he'll just make me birth another

child to inherit my money."

"And it'll all go into his little business investment with Hammer," Marx finishes.

"After he gets rid of me and Lovely, of course," I seethe. I cannot wait to end this man. Tav must feel my rage bubbling up because he holds me just that little bit tighter, the pressure making me feel safe, allowing my body to soften slightly.

Since Remy's revelation, Chewy and Wire have been tapping away at their keyboards frantically. I have no idea what they're doing, but it must be important because neither of them has looked up for a while.

"Bingo," Chewy whispers under her breath.

"Do you see it too, Chewy?" Wire asks, both of them with eyes on their laptops, before turning their wide eyes to me and Lovely.

"What is it?" Lovely asks, shrinking back into her chair.

"Well, I can see why Royal really wants Niko." Wire's eyes flick towards me and I feel like I'm going to storm across the room and beat the information out of Wire at any moment.

"If something were to happen to you, Niko, and in turn Royal would be $15 million richer,"

I think I just heard a record scratch. No, I'm certain I heard a record scratch.

"Come again?" I ask, my voice sounding tinny and distant in my own ears.

"Your inheritance is worth $15m. Way to go, Tav!" Chewy says, a wide grin on her face, her eyes still on her screen.

"Yours too, Lovely," Wire adds.

I stare at my sister who has gone deathly pale and looks like she's going to keel over at any moment.

"Lovely! Name 5 colors you can see!" I bark at her.

I watch as she takes a deep breath, then looks around the room.

"I-I see the green of the pool table top, Bee's pink blanket, Vic's blue Henley, the yellow of the kitchen wall and Marx's black leather vest." By the time she's reached Marx's vest her cheeks are pink, and she's looking a lot calmer.

"It's called a cut, sweetheart," Marx gently says, smiling at my sister.

"Oh, a cut," she repeats, smiling back at him, rocking her baby side to side gently.

Remy puts her hand up, indicating that she has something to say. All the men turn to her and Marx gives her a smile to go ahead. "If Royal really wanted Blanche's money and needed Niko to get it for him, why didn't he just take Niko when he was younger?"

"He tried. So many fucking times. We stopped him every time," Vic grumbles.

"By the time Blanche moved here she'd made some high up friends who signed a restraining order," Dom continues.

Marx's eyebrows raise, as if asking me to elaborate. I let out a sigh. "I'm a PI specializing in infidelity. I caught a certain judge's husband, and she owed me a favor." I shrug. The job itself was no big deal. "Having a restraining order against Royal meant he had to stop his harassment or face the authorities. And the one thing that man hates more than me is the authorities. He's the one that brings in all the new Keep members. He needs to look squeaky clean otherwise why the hell would they follow him?"

"OK, so now that we know Royal is an asshole, Hammer is a bastard, the Cartel are involved and we have two women sitting in our common room with money coming out the wazoo, what the hell are we going to do about our little problem?" Pops butts in.

"We need to divide and conquer," Chewy nods her head, happy with her plan.

"Chewy is right. Roman, you're handling the cartel?" Marx barks at the Russian.

"*Da*, I will take care of that pesky problem."

"You won't fuck us over, will you?"

Roman's hand flies to his chest as if he's absolutely disgusted that Marx would even think such a thing. It's not that hard. I'm not sure this guy is all that trustworthy myself.

"Marx, you know after having my daughter advertised in a fucking skin catalogue that I will do anything to put a stop to women being trafficked." His dark brows slash downward on his pale skin.

Marx squints a little before nodding once. "Very good Roman, glad to be working alongside you again."

Roman face splits into a wide smile, "Of course. I don't have a murder ban, so I'll make sure to kill enough for the both of us." With that, he leaves. Clearly, the rest of this little get together is of no interest to him.

"I really don't like that guy," Savage says under his breath.

"Hey! That's my bestie you're talking about!" Ana growls from Gus's lap.

Marx whistles to get our attention. "Here's what we're going to do,"

* * *

"You OK baby?" Tav asks, crawling into bed behind me. By the time we got all the details hashed out, it was past midnight. Lovely had already turned in, leaving the MC, the Tombs family and my brothers to all plan.

"Yeah, just a lot of shit to sort through, you know?" I roll toward Tav, resting my head on his shoulder and curling my body into his, the warmth of him seeping into me, comforting me.

"Yeah, it's crazy. Who would have thought I'd end up with a sugar mama?" He laughs, my head bouncing as he chuckles.

I tweak his nipple, startling a yelp out of him. "Shut up, you! That amount of money is fucking nuts to me. And I can't believe that asshole not only wanted my kid, but would knock me off to get that money. I'm amazed he never killed me all those years ago, choosing to bide his time instead."

Tav looks thoughtful. "I thought that too. But think about it, since you've been out of the Keep you've had your brothers for protection, and then you had a restraining order. He couldn't risk coming after you. But if he took Niko, you would have signed over everything to get him back."

"You're damn right there," I mumble back, swirling my fingers in his chest hair. "I still can't believe he would take my child or kill me. Or Lovely. How fucking evil do you have to be to do that to someone so, so, *lovely?*"

"She really does suit her name," Tav muses, making me snort.

"Yup. Probably one of the few that does. I mean, we all know that I'm the exact opposite of patience," Tav laughs as if it's the funniest joke I've ever told.

"Well, I love you just the way you are. But speaking of patience, are you happy with how this is going to go down?"

I nod, my face rubbing in the soft hair on Tav's chest. "As long as I get to kill the men I want, then I don't mind how this goes down. Although I have to admit Chewy's plan is diabolical."

"It's what she does best. Now baby, it's time for sleep. As much as I would like to fuck you into a coma, I'm too damn tired and we have too much shit to do tomorrow."

"You know, I would love to tease you about being old, but I agree."

"Does this make us lame?" Tav asks, his voice gentle and slow.

"Very, very lame,"

"I won't tell anyone if you don't,"

"Deal." I let Tav's warmth soothe me. His breathing evens out and I admire his strong profile.

This man has turned my life upside down and inside out, and I can't thank him more.

Chapter 16

Waking early, I decide it's better to get up rather than lie in bed thinking of everything that needs to happen over the next few days. Marx and Gus outlined the plan, and it makes me feel a little more relaxed knowing that Gus had a part in it. Not just because he's my brother, but because he's always headed up any dangerous jobs we've had to take with Tombs Security and we've never lost a man.

Wandering through the quiet clubhouse, I come to a stop in the kitchen when I see Pixie's brother leaning against the countertop, sipping from a cup.

"Hey man, trouble sleeping?" I ask, heading to the coffee machine, pouring myself a cup.

"Nah, it's my turn to check on the rescue," he answers. I'm pretty sure this one is Dom. He's slightly quieter than Vic and Chris.

"Lovely?"

He snorts before bringing his cup to his lips and taking

another swig of coffee, "No the baby gator."

The shock of his words causes my mouthful of coffee to go down the wrong way, leaving me spluttering and wheezing, tears running down my face.

"For the love of fucking God and all that's holy do not let my sister find out what you've got," I manage to croak out.

"Find out what?" Chewy says from the darkness, through the dining hatch.

"Holy shit! How long have you been there?" I demand, because I need to know it was after what Dom said.

"From when you said 'Don't let my sister find out'. Find out what?" She turns her large eyes on Dom whose gaze flits to mine.

"Oh, it's nothing. Look at the time! I gotta go somewhere," Dom says, emptying his cup into the sink and then whispering "good luck" to me before hightailing it out of here.

"Nothing," I assure Chewy. "What are you doing up this early, anyway?"

"I wanted to make sure everything is double-checked and ready. It's the first time the MC has been split, so I want to make sure all our people are safe," her disembodied voice says until she walks through the door to the kitchen.

She pulls a bottle of water out of the fridge, takes off the lid and guzzles the water down, like a thirsty toddler. She's always drunk water like this. I try to fight a smile as I take another sip of the coffee that will hopefully calm my nerves and wake me up.

"Are you worried, little sis?" I ask, watching her a moment longer.

She frowns at me, then rolls her eyes like I asked the dumbest question in the world. "Of course not. I trust everyone here.

What I don't trust are all the other factors. Hammer will always be an unknown. He's nuts. We also don't know what type of relationship he has with Royal or the cartel."

That's a good point.

"True. But I trust the intel, and I know you and Wire wouldn't send us in to an ambush,"

"Damn straight," she says, taking another long drink, then slamming her bottle on the counter with a long "ahhhhh". "I'm going now. I'll talk to you before you ride out." With that she leaves the room, in the abrupt way she does everything, and I try not to chuckle at her.

I finish up my coffee and think about making myself breakfast, but before I can fully open the fridge door to see what's in there Mama Debs slams it shut and tells me to get out of her kitchen.

"Good morning to you too, Mama Debs," I drop a kiss to her cheek and chuckle when she mumbles about people messing up her kitchen.

"You go get your family up, and I'll make breakfast."

"Yes, Mama," I draw it out like I used to do to my own mom, and then have to dodge the twisted up dish towel she flicks my ass with.

Laughing, I make my way down the hall. Stopping to peek into my room, I notice Pixie is already up, so I head down to the kids' rooms, surprised to find all four Landry kids in the same room, the two big kids in camp beds next to their siblings.

My Ol Lady is sitting on the floor between the two twin beds. The Littles are both lying on their sides, looking at their mom, the big kids sitting up in their beds so they can see her too. She's mesmerizing, softly speaking to them, rubbing their foreheads, leaning to kiss Elio on his perfectly coiffed hair. I don't know how she senses me in the doorway, but she does. Her soft eyes meet mine and she grins, warming me from the inside out.

"Are you going to join your family or are you going to stand there watching like a creep?"

I lean on the door jamb, crossing my arms over my chest.

"Family, huh? I vaguely remember someone telling my grandfather that we were just friends."

She rolls her eyes at me while Niko snorts, "Yeah, we all knew that wasn't going to last long," He says, grinning at me.

It's amazing how far this kid has come. He was a surly little shit. But drop him in the middle of the clubhouse surrounded by men willing to keep his mom safe and he's a different kid. An actual kid, not someone constantly worried about the safety of his family.

I walk into the room, and Pixie shuffles forward, inviting me to sit at her back like we did the other night when we read "And Tango makes Three." Settling in I wrap my arms around her as she tells the kids what the plan is for the next two days.

"You're all going to stay with Mama Debs and some of the brothers. Wire, Remy, Chewy and Rhodie will all be here with you. So will Gus, Ana, Pops, Jules, Nat, Judge, Jovie's grandpa Flack and Aunt Lovely. They'll all keep you safe."

"So will me and Sage. Pops got us hunting bows so we will be armed and ready," Niko says seriously. He catches my gaze and I give him a nod. He gives me a little smile back. He's almost 18, a man. If he wants to protect his family and the clubhouse, I'm not going to stand in his way.

Pixie sighs a long, tortured sigh. "I knew Mama Debs was dangerous." I chuckle at her words because she's not wrong. She's as much of a menace as the rest of the Ol Ladies. I'm just glad that we've been too busy for my woman to be drawn into girls' night. I shudder, Pixie twisting her head to look at me in confusion.

"Nothing babe, just thinking,"

She holds my gaze a moment before turning back to the kids.

"OK lazybones, let's get you all up and fed. The earlier we leave, the quicker we can get back to you all."

Blanche

I double check that I have everything in my bag. The case I normally carry when I stake out the Keep is staying here because Tav, my perfect, wonderful man, has gifted me with a case full of all the top of the line toys he uses. Gone are my older model night vision goggles, replaced with these sleek numbers that are now perched on my head like a headband.

"Look at you looking all sexy and dangerous," Tav smirks, holding my head in his big hands, moving me to where he can place a kiss on my head without the goggles getting in the way.

"Thanks, a hot man gave me these," I grin up at him. I know I should worry about what's going to happen, but somehow having Tav with me makes me feel ten feet tall and unstoppable. I never knew that having someone at my back while I do this was going to feel so good.

"You almost packed up there? The others want to get on the road soon."

"Yup. This needs to go in the car and I'm set." I close up my goodies and set the large case on the floor.

To stop any suspicion from the local PD, namely Officer Martin, we decided the best way for us to travel was to have me and Tav in my mom car, my brothers driving their vehicle, and the MC brothers on their bikes. They were going to leave two at a time, in different directions. Apparently, no one in the town will notice them given that they often ride together to work. The brothers will all meet up outside of town limits to ride as one, and those in vehicles will bring up the rear.

While we're gone, the others will put their plan into action. I'm still not sure what that all entails, but whatever it is, it'll get Officer Martin out of our hair. Marx has already lodged a complaint with the Rose Grove PD and gave Sergeant Davies the evidence that he was involved in some particularly sketchy stuff. Marx got word earlier this morning that he's been stood down pending investigation. Chewy says this is going to play straight into their hands. I'm hoping it does because Tav, Gus and Jules are all a little concerned that the torture and murder ban has her acting out of sorts. I don't know what she's normally like, but listening to Tav I'm guessing she isn't usually into crafting and planning baby showers.

Marx's whistle pierces the air, and Tav and I make our way into the common room where everyone has assembled.

"Fox and Nitro have left already. Judge and Tank, you're next." Both men nod, grab their things, and head out.

Marx then turns to my brothers but before he can continue with his orders Vic speaks up.

"Chris is going to stay here with Lovely and Bee. It's not that we don't trust your men, but she's scared, running from the only place she's ever known, and a new mom. She needs support from her family,"

Marx nods, "Good. I was concerned that she wouldn't be

ready to be here without her family. Having your brother here will make her feel secure and she can get to know the women."

Vic gives him a chin up and gives Chris a hug, before hugging Lovely. Then Dom does the same. Knowing how Dom feels about what my father has created, I think I might have competition for getting rid of the council members. They both grab their bags and head out to their vehicle.

"Tav and Blanche, you are bringing up the rear. Blanche, you're positive that Royal is at the Keep?"

Nodding I check my phone, "Yup. My contact inside said he's been having emergency meetings in the Keep. Mercy is not going to live for much longer, which means Royal's making his move to take over. He'll be there, so will the rest of them."

"Any eyes on Hammer?"

"Yup, he left the Keep for two hours yesterday, then returned. Hasn't left since."

"We need you to bring him back unscathed for Chewy's plan to work," Rhodie says.

Marx runs his hand down his beard. "Savage and Dex, I know Hammer was the reason you wanted to ride out. You happy to bring him in for Chewy to take care of?" Both men nod and then grin. I've never seen Chewy in action, but I've heard the stories.

"OK. All the players are in position. Let's roll out," Marx walks out, Rider following behind.

I hug Cove, whispering I love her before giving her a kiss and then doing the same with Elio.

Sage wraps her thin arms around me, squeezing me tight. "Be safe, Mom."

"I love you, Sagey," I kiss her on her forehead and then move to wrap my eldest in my arms.

"I love you Mom. Go get rid of the Devil and burn that place to the ground," I pull back from my son, so thankful that Royal never got to him. I make a note to contact my lawyer when all this dies down. Niko might well be my eldest, the child I grew in my body, but all four of them are my babies and they will be seen as such in the eyes of the law. I give them all one more hug each and blow kisses while Tav shakes hands and pounds on his brothers' backs, Gus lingering for a little longer. He hugs Ana and then waves at Chewy when she waves back at him.

"Where's Pops?" he asks, those thick black brows pinched.

"He's looking for a hooker," Chewy answers, a dozen heads all whipping toward her. "Trust me, it's all for a good cause."

My gaze flits to Debs who has a small smile on her face as if her boyfriend looking for a hooker is completely normal behavior. Tav stands staring at his sister for a moment before shrugging his shoulders.

"Right then," He goes up to the kids and hugs each of them. Cove, Elio, Sage and then man hugs Niko. "You relax and be kids. I'll take care of your mom," he tells them before taking my hand and leading me out the door, turning to wave once more.

Tav and I settle into the seats of my mom SUV. The booster seats have been removed and in their place are cases of surveillance equipment and weapons. I giggle at the sight, Tav turning to see what tickles me and when he sees what I'm seeing he rewards me with a beautiful grin. We watch Marx and Rider roll out while we sit in the idling car.

"Ready Pixie?"

"Ready."

Chapter 17

Tav

We traveled the three hours to the outskirts of Eden's Keep and the whole team have spent the last two hours setting up surveillance. I have to admit, I've worked security, people recovery, even search and rescue before, but never have I seen anything quite like Eden's Keep.

"The place is absolutely massive," Savage says, dropping into a seat in the motel room that we're all gathered in.

Adonner is a shitty little town close to Eden's Keep. Blanche's intel pegged Adonner as the best place to hole up because the Keep members never come here. They prefer to go further afield for their supplies. Well, that and Adonner locals dislike Eden's Keep with a vengeance, so the likelihood of someone from this small town ratting us out seems fairly low.

"It's massive and fucking creepy. Did you see how the women dress there?" Nitro asks the room. "Did you wear that shit, Blanche?"

Pixie's lips curl up in the corners, "Hells yes I did! I loved my floor length brown dresses and big white sneakers," she snorts then giggles, unable to keep up the lie. "Want to know what they wear on their wedding days?"

Rider leans forward, clearly interested in hearing more. Hell, he's not the only one. Most of my brothers are listening in eagerly.

"We get to wear pink versions of the brown dress. And big white sneakers."

Rider shudders, looking horrified, and rightly so.

"After the ceremony, everyone gathers in the hall, seated for dinner, while the bride and groom get taken to the bridal suite. They're not allowed to come out until they consummate the marriage. After that, they enter the hall and the members celebrate the fact that they just fucked. Then they get to eat dinner."

"That's fucked up," Tank grumbles, everyone else nodding along.

"There's a lot that's fucked up about the place. I was lucky. It wasn't so bad when I was growing up but, it got more and more fucked up after I left. At least I knew things weren't normal. Others, people that are born there, they don't know. Someone like Lovely will take a long time to get used to the outside world." Blanche says, her sister very obviously on her mind.

Marx frowns for a moment, then goes back to watching the small screens our video feeds are playing on. I have to admit, being able to bring a shit ton of security equipment is making our jobs a cakewalk. We spent two hours setting up a perimeter, and now we're chilling out, watching the coming and going of Keep people.

It's Saturday, so the younger kids are playing with balls and hula hoops in the middle of the compound. The older teenage kids are in groups, the boys playing something akin to football while girls huddle in packs on the sidelines watching. The women look tired as they push large baby buggys with two or even three babies sitting in them. There are no men in sight, at least not on our feeds.

"Pixie, where are all the men?"

She leans closer to the screens, then frowns at the smart watch on her wrist. "The men usually meet at 5pm on a Saturday. They're two hours early."

Marx runs a hand down his beard. "What does it mean if they're meeting early?"

Pixie's eyes look up to the ceiling, "I've only ever remembered it happening two or three times when I was there. The first one was when one of the council members died. One of my contacts would have messaged me if Mercy had passed away so it won't be that. Another time was when they thought they were going to be raided by the FBI and needed a plan."

"Fuck," Marx curses under his breath, "You don't think they got a whiff of us, do you?"

Pixie tips her head to the side, watching the feed for a moment, as if remembering. "No. The time that happened we weren't allowed out. Women and children were locked into the big hall with two councilmen. We were to keep quiet. The men even went around handing out candy to the little kids, which made them fall asleep. Us older kids were told that if the government came there was a special drink we would all take and it would take us somewhere safe." Looking around, she knows she doesn't have to explain what this special drink was.

"And your dad decided that?" Tank asks, incredulously.

"That's how the Keep works. The outside is evil, full of devils in disguise. Your soul will go to hell where you'll be punished for eternity. The outside people are dirty. They're all murderers and rapists. Ironically, so is the Keep," Vic answers for his sister.

"How come you turned out so normal?" Rider asks Pixie, his brow raised.

"I'm not an idiot? I don't blindly believe people just because they have a dick? I'm stubborn? Let's put it this way, I don't listen to salvation advice from someone who marries underage girls," Blanche says, her voice even, belying the fire in her eyes.

"Makes sense," Dex replies before something catches his eye. "There you are fucker."

Hammer can be seen on the screen, jovially joking with a few of the men as they leave the hall, looking so fucking out of place within their compound. The rest of the men are in collared shirts buttoned to the very top, neatly tucked into slacks. They too are wearing white sneakers and at this point I'm questioning if they own shares in New Balance or something. I can't tell what color the men's shirts and trousers are, but in contrast to Hammer's t-shirt, jeans and vest, it makes him stand out like a dog's balls.

Savage turns to Marx, keeping his eyes on the monitor for a moment before looking at Pres. "When do you want us to grab him?"

"Seeing the compound and the number of people milling around, I say we go in tonight. Blanche, any idea where his room is located?"

Pixie nods, before tapping away at her phone screen. "Just sent you the layout. It's been almost two decades since I was last there, but I can't imagine it's changed much. All 'outside' guests stay in the same place. The main office building has a hall that leads to the council members' rooms. There's one pokey little room at the end of the hall on the left-hand side. Hammer will be in there. There's a single door and one window, but the windows only open an inch before they lock. "

Savage and Dex check their phones, their fingers working on zooming in on their screens.

"You'll all have your watches and the earpieces to communicate and I've got the Tombs Security stash of night vision goggles and a drone I can fit in my pocket." To illustrate my claims, I unzip the side pocket of my cargo pants, pull out a khaki case and open it, showing it to my brothers who ooohhh and ahhh over it.

"Hold the fuck up," Sniper rasps in his measured way. "Is that the Black Hornet?" His eyes look like they're about to pop out of his head.

"Yup," I reply, popping the "p."

"No fucking way do you have one of those!" Rider adds, trying to get past Tank's big body for a closer look. "My buddy was telling me about these. These things cost a fucking bomb,"

"It's one of Chewy's perks. She helped an unnamed organization, and they paid her in three of these."

Dex's eyes get comically large before he whispers, "Holy shit how much does she charge?"

"Probably not enough for some of the information she finds," I wink at him.

"OK, so we have a fancy ass drone on the team. Savage and Dex, how many more men do you need?" Marx looks toward the men, who communicate purely with a look at each other.

"I think it's best to send in a small team," Savage answers. Marx agrees with the ex Death Riders Pres who continues, "With Tav having eyes on us, that decreases the number we'd need, so I'd say one more. That gives us one man sweeping and two of us dragging Hammer outta there." Savage looks around at the men in the room.

Sniper steps forward and knowing his background I'd say he is probably the best choice. Quiet, patient, hard to rattle. Marx nods at his MC brother. Savage and Dex look happy too, Sniper is who I'd want watching my back.

"Blanche, what time is lights out?" Pixie gives Marx a funny little smile, "We all know there's a lights out. No one runs a compound like this and lets people have an ounce of freedom," Marx reasons.

"You'd be right. Lights out is 10pm, on the dot. The electricity gets turned off at the mains, only the main perimeter alarms are left on. If anyone needs to get up for anything after that, they're instructed to use a torch."

"Fucking weirdos," Fox grumbles, Pixie turning to give the big man a huge smile.

"We go in at 11pm. Rider and I will take first watch on the screens. Tank and Tav you're next. Everyone else, rest up or get some grub. It's gonna be a long night."

Blanche

"How are you feeling, baby?" Tav asks, his warm breath skating over my skin as I lazily wake from the nap I swore I wasn't going to take.

It's weird, when I'm on a stakeout I never nap. Put me on the most important stakeout of my life and I sleep like a baby in the middle of the afternoon. I blame having the security of all these men around me. Never in my life did I ever think I would submit to a man, or even ask one for help, and yet here I am, relying on these men to help me take down the evil from my past life. It's a real trip.

Rolling over, I lift my arms over my head and stretch while Tav hovers over me with a soft smile on his face. Finishing my stretch, I reach up and cup his cheek.

"Thank you for coming with me." I rub his dark stubble with my thumb.

"You couldn't keep me away, Pixie. I'm your backup." He leans forward and his lips gently meet mine. He pulls back far too soon. "Speaking of backup, wanna come watch some feeds with me and Tank?"

I think about it for a moment, before deciding I'd rather eat something. "Nah, I'll leave that exciting stuff up to you. I might go grab something to eat."

Tav drops a quick kiss on my lips before bouncing off the bed. "OK babe, I'll walk you to Dom and Vic's room. You can eat with them, yeah?"

Nodding, I roll up and get off the bed a lot slower than Tav did, then gather the stuff I'll need. Once ready, Tav walks me to Chris and Dom's motel room. Knocking on the door gently, I wait until Dom opens it a crack. Instead of looking directly at my face, I have my middle finger up in the doorway's crack.

"You're a child, you know that?" he says, swinging the door open wider to let me in.

"Yeah, yeah, you love it. Whatcha got to eat?"

Both of my brothers roll their eyes at me.

"Aren't you too nervous to eat something?" Vic grumbles before shoving the pizza delivery menu at me.

"Weirdly enough, no. I thought I would be but the nerves haven't hit yet. If I'm being honest, I'm not sure if they're going to." I shrug and then mouth at Dom who's on the phone to the pizza place that I want a cheese pizza with olives.

"Well, I feel better knowing that the MC has a plan. I'd be shitting myself if you were doing this alone," Vic says, looking a lot less wound up than last night.

Vic has always been the one who liked to have a plan for things. He hates chaos and I guess it makes sense. Growing up as we did, it was a weird mix of regimented and chaos. We knew exactly what we were doing at what time of the day. That was easy. Eden's Keep has a program, so the same stuff every day for everyone. The chaos comes in the form of the adults we had in our lives growing up. Our mother worshiped the ground our father walked on. She loved us, but she loved him more. I remember when he first talked about having a second wife; she cried and fretted about what she did wrong. She became paranoid that he didn't love her anymore. She checked out from us emotionally, being too caught up in her own fear and grief. When she passed away, we were shunted around the Keep adults, but they all had their own issues. The nurture that children need to feel safe just wasn't there and because of that my brothers are almost codependent on each other. When they were kicked out, they were all each other had. So I get it.

"Are you coming in with me tomorrow?" I ask just as Dom hangs up the phone.

"Fuck yes. There is no way we'd let you go in there alone. I want to watch as you take down the Council and Father dearest," Dom growls.

"I made a deal with Marx that I got to take out all eight council members."

"Wanna split that three ways?" Dom asks darkly.

I look at my brothers. Vic looks keen to help as well, which is a surprise. We were raised as good God-fearing people, meaning we don't really go around killing people on the regular. When I shot my cousin Valor Landry in the back of that van in Rose Grove, that was pure rage burning through me. Like an angel of death, I let my weapon cleanse the world of one evil man. I cannot wait to stand shoulder to shoulder with my brothers, ridding the world of a few more.

A knock at the door signals pizza, so while Vic sorts that out I clear the coffee table of the boys' guns and knives and grab plates. Vic drops everything on the table and plops down on the couch next to me, Dom sitting on the floor closer to the food.

We eat in comfortable silence for a while before Dom breaks it. "What do you think the plan is with Hammer?"

Swallowing my mouthful, I think for a moment. "Well, she's one of two enforcers the MC has. Rhodie holds that title and VP, but from what everyone has said Chewy does all the enforcing these days. I've heard some stories. Savage and Dex say she's really scary and a little gross, so I'm looking forward to it,"

"It's so weird, because she's such a cute little thing," Dom replies.

"She didn't seem that sweet when she was busy poking Chris in the chest with that big black dildo," Vic chuckles, causing me to choke a little on my pizza when I recall the scene.

"She has 90 of them too," I laugh, covering my mouth with a napkin.

"Do you think all MC's are like DRMC?" Dom ponders.

"Judging by Savage, Dex and Flack and how bewildered they seem half the time, I'm going to say no," I answer him, with my mouth full of pizza.

Vic does a double take at me before throwing his greasy napkin at my face. "I don't know what Tav sees in you."

"Me neither. But I licked him, so I'm keeping him."

Both of my brothers give me grossed out faces before Vic's softens a little. "I'm proud of you little sis. You have a family and a man that loves you. You did good, kid,"

"I wouldn't have been able to do it without you guys," I say with a thick voice, my eyes stinging with tears.

"I guess we could probably thank Mercy for teaching us to thrive through hardship," he shrugs.

"I say we thank him by bringing down his paradise," Dom says with a grin.

"To bringing down the Keep!" I say, holding my soda up in the air.

"Bringing down the Keep!"

Chapter 18

Sniper

"Five minutes," Tav's voice softly informs us through our earpieces.

I wasn't too sure about Chewy and her brothers when they first turned up. Now, though, now I know they're good people. Their gadgets go a long way in helping, too. I have no idea how the hell they get their hands on military grade shit, and I don't care. As long as I know they're using it to watch our backs, I'm all good.

"Sniper, you'll lead?" Savage asks, turning to look at me in the back seat.

Savage and Dex may be ex-military, but I'm the highest ranking of the three of us and stealth is my strength. I nod my reply and flick my night vision down, my eyes adjusting to the digital images lit up in front of me. The lights went out 25 minutes ago, just as Blanche said they would.

All I want is to get in there, get Hammer and get back out. The longer I sit here on the perimeter the more antsy I get. The women and children in there have no idea the danger the cartel will bring them. The Cordozass don't care who gets hurt. They think nothing of destroying everything in their path to get what they want. More money, more drugs, more women. I should know. I've seen firsthand what they're capable of. If they're edging close to our territory, then they need to be put down. I have no fear that Roman and his Bratva are a formidable enemy. I can only hope that he's big enough and bad enough to send them on their way. Otherwise I'll have to step in, whether Pres allows me or not.

"It's go time, brothers."

Tav

After successfully playing eye in the sky for Savage, Sniper and Dex, I crawled into bed with my woman. Those men are lethal, and I'm glad they're on our side. We had originally planned for 40 mins to get into the Keep, locate Hammer's room, subdue the man, and get him out of there in one piece. We weren't allowed to beat him. Chewy gave us specific instructions on what we could and couldn't do with Hammer. Weirdly enough we could choke him, so with a very impressive choke hold Dex had him incapacitated within moments. Then they were allowed to cuff his hands and feet, ready for transport.

Savage and Dex didn't want to hang around with Hammer in their room, so they threw him in the back of an SUV for the night with a little bit of Pops' cocktail running through his veins. Pops assured us that the dose will have him knocked out for at least 16 hours, giving us enough time to finish our job here and head home.

"Did you get it done babe?" Pixie asks, her voice rough with sleep, not even bothering to open her eyes to look at me.

I lean over and kiss her gently. "Yeah, Pixie. We have Hammer in the back of the SUV off his nut on Pops' special medicine."

She snorts before turning toward me and snuggling into my side. "I'd fuck you, but I have a big day tomorrow." Eyes still closed she give me a big cheesy grin.

"What about if I do all the work?" I ask, tweaking her nipple, rolling the tight bud between my fingers.

She whimpers. "Go on, tell me about all this work you want to do?" she gasps as I bite the turgid peak through her cotton tank.

"Roll over baby, let me get that pussy ready,"

She grins, eyes still closed as she rolls, then nestles her ass into my hard cock. I slip one arm under her head, the other runs down along her juicy thigh, before running back up and squeezing her ass gently. Lifting her leg I place it over my hip, my cock close enough to feel the heat of her. My fingers search out her pussy, surprised to find her bare.

She giggles at her little surprise, eyes still closed as she sleepily moves against my hand.

"Don't fuck around, Tav, I need you inside me now." She reaches back to cup my face in her hand before adding, "I need an orgasm and then sleep. Chop chop!"

I stop messing around, pulling my fingers from her slick slit, gripping my cock and then rubbing the crown of my cock along her lips a few times. Notching myself at her entrance, the heat of her sucks me in. Groans are pulled from both of us at the pleasure.

We move as one, gently, softly, before both crashing together.

"Love you, Pixie," I smile down at her heart-shaped face, her body soft in slumber as she snores gently, safe in my arms.

Blanche

Standing on the edge of the woodland that blocks the view of Eden's Keep on the South, I take a deep breath of the early morning air. It's fall, so the air is a little crisp, but I find it invigorating, adding to the electricity running in my veins. After years of waiting, my plan is about to come to fruition, and instead of doing this alone, I'll be standing shoulder to shoulder with a group of good men.

"How you feeling Pixie?" Tav's deep voice settles some of the frenetic energy in me as he stands beside me.

I allow myself to lean into his solid warmth for a moment. "I feel good. We've gone over the plan. We know the women and children will be in their barracks for another hour and a half. Any of the non-council men will be in the hall ready for their meeting. Even without silencers on our weapons the men won't know what's happening in the meeting room. My father had that room soundproofed so his skeezy sex schools could run at the same time as the children's evening lessons." I shudder at the memory of seeing mothers dropping their children off and then entering the room where my father would tutor them intimately. "As long as we can keep them all separate, we should be able to get this done with minimal loss."

It's important that we make this as clinical and efficient as possible. If any of the council members raise an alarm, we'll have to shoot our way out of the Keep. These people, Mercy's followers, they've been brainwashed that Eden's Keep is the only way to get to heaven. They will willingly die for their Prophet, which makes them not only fanatical, but suicidal as well. The best-case scenario is that once I take out the senior members, Royal and my father; the Keep will be leaderless, they'll flounder and go off to find a new church to worship at.

"Team, check weapons," Marx rumbles, checking the guns and knives he is carrying.

I follow suit, checking the two handguns and two knives that I have on my body. I also have a garotte that my brothers thought I might like, and my self defense ring that has a razor blade in it. My pockets are full of ammunition and the men around me assure me they are packing enough heat to take out anyone I can't. I know it's probably overkill, knowing that I will have two brothers and my Ol Man with me, but better to be prepared. Besides, I want this to hurt, so I might need to use all my goodies.

Checking my watch, it's 5.29am. The lights come on in the compound at exactly 5.30am, lightly glowing through the trees. Marx raises a finger, circling it in the air. He moves first, the rest of us following silently.

Rider is walking forward angling out and away from the group, Tank doing the same thing on the other side. Soon they'll pull back so they'll flank me, Tav, and my brothers. Savage and Dex are somewhere in the trees, circling even further around, as are Fox and Nitro, and Sniper is somewhere looking over us. He never returned last night with Savage and Dex, saying something about setting up a nest.

Within a few brief minutes, Marx, Tav, my brothers, and I are all on the edge of the compound. It's been years since I was last here and nothing has changed. Glancing at Vic, I know he feels the same.

Marx looks at us, and I tip my head toward the main hall. The room the Council meets in is off to the side. There is an internal door and an external door. We'll be coming in the external door and I'm betting on Royal's cockiness that he will not see me as a threat. Not until it's too late.

As a group we make our way to the meeting room, Marx in the lead, the men flanking me, alert for any threats that may come our way and yet there are none. As far as my father's followers are aware, it's just another day in paradise.

Reaching the door that separates me from my nightmares, I motion toward Marx. I want to be the one to walk through that door first. The men won't see me as a threat, either. Why would they? I'm just a weak woman who walked away decades ago. Marx steps back and I grip the handle, my heart pounding. One hand on the handle, and one on my gun I swing the door open and step inside, my brothers, my love and my Pres at my back.

"Well, well, well, if it isn't my little wife. Come to beg for forgiveness?" Royal leans back in his chair, his dark eyes taunting me as his lips curl.

Nausea swirls in my gut, but I don't let it show. This man thrives off the fear of others. Every tear, every scream, every beg uttered through cracked lips is like an aphrodisiac to this man, and I will not give him what he craves.

"One of us will beg for forgiveness, but it won't be me."

Turning to my right I raise my gun and without thinking twice I squeeze the trigger, hitting Peaceful Landry square in the chest.

Any council member that gathered themselves quickly enough to raise a gun at me all hesitate at the sight of the four men behind me with their weapons raised. Clearly wanting to live a little longer, they sit their asses down waiting to see what command Royal will give.

Royal tilts his head at me, his eyes cold even as his eldest son lies bleeding out on the floor.

"Do you feel better, Patience? Do you feel good knowing that you will rot in the depths of hell for your sins? Your lust, greed, gluttony," he sneers, his eyes drifting over my body. He always said I was too fat. Well, fuck him. "God will strike you down for what you've done, Patience, you will spend eternity burning in hell." By the end of his tirade his face is red, spittle flying from his angry mouth.

"Well, I guess I'll be seeing you there," I smile at him and then point my gun directly at him.

Moving my aim slightly, I squeeze the trigger, my bullet nicking Royal's ear but hitting my rapist cousin behind him. His head flies back, and he falls out of his chair, brain matter on the wall behind him.

"Here's what's going to happen. Each and every one of you is going to kneel and repent your sins. Blanche will give you the forgiveness you all preach so fervently," Dom growls, his gun trained on Discretion Clark, the man most likely to blast his way out of this room.

With their hands on their heads, they all kneel before us. All except Royal, who I let sit on my father's throne a little longer, Marx standing sentinel behind him. I want him to feel his power slipping through his fingers. Five members kneel before me and my brothers. Some crying, some cursing, some whispering to their God to save them, but he isn't coming.

Where was He when their child brides were whispering for help under their heavy, sweaty bodies? Where was He when they forced their wives to bear child after child after child? Where was He when Royal was selling their daughters? My hands shake with rage as I hold my gun at the head of the man in front of me. Leaning forward to see his face through his snot and tears, I almost feel giddy when I recognize him.

"Worthy Williams, how do you plead?"

"Not guilty of whatever you're blaming me for you harpy!" he spits out.

Tav moves to stand directly in front of him, staring down at him like he's a piece of shit on his shoe. He grabs Worthy's chin in his hand and then squeezes tightly. "The woman asked you a question. If I were you, I'd confess my sins and beg her to let you live."

"I have no sins! I do what our Prophet and Savior tell me to do! You know nothing!"

"Oh, you are so very, very wrong. I hear things, whispers from the women I've saved. I know you raped three little girls before raping your own wife on your wedding night." I say, pressing my gun harder into the back of his head, him angling forward to get away from the metal. He remains silent, so I press even harder, "I know you raped your own daughters before marrying them off at 12 years old to your buddies here. I know you and every other man here is helping Royal sell women to the cartel." I flick my gaze to Royal who looks a little surprised that we know that little nugget of information. "Surprise Royal! We know all about your little venture." I tap

Worthy on the head with the muzzle of my gun. "And I know all about you, Worthy Williams." His shoulders slump and he cries in earnest. In my peripheral Tav steps aside.

"I have no time for your tears, just like you had no time for theirs," I whisper in his ear before sending him to his maker.

Two more guns sound out thanks to my brothers, the men in front of them hitting the ground with dull thuds. Worthy Williams's body slumps in a heap at my feet, my gun still in the same position, now pointing at nothing in the air. Tav's feet step back into my line of sight, but I don't want to look at him. He's just watched me kill, no murder, three men. It's one thing to say he'll stand beside me to stop these men. It's another to watch your woman so filled with rage that she'll put bullets in men without blinking an eye. I'm afraid that if I look up, all my fears that Tav will see the real me and be disgusted will come true. Inhaling a breath, I let it out slowly before raising my eyes to look at the man I love, and I'm taken aback by what I see there. Instead of disgust, I see pride and love shining back at me. A soft smile plays on his lips.

"Five down, three more to go, Pixie."

Chapter 19

She's like a valkyrie. But better because she's mine. All these men are pissing themselves. They have nowhere to run to, nowhere to hide. All of them except Royal. Every man who snivels, begs and cries has him lighting up on the inside. This man gets off on fear and power.

Marx leans forward, murmuring something in Royal's ear. Whatever it is has him stiffening, the glee on his face replaced by pure unadulterated anger.

"What's the matter, Uncle?" Vic asks, feigning concern as he steps over the man that he put down, "accidentally" standing on his pudgy pink hand. "Worried that our little sister is bringing an end to your dreams?"

Royal stares at Vic for a moment, before his gaze moves, stopping when it hits Dom. His lip curls up into a sneer-like grin. "My, your mother did make beautiful children, didn't she? Pity she died before she could watch me break you all."

A pop from Pixie's gun, followed by a dull thud has us turning to look at the newest victim.

"Oh yeah, you're doing a great job of breaking us," Vic answers, not taking his eyes off the man on the floor.

"I wouldn't be so sure if I were you. Let me guess, you and your brothers have been taking turns looking after Lovely? Helping her with the night terrors as she screams and cries, begging for it to stop?" He smiles when neither Dom nor Vic answer. "You stay up all night watching that beautiful baby girl I made by forcing my seed into your sister's belly, protecting her from people that won't think twice to put a bullet in you before selling her to her new owner. I hear he likes to break them in before they're 6 months old."

Pixie wipes his grin off his face, moving fast as lightning and backhanding him across the face, his head flying sideways. Instead of looking at her he laughs maniacally as if he is the funniest fucker on the planet.

"Oh my dearest Patience, is that all you got? I'll tell you what, I'll let you continue your little crusade. Get this out of your system. Then, well, that's when the fun will start. You think you're so smart, coming here with all these big tough men. Let's see how they fare when the Keep finds out what you've done, huh?"

Pixie's eyes narrow before widening. She spins to look at her brothers who all seemed to have figured out what the hell he's talking about. They communicate without words, and I'm getting antsy at the look on her beautiful face.

"We've got this, sis. Marx, please stay with my sister. Tav, I need you with us," Vic murmurs..

Marx takes one look at Pixie's brothers. His jaw clenches and yet he still nods in understanding. I can feel the bewildered look on my face that my Pres is agreeing with them.

"Wait, no I'm not leaving my fucking Ol Lady -" I start. Pixie steps up to me, her small hand cupping my cheek, the warmth of her stopping me in my tracks.

"Baby, if you don't go with them we'll never make it out of here. Royal has a failsafe, and I think he's put it into play. If you and the boys don't get out there soon, we're going to have the weight of the Keep bearing down on us, and those men will have a fuck ton more weapons on them than we do."

I open my mouth to argue with her, but she presses her fingers against my lips, "Octavius, listen to me. I need you to go. I need you to make us safe. I need you to get us home to the kids and we can't do that if we're both in this tiny room."

I study her face, and I know I have to do what she asks of me. I need her focused. The only way I can do that is by listening to her. She can't complete her mission if she's fretting about me and the kids.

Pressing my forehead to hers, I breathe in her scent. Telling her I love her isn't enough. The word just isn't big enough to describe how I feel. I say the only thing I can think would make sense to her, my woman who survived a fucked up religious cult who thinks having people submit to them is what makes you powerful. "You own me, all of me."

Her quick intake of breath lets me know I hit the mark. "I love you, Tav."

She grips my head and kisses me roughly, then pushes me away from her, stepping up to the next man in the line, the very last one before it's Royal's turn. I hesitate to follow Vic and Dom, who wait impatiently by the door.

"Prospect," Marx barks, bringing my attention to my Pres, "I've got her. Go fuck them all up so we get out of here in one piece." I nod at my Pres and turn to leave the room.

My legs feel like I have lead in my boots as I follow Vic and

Dom.

"I need you to get your shit together. We'll take care of the men and then be back in time for Blanche's big finale," Vic says, gripping my shoulder and giving me a shake.

I scrub my hands down my face, getting into gear, but I still can't shake the feeling that is in my heart. I know why she wanted me gone. She thinks that by splitting up one of us will have a better chance of survival. She has another thing coming because there is no way I'm leaving this place without that stubborn woman of mine.

"Who do we have to fuck up so I can get back to my woman?"

Matching grins spread across their faces.

"Why Tav, I didn't think you'd be so bloodthirsty," Dom coos under his breath.

"Royal's looking cocky in there. Either he knew we were going to strike, or he's had the fail-safe in play since Hammer's arrival in case something like this happened," Vic explains, back against the building as we move quietly toward the entrance of the main hall, where all the men will be. "If that's the case, he's had a camera in the meeting room the whole time."

"Wait," I stop to look at them both, "If that's true, why hasn't anyone burst in?"

"He would have given them strict instructions to wait. He'll have a signal, trust me. When that happens, there'll be an ambush. But it won't be us who'll be in the hot seat."

We reach the main doors at the same time Rider and Tank come crouch-running toward us, guns drawn.

"Marx sent us. I say we smoke the fuckers out and pick them off," Rider says, waving a smoke bomb canister in his hand.

The Landry brothers look at each other before shrugging.

"You gonna be OK with this? I'm guessing you'll know some people in there," Tank, ever the voice of reason asks, his head tipping toward the door.

"They're traffickers. Fuck em," Dom answers darkly.

"Grab whatever cover you can. Rider, you're it," Tank's deep voice commands and we scatter.

"Fire in the hole!" Rider grins, then pulls the pin off the gas canister with his teeth, kicks the door in and throws it, running to stand with his back pressed against the wall at the front of the hall. Dom is crouched behind a tree, Vic is across from me behind some type of outbuilding, Tank behind what looks like a kids' playhouse. A quick sweep of our surroundings shows Nitro on the left of the hall, Fox on the right, with me sheltered behind a small shed. I have no fucking clue what is inside, but I'm hoping it doesn't house some well-armed women willing to take me out.

Within moments smoke billows out of the hall doors, and with it men come flooding out. They may be coughing their guts out but they are also pulling weapons, holding them at the ready for a gunfight. We don't have the luxury of counting how many men we have to face off with, or talking them down in the hopes of a peaceful resolution. The first shot rings out from one of the Keep members, who has spied Tank's giant body in the playhouse. That single shot is exactly what we need to get this party started.

With the men surrounded, we start picking them off, one by one. Rider is proving lethal with his rear attack, confusing the dumb fucks. They fire wildly, no rhyme or reason. Some even take down their own brethren in a clusterfuck of bullets. It's like shooting fish in a barrel, and if I was a better man I'd feel bad about that. But I'm not, so I shoot at anything in white sneakers. I have kids to get home to.

The crowd starts to thin. Fewer men come charging through the doors, and I don't want to get too complacent thinking we have them all. There is only one door into the hall. There is an entrance into the meeting room where Marx and Pixie are, and the outside door to the meeting room, meaning there could well be men out the back of the hall if they've managed to make their way through Marx, which let's face it, he's a massive, feral fucker so their chances are pretty low.

Rider waves his hands around, first pointing to his eyes, then making a karate chop movement toward the door of the hall. Tank answers back in kind. It's easy to forget that these men are trained for missions like this with long histories in the military. To me, they're good men, family men, men who want to protect those they love. Remembering that I have these men at my back makes me want to call my sister and thank her again for stumbling into their compound that day.

Tank waves at me and the Landrys to stay put and watch their backs, Rider staying low and entering the hall, Tank going high, following in behind him, Fox and Nitro flanking the sides. I watch and wait, although I can't help the prickling feeling that I'm being watched myself. Turning from my place I'm met with a group of women huddled together, children clutched to them.

A tall woman pushes her way to the front of the group, holding her arms out to the side, as if to stop me from rushing them, or taking an interest in the children behind her.

"I'm not going to hurt you," I say in a gentle voice, trying hard not to scare anyone. Although I'm guessing with the gunfire, it's probably too late.

"Save it, we've heard it all before," she scoffs, before looking me up and down. "Did Blanche send you?"

"Blanche is my woman." She narrows her eyes at my words and takes a step back, pushing the other back with her movements. "Shit, I mean, I belong to her. I'm here to help her achieve her vision."

"To get rid of the council and her father?"

I nod, slightly afraid I'll say something and fuck up again. She smiles, her stance relaxing slightly. "What of the men?"

Looking behind me, I watch for a moment as Tank and Rider exit the hall, giving us the thumbs up. "Looks like they're gone."

A brilliant smile crosses her face and murmuring behind her sounds more excited than afraid. Her smile falters when she looks over my shoulder, before she steps to the side, to get a better look behind me.

"Vic?"

"Loyal? Holy shit, I haven't seen you in years!" Vic steps forward in a rush, as if to hug her, but stops as soon as she flinches. "Sorry, just, I didn't know you were still –" He waves around before rubbing the back of his neck.

"Well, someone had to help your sister get these women out," she says with sass. Well, OK then.

"You've been her contact all along?"

She grins up at him before it falters slightly, "I, um, with everyone gone, I'm not sure where we should go," she points to the group behind her.

"We have networks, people and places that can help. Let me take care of it?"

She nods in reply and Vic looks toward me, and then his brother, before finding Loyal again. "Can you still remember what I taught you?"

She rolls her eyes, "Of course."

"Good, grab all you need, get in the Keep van and drive to the nearest town. We'll meet you there." They share a look, then Loyal rushes away, urging her group to follow her.

"Right boys, let's find my woman, get rid of Royal and Mercy and burn this fucking place to the ground."

Blanche

I have one councilman left sniveling in front of me. There's been no rhyme or reason to the order in which I've sent them to their maker, but I have to admit, leaving this one for last gives me a little thrill. Steadfast Cormier was the most vicious of all the men in Eden's Keep. His wives were always sporting bruises thanks to his "correction."

"Any last sins to repent, Steadfast?"

He turns to look me in the eye, then spits at me, hitting me in the cheek.

"You're a fucking slut, Patience, and you'll be treated like one when the Keep men come for you," he sneers at me, eyes burning brightly. I see the exact moment he realizes his words don't hit their target.

"May the Lord have mercy on your soul," I whisper in his gross, hairy ear, his head snapping back when my bullet hits it.

"Well, girl, you've got your eight men," Marx says, his hand gripping Royal's shoulder, keeping him in his seat.

He still has a cocky smile on his face, and I cannot wait to see that disappear. A bang sounds out in the hall, on the other side of the door. We wait for a beat and then gunfire surrounds us.

"Blanche," Marx barks, "Stand down. It'll be over soon,"

I stand stock still in the middle of the room. Marx yanks Royal up by the collar, bodily moving him and then shoving him into another chair, this one with a good view of the connecting door to the hall. He raises his gun and holds it steady. I move to the right side of him, aiming mine as well. If anyone decides to escape out the back, we'll pick them off as soon as look at them.

Holding strong the sound of gunfire lessens until it comes to a stop. My heart thuds in my chest, hands sweaty. What if we didn't win? What if something happened to Tav? To the rest of them? Shit, I feel dizzy. Fuck, get it together, Blanche! My mind screams at me to find three things that are blue in the room. I look around wildly, but all I can see is red. The red of blood, on the floors, on the wall. On my hands.

My body jolts like it's touched a live wire when someone thumps twice on the connecting door, "All clear, Pres!" a gruff voice calls out. I think it's Tank.

All the tension leaves my body at once and I try to lock my knees, to stop myself from falling to the ground in relief. Strong hands wrap around my biceps, Tav's smell invading my senses, calming me even before his voice reaches my ears.

"I'm here, Pixie, I'm here." Turning to look at my love, my eyes dart over him, wanting to check for injuries. When I see that he's unharmed I lean my forehead against his hard chest.

"I hope you have a backup backup plan," Rider sasses Royal, walking in with a cocky grin on his face. My brothers and the MC brothers all cram into the meeting room, all except Savage and Dex.

"Where are the other two?"

"Here Pres," Dex says, followed by Savage, silly grins on their faces.

"Where the hell were you when we were facing off against those brainwashed hillbillies?" Tank asks, flipping Royal the bird when he turns to glare at Tank.

"I had a feeling that he had something else up his sleeve," Savage answers, tipping his head toward my uncle dearest.

"And?" Marx growls,

"Threat neutralized. These fuckers had this place wired to blow fucking sky high," Dex throws a pile of wires and metal parts on the floor, and for the first time Royal is looking nervous.

"Are you ready for your turn, husband dearest?" I taunt, ignoring Tav's growl behind me. "I have something extra special planned for you."

Vic and Dom grab an arm each and yank Royal to standing. "Come on old man, let's go visit the Prophet, huh?"

They frogmarch him out the door, his feet cooperating before he decides to be a pain in the ass. He kicks and goes limp, my brothers almost dropping him.

"Fuck it," Dom growls and using their brotherly telepathy Vic takes hold of Royal's legs, Dom the top half.

They carry him through the compound to the Prophet's house, leading the way for the rest of us. There are women standing around, obviously having come out of hiding. They're looking bewildered, children cuddled into their bosom. They stare at us as we walk through, none of them asking who we are or what we're doing.

"This place gives me the creeps," Fox mumbles to Nitro,

Nitro nodding his head in agreement.

"Not a tear has been shed for these men, either."

"Why would they? The bulk of their husbands were bullies and rapists," I say, catching the eye of one woman in the crowd. She gives me a smile and mouths, "Thank you." I give her a nod in return. I'm not sure what will happen to them without the menfolk, but that's a problem for a later date.

We round the last bend, following the path that my mother laid herself, the one that leads right up to the Prophet's front door. My brothers wrestle with Royal who hasn't stopped wriggling and sneering. I mean, I don't blame him. We've killed his men, his followers. His bombs have been found and Hammer is tucked up safely in the SUV. Unless he has the Cordoza Cartel hiding up his ass, there's no one to save him.

Finally, Dom has enough, wrestling Royal into a good enough position to punch him in the gut. "Stay still, fuckhead."

Vic snorts and then tips his head toward the door, his hands still full with Royal's kicking, twisting feet. Following Vic's head tilt, Tav steps forward and kicks the door in.

"Oh Daaaddyy! We're hoooome!" Vic calls out in a silly voice.

Dom and Vic carry Royal into the house, followed by Marx, Tav, and myself.

"We'll wait outside and watch the perimeter. There were some women out here I don't like the look of," Tank mumbles, turning to the rest of the men who nod.

Stepping into the living room of the house I grew up in, my eyes are drawn to Mercy Landry, lying in a hospital bed. There's a young girl next to him, clutching at a glass of water with a straw in it.

"Darling, why don't you go wait outside, yeah?" Marx offers, smiling at the terrified woman. She glances at Mercy, then

Royal, before scuttling past us, headed for the door.

Tav brings forward one of the stiff wooden chairs from the dining room, placing it at the foot of Mercy's bed. My brothers dump Royal into it. Vic stands behind him and grips both of his shoulders, holding him down.

"Patience?" My father's voice is thready and weak, his eyes barely open as he peers at me from the angle at which he lies.

"Fuck, this is depressing. Dom, sit his bed up so he can see what's going to happen," Marx demands.

Dom nods once, then moves to look at the controls on the remote attached to the bed on a curly wire. His brows furrow, and he presses something. We wait for Mercy to sit up, however his legs raise up instead.

"Shit, wrong button, hold up," Dom mumbles, pressing something else.

"Dude, you've turned him into a V," Tav snorts, then coughs, trying to cover up his laughter when Marx gives him a stern look.

We watch for probably too long as my stupid brother fiddles with the settings, none of them putting Mercy in a good enough position.

"Fuck's sake," Marx growls under his breath, snatching the remote away from Dom, throwing it across the room only to have it come boinging back on the curly cord it's attached to. Thanks to their quick reflexes Marx and Dom both duck away. Mercy isn't as lucky.

I roll my lips between my teeth and try to ignore Tav's shoulders shaking. Even Vic is trying hard not to laugh, his mouth is tight, and he looks constipated.

Marx grabs some cushions off the couch, grips Mercy by the front of his shirt, pulls him forward, and ignoring the old man's protests he shoves the cushions behind his back.

"There, now get to it. We have more fuckers to deal with once these two are done."

My father wheezes before squinting at me. "It is you, my little girl. Patience. You look just like your momma."

"Who I imagine looks just like Lovely's momma," I mumble back.

"They were beautiful women, who created more beautiful women,"

"That you then passed on to your brother you sick fuck," I retort.

His white eyebrows fly up his forehead. He looks as if he's about to wind up and preach to me about how swearing is the devil's language or some shit.

"We're not here for a family reunion. I just wanted you to know that in a few moments, Eden's Keep will be no more," I indicate to Royal.

"What are you talking about? Royal will be the next prophet. I've been grooming him since I became ill. He will lead Eden's Keep, make it stronger, save more lost souls. It will be glorious," the old man smiles, a faraway look in his eye as if he can see this kingdom on earth he dreams of. The one that enslaves women and then sells their children.

"Are you sure Royal will be the next prophet, Father?" I ask innocently.

"Of course! The angels told me Royal will be the next to lead our people."

Standing behind Royal, I run my hands through the hair on his head before I grip it and yank it back. "Say goodbye, motherfucker," I whisper to him.

His eyes blaze at mine and he opens his mouth to spew vitriol, but he's interrupted by his brother and Prophet. Letting go of his hair, he straightens up, looking at Mercy.

"I always knew you would be the one who would lead my flock to salvation," he smiles at his younger brother softly, then his eyes widen in horror.

Mercy's mouth opens and closes and nothing comes out except an awful wheeze as he watches the scene in front of him. Royal struggles and scratches at my hands, trying to remove the garotte from cutting into his fat neck, but it's no use. With my knee propped on the back of the chair I'm leaning back with my full weight, the thin wire cutting through skin, fat, muscle and ligaments, stopping when it hits bone and Royal's hands drop to his sides.

An awful mewling sound leaves Mercy, his eyes wide, staring at me. I watch as his dreams, my nightmares, turn to dust in front of him.

"You, you, you–" he points a bony finger at me, too lost to even form the words he wants to say.

"Where are your angels now, father? Hmm?" I step up to the bed and grip his hand in mine, turning to look at my handiwork. "You disowned your sons, threw them out like trash, calling them weak and useless. You wouldn't stand up for me when I came to you time and time again to tell you of the horrors I endured at Royal's hands. No, instead you gave him another of your 'precious' daughters. You blamed our stubbornness on the devil and called us weak. Well, daddy dearest, who's weak now?"

I tilt my head until I'm looking into his dark, soulless eyes. My hand finds the textured handle of my gun, the weight feeling right in my hands. I press the muzzle against his temple and look deep into his eyes, waiting for recognition that it was me, me who ended him.

"Goodbye Father. Give my regards to the devil."

Chapter 20

Tav

"Babe, Pixie, wake up, baby. We're home." I gently brush her short bangs away from her forehead, trying to gently wake her.

She's been crashed out since she got in the car. She held it together after getting rid of Royal and her father. She even held it together when a lone sniper came out of the trees behind the Prophet's home. Luckily, she recognized him as her male contact, Justice, otherwise he would have felt the cold steel of a fuck ton of bullets. He set to work cleaning up our mess and assured us he'd keep an eye on the women and children at the Keep until they decided what they wanted to do.

I'm fairly certain that without a Prophet a lot of them will leave, either go home to their families or find a new church. Others were in so deep that I'm unsure they'll ever leave the Keep. Tombs Security has a few contacts within the services we sometimes contract to, people who have worked on deprogramming cult members and the like. I passed their numbers onto Justice. He'll need it if he's serious about helping them move on.

"Pixie, we're home. The kids will be waiting," I kiss her temple, damp from where she's been smooshed up against the headrest.

She mumbles and tries to shove me off. I smile into her temple and press more kisses to her face, moving on to her cheek and neck, snorting when she whines.

"Alright, I'm awake!" she grumbles, blinking owlishly. "Oh, we're home!" She unbuckles her belt and flies out of the car.

Chuckling to myself, I get out and stretch, feeling how good it is to have this chapter behind us. Well, almost. Savage and Dex have a woozy Hammer balanced between them, leading them to Chewy's favorite place in the world.

"Come on prospect, may as well enjoy our heroes' welcome," Rider says, clapping his hand on my shoulder far harder than needed.

Following behind Rider, Tank, Nitro, and Fox into the club-house, I come to an abrupt stop when they do. Marx is standing in the doorway, hands on his hips, head hanging, mumbling to himself.

"Two days. I was gone for two fucking days." he shakes his head before straightening, and I'm very sure glaring at his brother. "Rhodie, I left you in charge. What the fuck is this?"

Marx moves further into the room, allowing the rest of us to make our way into the room, where we too come to an abrupt stop.

Everything looks as it always does, well apart from what appears to be dildo coat hooks dotted around the room. But no, that's not what has Marx gaping. That would be the sight of my sister standing in the middle of the room, the two moms-to-be and Lovely gazing up at her as she wears a baby carrier on her front. A baby carrier complete with an alligator in it.

"It's my baby, Marx!" Chewy coos, patting the head of the thing, which is sticking out dangerously fucking close to her face if you ask me.

Dom side eyes me and then rolls his lips between his teeth, trying not to laugh. Chris also has eyes on me, a smirk on his lips. Fucker. Pixie wanders over to look at Chewy's baby, but instead of cooing over the gator, she instead looks as though she's examining it. She pries its mouth open before closing it and running her hand over its snout.

"He's malformed. This is the one you were hand feeding?" Pixie asks her brothers.

"Yeah, his upper jaw is too short. He has polydactyly and his toes are curled up," Dom answers.

"Chris said he'll never be able to feed himself properly, nor will he be able to survive in the wild," Chewy adds, looking unusually sad about this.

"He may not survive in the wild, but he sure as hell will scare the shit outta people in the Rev Room," Pops adds with glee.

Chewy places her hand on the gator's back as he rests in the carrier on her front, her eyes huge as she stares at Marx.

"It's like when a kid asks their dad for a pet," Tank mumbles to someone behind me. Whoever it is snorts in reply.

Rhodie steps up next to his Ol Lady, pulling her into him. He, too, gives Marx the big eyes.

"You've already named it haven't you?" Marx accuses his enforcers.

"Yeah, his name is Chomper," Chewy beams, clearly not seeing the irony in the name given the fact her gator is essentially disabled. Or maybe that's exactly why she named him that.

"Fine. But he's your responsibility! And get rid of the fucking dildos!"

Cheers ring out from everyone in the room before Marx waves his hands, telling us to settle down.

"One round of drinks and then we take care of the piece of shit in the shed. I want this whole thing wrapped up," he barks out then heads for his office.

The Landry brothers head for Lovely and little Bee, my MC brothers all head to the bar, and I make a beeline for my family. I'm ready for a Cove-hug, but I'm stopped by Niko first, who shocks the shit out of me by holding his hand out to me. As soon as I clasp it, he pulls me in for a half hug.

"Thank you for helping my mom and keeping her safe."

I place my hand on the back of his head, pulling him into me tighter. "Thank you for trusting me to keep her safe. I know it was a big deal, since you've been doing it all this time."

He pulls back to look at me, a smile playing on his lips, "It's your turn now, old man,"

"Hey! She's older than me!" I retort, not that he gives a shit as he gives me his back.

Not that I take it to heart because the Littles run up and hug both of my legs while Sage wraps her thin arms around my waist, giving me a quick squeeze.

"Thank you for coming home," she says, before moving back so I can pick up Cove and Elio.

"Tav! Did you know that Ana and Nat both have babies in their tummies?" Cove yells in my face as Elio rests his head on my shoulder.

"What!? I thought they just ate too much ice cream!"

Cove stares at me like I'm crazy and Ana shoots me daggers before flipping me the bird. I settle on the couch with my family surrounding me. We catch up, the big kids keen to hear that

Royal will never bother them ever again, the Littles wanting to know if we got them gifts.

Before we know it, Marx is whistling to get our attention. Mama Debs, Lovely and the Ol Ladies minus Chewy and Pixie, bustle the children into Mama Debs' suite for movies and junk food, and we all wait for Marx's orders.

"Chewy, it's time. Is everything set?" Marx asks my sister, her nodding enthusiastically. "Good, let's do this,"

Blanche

I follow the men out into the Rev Room, which once again has snacks on the table laid out for us. Rider, Fox and Nitro all fight for space on the couch, while everyone else seems to lean on the walls or anything else that can prop them up.

Hammer has already been strapped to the bright yellow chair, and the man looks completely mellow thanks to whatever Savage and Dex dosed him up on. He stares wide-eyed at Chewy as she fusses about, then jumps back, struggling against the cable ties on his wrists and ankles.

"That's a fucking real alligator!" he yells, wriggling so much he rocks the chair, falling back onto the grate on the ground. He stops yelling and wriggling to stare at something, before screaming, "Those are teeth in there! Whose teeth are those!"

Rhodie lifts him up, setting him back to rights as Chewy bends over, looking into the grate. "You need to learn how to clean better, Tav," she shakes her head in disappointment.

"Sorry sis, I'll try better with this one." He grins back, moving up behind me, wrapping his thick arms around my waist and pulling me into his front, like he always does.

"No need, this one is gonna be almost mess free," she wags her eyebrows and then pulls out a large black dildo, thumping it down onto a conveniently placed metal table so it wobbles slightly. "Babe, my soundtrack please," she puckers up and Rhodie drops a kiss on her lips then presses something on his phone.

"Is this sex music?" someone grumbles. I'm not too sure who it is as basically the whole MC, Tombs Security and my brothers are all crammed in here.

"Yeah, I need to set the scene. Get Hammer all raring to go,"

I see a lot of side eyes happening. I mean, I was bracing for torture, some blood maybe, a lot of crying and sniveling, not a seduction. Chewy is warming up what looks to be massage oil while Pops is lighting scented candles.

"Can you two hurry it up?" Marx growls.

"Marx, good things take time. We gotta romance him," Pops snorts.

Chewy nods at Rhodie, who cuts the ties restraining Hammer. He slides his knife down Hammer's clothing, cutting them all away until he's standing nude, his small dick on show under his pasty belly. Savage and Dex step up, helping Rodie manhandle him onto the St Andrew's cross, which seems to be a favorite of this bunch. They all secure him and Chewy steps up, gloves on, massage oil in her palm.

She covers his torso with the stuff, moving down to his legs. She has purposely avoided his junk, and I don't blame her. I would too. However, she must have a plan because she reaches her hand back, Pops slapping a rubber scraper into her hand. She squirts oil in it and then paints his dick and balls with it.

"That's an interesting use of that," Switch says loudly, his eyes glued to what's happening to Hammer's balls.

"Turn him, boys!" Chewy demands, and the boys jump to attention.

Well, they try. Now that Hammer is all oiled up, he's also really damn slippery. Meaning Rhodie, Savage and Dex are having a hard time maneuvering him.

"Fuck's sake, get a grip on him!" Pops yells from his position in a chair next to the dildo table.

There's a lot of grunting happening. Hammer is trying to wriggle his way out of their hold, the other three frantically trying to wrestle him onto the cross.

"Ew fuck! His balls touched me!" Dex grunts and then shoves him off of him, right into Savage.

I know I shouldn't laugh, but I can't help the honk that comes out of me, followed by giggles and a snort. I'm not the only one. Rider has just spit out a mouthful of brownie and is clutching his stomach.

"For fuck's sake," Pops says under his breath before he storms over, grips Hammer in the soft spot under his arm, swings his leg out and brings it down onto Hammer's, causing him to stumble face first into the cross. "You're welcome," Pops grumbles.

Rhodie secures him finally, and Chewy gets to work, oiling up the back of Hammer. "Might want to put your coveralls on when you dump him," she says, not looking at anyone in particular, just concentrating on getting Hammer all lubed up.

"Savage and Dex, you guys wanted to be hands on with his one, huh?"

They both nod at Chewy, jaws clenching.

"Awesome. Would you please hold his ass cheeks open for me?" She asks so sweetly, just as a Barry White song starts up.

"Uuuummmm," Savage and Dex look at each other in bewilderment. Actually, everyone is. There isn't even a smart ass comment from Rider.

"Come again?" Dex squeaks out.

"That's what she said," Pops adds, elbowing Marx and grinning. Marx just rolls his eyes and crosses his arms over his broad chest.

Chewy pushes her goggles up on to the top of her head, her curls sticking out all over the place. "I need you to spread his ass cheeks. Please." She says this patiently, as if talking to children.

"Um, and if we don't?"

"Then I won't be able to lube his asshole. It's really an integral part of the plan," she stares at them, and then at Hammer's shiny ass.

"Listen boys, that asshole holds the key to getting Officer Fuckwit off our cases. If you want him gone, you'll spread that ass,"

Hammer must hear the growl in Pops' voice because he whimpers a little. Savage and Dex share a look, then a glare around the room.

"This doesn't leave this room. And not one word to my Ol Lady because I'll never fucking live it down, got it?" Savage gives everyone the stink eye.

Everyone nods, Rider even goes so far as to zip his lips, lock them and then throw away the key. Both men step up to either side of Hammer, grip a cheek each, and pry them apart. I turn my head, because the last thing I want to look into is a hairy asshole.

"Pops, my beautiful assistant, can I please have our secret weapon?" Chewy coos at Pops, who bounces up and shuffles to the table.

He busies himself putting gloves on. "What do you think is in there?" I mumble to Tav, turning my head slightly to look at him.

"Babe, it's Pops, it could be any-fucking-thing," he whispers back, his hot breath on the shell of my ear sending a bolt of electricity straight to my panties.

"What the fuck, is that a used condom!?" Tank yells out, as Pops holds exactly that. A used condom pinched between his thumb and forefinger.

"Yes, yes, it is. Jules helped me find the hooker that Officer Fuckface frequents. All I had to do was sweet talk her into throwing the used Jimmy out of the car window into my waiting hands and 'Operation Fuck Officer Martin' was put into motion," Pops says proudly.

"I did not see that coming. Did you?" Vic asks Chris and Dom who both shake their heads.

"OK. So the plan is I'm going to fuck his ass with this," Chewy waves the black dildo around in her hand, "Then I'm going to place the condom in his ass."

There's a collective intake of breath and even a few hisses.

"That's fucking diabolical," Marx grins as Chewy gently takes off the front pack with Chomper and hands him over to Pops who straps him on way too easily. It's as if he's been practicing or something.

Once Chewy is Chomper free she takes her dildo, moves behind Hammer and does exactly as she said. It's brutal and disgusting and yet there's a feeling of righteousness about the whole thing. This man has done unspeakable things to women and children. He deserves this and everything else Chewy's genius can come up with.

Stepping back from a broken Hammer, Chewy removes her gloves and blows her hair out of her face.

"Savage and Dex, he's all yours. Gag him, whip him, paddle him, do whatever you want, as long as you finish by choking him. This needs to look like rough sex gone bad, got it?"

The men share an evil grin. "Yeah, we got it," Dex says, rubbing his hands together.

"What do you say we get outta here, Pixie?" Tav whispers, then sucks on my neck softly.

"I thought you'd never ask,"

Tav

I give Gus the eye, who then rolls his, gives me a nod and then tips his head at the door.

"Was that some type of weird Tombs language?" Pixie teases as we hold hands, swinging them as we head into the clubhouse.

"Yup, very special. We mainly do it because Chewy can never figure out the code. Makes it easier to surprise her."

"Why would you want to?" she asks, tipping her head up.

"Chewy believed in Santa for a really long time. In her mind, parents don't lie, so Santa must be real. When they died, it landed on me and the boys to become Santa. The problem being you cannot hide ANYTHING with Chewy around. She'll find whatever it is you've hidden. We had to come up with a secret language and work as a team to make sure we could keep everything a secret. It was fucking exhausting." I chuckle, thinking back to having to distract Chewy and then head nod at my brothers to move shit to a different hidey hole because she was on to us.

"You are such a good man, Tav. You love your family so much, and I am so glad that me and the kids are a part of it."

We stand in the common room, surrounded by rubber dicks, and I cannot think of any place I'd rather be. I cup her face and then gently press my lips to hers.

"Oh finally, you're back! We've been waiting. Can we have a sleepover in your room?" Cove asks, jumping up and down on her toes.

I snort when I see the look on my woman's face, then hide my smile in her neck as I cuddle her to me. She's having none of that, pinching me in the soft spot under my arm.

"Ow! You learned that from Pops!" I accuse her.

"Damn right," she grins. "So, what do you say Ol Man?"

Looking at Cove's bright face shining up at me, and Elio's little smile, I can't help it. "Yes. But first showers and then PJ's." They run off screaming, well at least one of them does.

"You're a good man, Tav, and I love you,"

Later on, in the early hours, I try really hard to remember those words as Elio's knobbly foot rearranges my balls inside my sack. Lifting my head, I see the reason. Cove is sleeping across the bed, her head on Pixie's shoulder, her feet in Elio's back. The poor kid is arched around her foot, his toes in my junk.

Realizing that I'll probably end up neutered if this carries on I roll out of bed and rearrange the kids. Checking the time and realizing that it's essentially the early morning I decide to get up and get my day started, knowing full well I won't get back to sleep.

Throwing on some clothes and my cut over the top I head into the kitchen to get a head start on the coffee machine. Instead, seeing Vic already leaning against the counter, cup in hand, his phone in the other.

"Hey man, you're up early," I say, grabbing the pot and pouring myself a cup.

"Yeah, we're wanting to get on the road early. Justice called. He has a number of women and children to be homed, so we've been talking to our contacts. Loyal is going to help us." He smiles at the thought.

After we left the Keep, he and Dom met up with Loyal and gave her the keys and directions to their place, promising that he'd be away overnight and then head back.

"She's a tough woman to survive in there."

"Yeah, she is. But she's a real sweetheart too. I'm looking forward to working with her."

I grin at him before addressing the elephant in the room. Or gator. "Soooo, are you going to take your gator with you?"

"Like hell Octavius Tombs! He'll have to shoot me and then claw Chomper from my cold, dead hands," Chewy growls from somewhere in the dark.

Vic just grins at me.

"How long have you been standing there?" I sigh out.

"Wouldn't you like to know?" she sasses.

"Yeah I would actually," I reply. No answer. "Chewy?"

"She's an odd little woman, and I can say that because Blanche is my sister."

"Yup. And she's perfect."

Epilogue

Tav

It still feels weird for me to be sitting in Church. Usually Prospects aren't allowed, but I'm guessing this has something to do with my Ol Lady bringing down a religious cult, so I'm sitting around the table with my brothers. Marx invited Pixie, but she told us she had better things to do. Namely, help the Ol Ladies set up for the triple baby shower happening in the common room after Church.

"So, you'll never guess who I had in my office earlier," Marx starts, leaning back in his chair, "Sergeant Moss Davies. Would you believe that Officer Martin has been taken into custody on suspicion of murder?" Marx's eyes get comically wide as we all gasp and clutch our chests.

"Seriously? So Chewy and Pops' plan worked?" Judge says, clearly shocked.

"It seems so. Word is that Officer Martin was questioned over his involvement in the trafficking ring and the failed abduction of Lovely. He was then cut loose, and they suspect it was during this time that he met up with Hammer for a little fun. Davies says that they have little fingerprint evidence because of the massage oil on Hammer's skin, so it was lucky that they found biological evidence inside Hammer's body."

"Fucking gross," Rider mumbles.

"Maybe so, but Chewy and Pops got rid of two thorns in our side," Marx finishes.

"Are we calling in a favor from one of our contacts on the inside?" Judge asks quietly.

"No need. Officer Martin was an asshole and put a lot of guys away with little evidence. I don't think he's going to last long in prison," Marx grins as we all cheer.

Pres bangs his fist on the table to get everyone to settle down, then looks at Sniper. "Roman has handled the Cordoza Cartel."

"How?" Sniper asks quietly.

"He's cut the head off the snake, and the next three in command."

"Carlos Jr?"

"He's seven years old. His mother wants nothing to do with the cartel. If the kid ever wants to avenge his father, it'll be fucking years away, by which time Roman could well have died of old age," Marx leans forward, looking directly at Sniper across the table. "It's done."

Sniper doesn't look entirely convinced, but he nods and relaxes slightly in his chair.

"Anything else to report?" Marx looks around the table.

I clear my throat, "Um yeah, I have an update on the Landrys at the request of my Pixie. Lovely will stay in town with Pixie and the kids, so you may see her around the clubhouse at family things." The brothers all nod their heads. They've been really gentle with her since she arrived, although I'm not sure she's as soft as everyone thinks she is. Quiet and shy, yes, but she found the strength to walk away from a cult, so I think she has it in her to thrive now that she's here in Rose Grove.

"What about the Keep?" Tank murmurs.

"Pretty much abandoned. Justice hung around long enough to make sure all the women and children found new homes. Some returned to family, others were farmed out to the Landry brothers' contacts. Pixie and my sister may or may not have had a word with a few of the older women who helped Royal," I tell them, trying to keep the smile off my face.

All my brothers smile back, knowing full well what a talk with my sister and my Ol Lady would entail.

"Good. Any chance the Landrys might want their gator back?" Marx asks and then jumps in his chair a little, "Keep your feet to yourself fucker," he growls at his brother.

"Nope, that gator is Chewy's baby, Pres," Tank says, crossing his arms over his chest.

Marx lets out a bone weary sigh. "Fine. What about getting rid of those fucking dildos?"

"Well," Rider starts, "So far 10 went on the walls, 10 on Officer Martin's cruiser -"

"A fair few in the Dongsai Garden out back," Tank adds with a smirk while Marx rolls his eyes.

"Oh, she also 'gifted' some to the Eden's Keep women too. Something about 'breaking the shackles with orgasms'," I shrug.

Marx runs his hand down his beard thoughtfully, "Good, that's good. There were a shit ton of women there, so we must be done with the dicks. Alright. Anyone got anything else to bring to the table?"

Looking around, the brothers all shake their heads.

"Not a word, brothers. I have a baby shower to get to,"

Savage says. He's so into becoming a father that Nat has had to threaten his balls just so he would go to work and stop hovering around her.

"You do know that a baby shower is for the mom and not the dad, right?" Flack points out.

"Shut up, it's my special day too!" Savage growls back and then tosses a pen at him.

Before they can start scuffling in earnest, Marx slams down the gavel, "Church over, now get out!"

We all stand to leave the room, coming to a bottleneck in the doorway behind Rider.

"Dude, get out of the way." Savage elbows him and moves into the common room, "Holy shit,"

We all side eye each other and then push to leave the room, wanting to see what the hell is going on. The common room is a sea of pastel colors. But not in any type of tasteful way. More in a "Chewy bought all this stuff, and it exploded everywhere."

"What the hell happened in here?" Fox whispers, wide eyed.

"Are those dicks ejaculating streamers?"

My gaze follows Judge's finger to the corner of the ceiling where yes, that is a dildo with streamers coming from the knob. It's not the only one either. There are all sorts of dicks dotted around the room ejaculating pastel crepe paper. On the walls, on the ceiling. There's some type of weird cake thing made of diapers sitting in the middle of one of the long tables, and I'm sure that's a black knob sticking out of the top.

"Jesus H Christ, that's a lot of dicks. And a fuck ton of pink and blue," Flack whispers under his breath, in awe of the sight. He opens his arms as Remy leans into him for a hug, not taking his eyes off the room he's standing in.

I look at my Pres to see how he's handling it and it's safe to say he's doing pretty well. If chewing frantically on antacids is a good thing.

"Welcome all, today we celebrate the incubators and the ex-incubator!" Chewy announces, indicating Ana, Nat and Lovely who are sitting in recliners wearing crowns. The back of the chairs are decorated with rubber dongs, giving it a whole Game of Thrones vibe. But with dicks.

A soft hand squeezes my ass before moving up my back, gently rubbing between my shoulder blades. I lift my arm and my Pixie snuggles in.

"So, what do you think?"

I stare down at her wide eyed, "Are you fucking with me?"

"No way! I helped decorate, and it was so much fun. I never had this with Niko, and Lovely obviously didn't have it with little Bee either. The girls decided Lovely shouldn't miss out on something so, well, lovely, so they added her into the mix." She beams up at me, a little teary.

"What's wrong, baby?" I ask, swiping the tear that falls from her lashes as it makes a trail down her cheek.

"It's just, I never wanted to be anyone's Ol Lady." Uh oh. "I never wanted to belong to anyone. And then you came along with your stupid sexy face and your soft heart and you gave me this. A place filled with people. Crazy, beautiful, kind people that have helped my kids to thrive. People that have accepted Lovely as their friend." She waves around the dick covered room before turning to me. "You, Tav, gave me a place to belong."

I cup her face as she looks up at me. "You own me, Pixie. Body and soul."

She rises to her toes and gently presses her lips against mine, tenderly. "You own me, Tav. Body and soul."

We turn and watch for a moment as Chewy brings out a cake shaped like a very realistic vulva.

"Ah, Chewy, what's with the vag?" Ana points to it, looking weirded out.

"The baby could have a vag," she replies, shrugging, jiggling Chomper in her front carrier.

"Of course," Ana mumbles, Gus interrupting further questioning by kissing her.

Chewy cuts the cake and tells us to all dig in. Rider and Nitro fight over who gets the clit, which causes us all to dissolve into raucous laughter when Pops realizes neither of them has it.

"Listen boys, do you both need a little sex ed in the Rev Room? I'm sure I have just the thing to help you both out." He waggles his eyebrows as he wanders over to sit with Ana, Nat and Lovely, the cake shaped like a clit in the center of his plate.

"Gift time!" Chewy yells, while covering Chomper's ears, or where she thinks his ears are. Hopefully, he has ears. That gator is already disabled enough as it is. The last thing Marx wants is a deaf gator with an under-bite and funny toes running around the clubhouse.

Standing behind Pixie, I wrap my arms around her and pull her into my chest. We watch the ladies of honor open their biker themed gifts - baby-sized leather cuts and tiny boots. Lovely oohs and ahhs over everything, and I'm sure it's overwhelming for her. I saw what the children at the Keep wore, so dressing Bee as a biker must be mind-blowing for her. Even Ana is given DRMC merchandise. Which Roman bitches about until she opens his and Sasha's gift - a tiny bratva suit.

"What are you guys gonna do if this lot has girls?" Pixie murmurs.

"What do you mean?" I ask her, brows pinching together.

"Ah, you guys have all essentially given them all stuff for boy babies. What's gonna happen if they're girls?"

I stare down at her, at the same time those brothers who heard her question all stare at her.

"I guess we'll come to that bridge when we cross it," she says before snorting.

"Ah Pres, you have a visitor," Jimmy calls out to Marx, everyone's heads turning to the door.

"Moss? Did Chewy invite you?" Pres asks, shaking hands with Sergeant Davies who seems slightly distracted.

"Are those penis decorations?"

"Yup, and a vag cake," Chewy answers.

Sergeant Davies stares at her and then points, "Is that a gator?"

"Yup. His name's Chomper. Cute, huh?"

He squints at her before shaking himself off. "Sorry, Marx, this isn't a social call. I need to take in one of your men."

Marx stands straight, larger than ever. Savage nervously looks toward his wife and then moves to stand, Dex coming to stand next to him.

"Who?" Marx demands.

"Tyson Sword. He's been accused of assault and battery."

There's an uproar as the room loses it. My hands shake with anger and it's only Pixie wrapping her arms around me that calms me. Marx lets out a piercing whistle, calling us to order.

"Tank?"

Tank walks toward Davies, staring at Pres. "I didn't do whatever I've been accused of,"

"I know, brother, we'll get this sorted out."

Marx turns to glare at Sergeant Davies who raises his hands, placating the Pres. "I know Johnny, the source sounds sketchy, but we have to investigate no matter if it's a nuisance call or not."

"Take care of my man, you hear me? Anything less and I'll be coming for you," Marx says in all seriousness, holding Davies' gaze.

A lesser man would have shit themselves by now. Instead Davies just smiles, "I know you will," He turns to leave, indicating Tank take the lead, not even cuffing him. "Oh Marx? Better call Maxine so she can have my balls. Again," he rolls his eyes as he follows Tank out the door.

"Wire –"

"Already on it, Pres," Marx scrubs a hand down his face. "OK ya'll, it'll be hard to party without Tank, but we all know he wouldn't want this ruining the ladies' day. Chewy? You said you had games to play?"

"How does everyone feel about bobbing for dongs?"

There's a collective groan and I lean into my woman, who chuckles into my chest.

"I love this place, and I love you."

"I love you too, Pixie."

Tank

I can't fucking believe I've been dragged downtown to face questioning. Maybe dragged isn't the correct word. Sergeant Davies was actually really good about it, didn't cuff me and let me ride shotgun. I get a feeling the man knows this is bullshit, but is just doing his job. That's why I don't give him too much shit and decide to listen like a good little boy and follow all the instructions.

Which is why I'm sitting here in a holding cell minus my wallet, my knives and my boots.

Staring down at my feet, I decide that I'll purchase new socks when I get outta here.

"Oh, hey, what are ya in for?" A peppy voice to my left asks. "Lemme guess. Hmmm, did you murder someone?"

Letting out a sigh, I don't even look up. "Do you think it'd be a good idea to make small talk with a murderer?"

"So you DID murder someone? I knew it! How did you do it? Gun? Knife? Expanding foam in the rear end?"

My head snaps to the side. "What the fuck?"

"What?" Wide green eyes stare back at me. "People never think to use mundane DIY products in their murders. It's always the same unimaginative carp."

"Did you just –"

"Yes sir, clean mouth here. No cursing, that's what my nana taught me. Well, no cursing out loud. In my books, I curse all the time."

I raise an eyebrow at her, and she raises one back. This woman is probably crazy. Which would make sense because she's the hottest woman I've laid eyes on in a long ass time. She's sitting on the crappy wooden bench in the cell next to me, so I can't tell how tall she is exactly, but from what I can tell she's curvy as hell. Big tits, cleavage peeking out from the top of her pinup type dress, thick thighs, soft belly. Blonde curls, those big green eyes and pink pouty lips.

"I write romance novels. But not the usual stuff. My ones have murder in them. Sexy murder romance. Or romantic, murder sex." She frowns at this.

"So, which one is it?"

Her head snaps up as if she forgot I asked her something. She squints at me, then waves a hand dismissively. "All the above. Maybe?" She shrugs and keeps talking. "So, was I right? Did you murder someone?"

The amount of words that keep spilling out of her is a little overwhelming, but I can't imagine she's going to be quiet anytime soon and I have no idea how long I'll be in here for, so I may as well make the best of it.

"I was accused of assaulting someone."

She nods as if that all makes sense. "I mean I get it. Your hands are the size of hams. The ones with the bones in."

"Thanks?"

"You're welcome," she beams at me. "Wow, you're really good looking. Such a sharp jaw. I bet you could grate cheese on that jawline. A total grater face. And your body looks like the muscles are really meaty. Like whole slabs of muscles instead of little piddly individual ones. What size are you exactly?"

"Excuse me?"

"Like how big are you? Height, weight, all that stuff. You'd make a great book character."

I gape at her. There is no way in hell I'm going to be a sexy murder romance character. Instead of giving her my stats I decide to distract her.

"So, what are you in for? Did you murder someone?"

She snorts as if that's the funniest thing in the world, "Puhlease. I'd never get caught if I did. But no, I'm in for harassment and indecent exposure."

My brows hit my hairline. This somewhat sweet looking, maybe crazy lady went down for harassment and indecent exposure?

She lets out a sigh, her breasts heaving under her pretty dress, "Yeah, I approached a man, big, like yourself. I wanted to know if he'd be strong enough to lift me up and bang me against a wall, with clothes on. It was strictly for research, to see if it could be done. Anyway, I may have gotten a little dog and bone-ish and may have not taken no for an answer. So I followed him a little pleading my case and then, THEN when I finally decided to give up I slipped on an actual banana peel, ramming into him, taking him down landing with my face in his junk."

I try not to laugh at the visual, but she keeps going.

"And to make matters worse this dress was not built for falling and my girls popped clean out of the top."

"Hence the indecent exposure?"

"Bingo." Her shoulders slump a little at this before she brightens. "Hey! So we're both in the same boat! Wrongly accused! This could make a good story."

She pulls a notepad and pen out of that amazing cleavage

and starts mumbling to herself, taking notes.

"Tyson? You're up," Sergeant Davies steps up to my cage and unlocks it, looking over at the blonde next door. "Back again, huh, Mira?" He smiles at the bombshell still muttering to herself.

She looks up at him before grinning, "Yeah. You know how it goes." Her eyes flick to me standing outside my cell. "Good luck biker man!"

"You too writer lady."

Thank you!

Thank you so much for reading! I hope you enjoyed Tav's book, and don't worry, I won't leave you hanging. Tank's book is on its way!

Want a bonus scene of Chewy finding out what the Landry brothers were keeping outside? Click here for the bonus scene

If you want to know more about me, what I'm up to or whose book is next be sure to follow me

Follow me at my author page on Facebook

Friend me on Facebook

Join my group Cleo Browne's Babes

Follow me on Instagram

What did she say?

Pepi - Baby
Ae - Yes
Kei te pai - Good, it's good, it's all good
Ne - OK

Cleo Browne Books

Rhodie – Devil's Rose MC Book One

August – A Tombs Security + Devil's Rose MC Crossover

Wire – Devil's Rose MC Book Two

Tav Devil's Rose MC Book Three

Devil's Rose MC Christmas Novella
Coming soon

Tank
Coming soon

About the author

Cleo Browne is the pen name of a neurospicy geeky girl from Aotearoa New Zealand. As a child, she realized very early on that she wasn't a people person, so she would spend all her time reading and writing her own stories. These stories usually ended with the line "and then they died." As an adult, she has gotten slightly more people-y (not much) and better at not killing all her characters off when she writes.

Cleo loves to write about women who don't need a man to do their dirty work and the hot alpha men who turn to mush when they watch their women handling business.

When she's not writing romance novels about strong, curvy women and the men who adore them, she hangs out at home with her hubby, her boys, and her ancient greyhound who likes to creepily watch her write.

Acknowledgements

First off, I'd like to thank all the wonderful readers who continue to keep taking chances on a kooky little woman from New Zealand. Without you all reading my books and loving my characters, I would have just faded away into obscurity, never to be seen or heard from again. So, thank you. I appreciate you all.

Second, I'd like to thank my author bestie and all round good biartch Shaye Torrel. Thank you so much for talking me off the cliff when I would freak out that I didn't know what I was doing. I still don't, but at least I'm not freaking out about it. I wouldn't be here without you, chick!

Thanks to the lovely Gabi Brockelsby and her eagle eyes to make sure you get a typo free book.

Thanks to the wonderful Sally Howells who gives the BEST chapter breakdowns, and found a buttload of gator merch that I need in my life.

Thanks to my betas and my ARC readers, you are all amazing and so very much appreciated.

Thanks to my partner PN. Without his constant words of encouragement, "I really didn't think MC books were a thing," I would never have finished this book. Thanks also go to my boys. Ronnie, for being completely disinterested, and Louis for your two hour long phone calls that would eat into my writing time. Love you guys.

Last but definitely not least, thank you so much to Suzanne Strickland Henry for sharing her beautiful memories, for the late-night chats, and for being a great friend.